THE ABANDONED CHASE

THE ABANDONED CHASE

CHASE FULTON NOVEL #20

CAP DANIELS

ANCHOR WATCH
PUBLISHING
** USA **

The Abandoned Chase
Chase Fulton Novel #20
Cap Daniels

This is a work of fiction. Names, characters, places, historical events, and incidents are the product of the author's imagination or have been used fictitiously. Although many locations such as marinas, airports, hotels, restaurants, etc. used in this work actually exist, they are used fictitiously and may have been relocated, exaggerated, or otherwise modified by creative license for the purpose of this work. Although many characters are based on personalities, physical attributes, skills, or intellect of actual individuals, all the characters in this work are products of the author's imagination.

Published by:

**USA **

13 Digit ISBN: 978-1-951021-40-5
Library of Congress Control Number: 2022922536

Cover Design: German Creative

Printed in the United States of America

The Abandoned Chase

CAP DANIELS

Chapter 1
Unfired

March 2009

"To say we were under fire would be like saying the Titanic is underwater. It's true, but far from completely accurate. Seven point six-two-millimeter rounds were hammering us from every direction. I'd never seen a firefight like that one. I don't think anybody's ever seen a gunfight like that and lived to tell about it. I was hit, but I didn't know it 'til the fight was over. I guess I was in shock, right, doc? Doc? Dr. Fulton, are you listening to me?"

I shook myself from the stupor into which I'd fallen. "I'm sorry, Sergeant Grimley. Of course I'm listening."

"It had to be shock, right?"

I adjusted my position in the Herman Miller Eames Lounge Chair that had been my seat of choice since I stepped away from the world where bullets flew in every direction and the line between good and evil vanished like an apparition. My education and experience combined to make me one of the few psychotherapists who'd actually experienced the world through their patient's eyes. I knew exactly how it felt to be outgunned, surrounded, hopeless, and ten thousand miles from home. When I hung up my boots and hung out my shingle proclaiming the office of Dr.

Chase Fulton to be open for business, I didn't know how much more terrifying it would be to relive someone else's trauma than to actually crawl into a foxhole and fight it out with an enemy bent on leaving me a lifeless pile of bloody flesh. Shooting back was easy, but walking alongside a traumatized warrior—on his path to recovery from the hell in which he'd made his home—stung and cut deeper than feeling my own blood stain the soil at my feet.

"It wasn't shock, Sergeant Grimley. It was adrenaline. Before the days of gunpowder and lead, we had sticks and sharpened stones. When the inevitable predator—we'll call him a tiger—stepped in front of us and was determined to eat our whole family, we stood and fought while the ones we love escaped. The tiger was motivated only by hunger, but our motivations were based on the immediate preservation of life: our own, as well as our family's. The tiger had no fear of us. To him, we were just a meal, but to us, the next few seconds of our lives could be, in all reality, the final few seconds of our lives. When our brain believes we're on the verge of dying a horrific death, it releases several chemicals into our bodies. The most powerful of these is adrenaline or epinephrine."

He raised his head. "Yeah, I know a little about that."

"You probably know more about it than you realize," I said. "Adrenaline does four very specific things to our body. It increases heart rate, breathing rate, and alertness. Interestingly, it also stops digestion so the muscles we need to fight can use the blood and oxygen that were previously being used by our stomach and intestines. There is one other effect of adrenaline that's not always present, but in extreme cases, such as yours in combat, it diminishes the body's awareness of injury and pain. If you sustained an injury that didn't immediately kill or disable you, your mind may choose to ignore that injury to keep you in the fight. We humans are amazing, and humans who've been trained to the degree you have are even more amazing. Even though you were wounded, your mind kept you in the fight. So, it wasn't shock you were experiencing. It was adrenaline, and it worked. Your body survived the fight and the injury, but your physical injuries weren't the extent of your wounds. Not all cuts bleed, Sergeant, and those are the wounds that are often most painful."

The young warrior rolled his eyes. "This is the part I think is a waste of time, doc. It's all psychobabble, touchy-feely garbage."

"Then why are you here, Sergeant Grimley?"

He stared between his boots and shrugged. "It's Bobby."

I cocked my head and met his gaze, but I didn't speak. Sometimes, in therapy, listening is the most meaningful gift we can give our patients.

Finally, he said, "My name, doc . . . it's Bobby. I ain't a sergeant no more. Those days are behind me, so maybe you could call me Bobby instead of Sergeant Grimley."

I tried my soft-spoken approach—the one I learned in clinicals but had never been very good at pulling off. "Okay. Bobby, it is." I paused again, using subtle silence as a tool to pry open the top of Bobby Grimley's skull and peer inside. And it worked.

The former soldier leaned back and stared at the ceiling as the corners of his eyes glistened with the tears he'd never let the world see. "I think maybe I'm a coward."

Bells rang and fireworks exploded inside my psychologist's head, but I didn't flinch. "What makes you believe you're a coward?"

He leaned forward, slammed his elbows onto his knees, and bit his bottom lip. "Why else would I wake up screaming every night of my life and pour a gallon of whiskey down my throat every other day? Huh, doc? Can you tell me the answer to that one?"

I wanted to recoil as his voice rose, but I feigned calmness, trying to maintain the tone I worked so hard to establish inside the office. "Tell me about Force Recon training."

He huffed and almost threw himself against the back of the chair. "Here we go again. I knew it. I knew you were just like all the rest of 'em. You'll tell me how cowards don't make it through hard-core training courses like Force Recon, and then you'll try to convince me that I'm not a coward because I made it back from half a dozen deployments and kept jumping back in the fight. It's a waste of time . . . Yours and mine. People like you just don't get it, and you never will."

"People like me, huh? Why don't you tell me about people like me, Bobby?"

The time for the quiet, calm tone in the office was over, and Sergeant Bobby Grimley marched right down the primrose path I'd laid out before him.

His face turned red, and his fingernails dug into the arms of his chair. "Okay, doc. If that's what you want, here it is. Until you've lain in the mud made from the blood of your brothers and smelled that stench and tasted that rancid air, you don't know anything about what I've been through. Until you've lain awake for a thousand nights because you can't stomach what you see when you close your eyes, you don't get to judge me. You don't get to say that you know how I feel. You don't get to—"

He paused as I lifted my pant leg to reveal the robot attached to the stump of what used to be my leg. I laid down my pad and pen and checked my watch. "Our time is up for today, Bobby."

He slammed a hand on the chair. "No! You don't get to do something like that and then tell me we're done. Ain't no way. Whoever's out there in the waiting room can just keep waiting."

I sighed. "Our time's up. If we're going to keep talking, it can't be as counselor and patient."

"Fine. Whatever. But you're *going* to tell me what happened to your foot."

I let my pant leg fall over my prosthetic, and I stood. "It's unethical for a psychologist to have a personal relationship with his patients outside the office, but I have a theory that you were planning to fire me anyway."

He exhaled in exasperation. "I don't know if you call it 'getting fired,' but I wasn't planning to schedule another session—or whatever you call these appointments."

"Yeah, from my perspective, that's pretty much the definition of getting fired." I motioned toward the door with my head. "Come on. There are a couple of people I want you to meet."

"What about your leg?"

"It works just fine. Come on."

I locked up the office, set the alarm, and headed for the parking lot. "You can ride with me. It's that brown VW Microbus."

He studied the thirty-five-year-old bus. "I should've guessed that was yours. It looks like the kind of thing a psychologist would drive. Where are we going?"

"Just get in. You'll see."

I slid onto the perch that Volkswagen called a front seat and sent a pair of identical texts to different numbers.

Eight minutes after the microbus buzzed to life, we drove up the pecan tree–lined drive toward the three-story brick house that looked—at least on the outside—a lot like the original house that first graced the property.

"What is this place, doc?"

"My name is Chase, Bobby. You fired me, remember? I'm not your psychologist anymore."

He twisted his mouth into an odd shape I couldn't describe, but I thought I understood what it meant. "All right, then. What is this place, Chase?"

"It's called Bonaventure Plantation, and it's been in my mother's family since before the Civil War. It used to be a pecan plantation. Now, it's just a place I go when I'm not being a doctor."

He examined the house and front yard. "Cool."

I rolled to a stop and threw open my door. "The cool stuff's out back. Let's go."

I led him across the backyard to my sanatorium, the place I loved more than anywhere else, the gazebo overlooking the black water of the North River.

Bobby stepped up into the gazebo and ran his hand across the centerpiece. "Cool cannon, doc. Where'd you get it?"

I raised my chin to point down the river. "About three miles that way, from the muddy bottom of the Cumberland Sound. It's British or French—probably French, but it came from a British-flagged warship during the War of Eighteen-Twelve. The ship burned and sank out there in the sound thanks to the handiwork of some of my ancestors and the men who worked the plantation."

"Slaves, you mean."

I shook my head. "No, they were slaves when they left the market in Charleston or Savannah, but when they got to Bonaventure, they became partners in the business and freemen. They had the option to leave any time they wanted, but life here at Bonaventure was better than almost anywhere else in the country in the eighteen fifties and sixties. Here, they were housed, fed, educated, cared for when they got sick, and paid well. My family has always believed in that oft-forgotten line about all men being created equal."

He traced the lines in the surface of the aged weapon of war while I deposited myself in one of the Adirondack chairs on the perimeter of the gazebo.

"Why'd you bring me here?" he asked, still caressing the cannon.

"I told you already. There are a couple of people I want you to meet. They'll be here soon."

"Is this going to be some kind of group therapy or something? I've been there and done that, too, and that didn't work, either."

I shook my head and checked my watch again. "No, I told you, therapy is over. You fired me. We're just a couple of guys hanging out by the river."

Before he could protest, I heard a vehicle pull up the long driveway and stop in front of the house. "Just in time."

Two of the men I loved and trusted more than any others rounded the house and joined us. Bobby shook both of their hands, and the men nodded and settled into a pair of chairs.

Bobby looked confused, proving my plan was working perfectly. He asked, "So, what's this about?"

The first man who joined us in the gazebo slid forward in his chair and peeled off his shirt. His muscled physique was speckled with scars the size of silver dollars. "Bobby, my name is Jimmy Grossmann, but you can call me Singer. Everybody does."

Bobby looked between me and Singer as if he were watching a fast ping-pong match.

Singer said, "They call me Singer 'cause I sing old Southern Baptist hymns when I work."

Bobby said, "Okay. What's that supposed to mean to me?"

"Nothing, really," Singer said. "I just thought you'd like to know what I do when I'm killing people."

Bobby recoiled and shot a glaring look toward me. "What?"

"I'm a sniper, Bobby. One of the best snipers in the world. I'm not telling you that to brag. I'm telling you that as a precursor to telling you about these scars. I've been shot six times above the waist, once in the thigh, and once in the butt. I've put a bunch of men in their graves, and there's not a night of my life when I don't see every one of their faces when I put my head on the pillow."

Bobby leaned in as if hanging on Singer's every word, but the sniper was finished for the moment. He pulled his shirt back over his head and stuck his arms through the sleeves.

The second man said, "My name is Stone W. Hunter. I used to

be an Air Force combat controller, and I got blown off the side of a mountain calling fire danger close. Do you know what that means, Bobby?"

"Yes, sir, I know what it means. It means you were calling down artillery fire or airborne bombs on your own coordinates because enemy forces were overrunning you."

Hunter nodded and shrugged. "That's close enough, but there's more. The Air Force decided I was too messed up to keep wearing the uniform, so they retired me. I went to work as a cop for NCIS until that man"—he pointed at me—"put me back to work doing what I was trained to do."

It was Hunter's turn to pull off his shirt. He turned, giving Bobby a good look at the dinner-plate-size scar on the back of his left shoulder. "That's what an exit wound from an AK-forty-seven round looks like. I was standing a foot away from your shrink when I took that round, and Singer stuck his hand in my shoulder and pinched off the bleeders 'til they could get me into the sick bay on our support ship."

Bobby swallowed hard and stared down at my boot.

I nodded. "I lost my foot by winning a gunfight-turned-fist-fight on a ladder aboard a ship off the coast of Western Africa. I killed the guy I landed on, but he got his licks in before I did. We caught the bad guys that day, but now I have to drag around a metal foot for the rest of my life. I don't have as many as Singer, or any as big as Hunter's, but I've got plenty of scars of my own. Believe it or not, I even had a Russian assassin cut my tongue in half with her fighting knife. Some of our scars are from bullets, and a few others are from knives, but the ones that hurt the most are the ones nobody can see, even when we take off our shirts."

Bobby chewed his bottom lip. "You know something, doc? Now that I think about it, maybe I don't want to fire you after all."

Chapter 2
Two out of Three Ain't Bad

Singer took Bobby Grimley fishing, and I don't know what they talked about, but I knew one thing without a doubt: whatever Singer told him came with the authority of the Almighty, and I'd never come close to giving that young man the comfort he'd receive from above.

Hunter leaned against the cannon and sighted down its long barrel. "Do you think it could still shoot, or has it been out of the game too long?"

I said, "Are you talking about the cannon or us?"

"Maybe both."

I gave the cannon's cradle a gentle tap with the toe of what used to be my foot. "This thing has seen its last battle, and now it gets to rest knowing it gave everything in its time."

He slapped his palm against the four-hundred-year-old warhorse. "Do you ever wonder if it misses the fire and smoke?"

"It's just a cold, dead piece of iron, Hunter. It doesn't have the capacity to experience emotions like that."

"How about you, Chase? Is the same true for you?"

I reclaimed my seat and propped my boots on the cradle. "It's corrupted to its core."

"What is?"

"The whole world," I said. "I used to believe we were the good guys doing the right thing, but that was just me being naïve. When was the last time your shoulder didn't hurt?"

He cupped his right hand over his scarred shoulder. "I don't remember."

"And what about Tony? When was the last time he remembered his high school prom or the day he met Skipper? He got blown as near to death as any man can survive and lost every memory he had packed away in his head. And you, you almost bled to death on a mission in which we were nothing more than mercenaries waging a private war of revenge on behalf of two rich, powerful men who were too important to get their own hands dirty. We weren't the good guys on that one."

He picked at his fingernails. "Who's to say we weren't the good guys? We avenged the murder of two innocent little girls."

"Avenging their murder doesn't bring them back. It doesn't undo the evil, and it's entirely my fault."

"Your fault? What are you talking about?"

I said, "We went into that mission under false pretenses. We thought we were chasing a guy named Marcus Astor for piracy. The Board lied to us and threw us in the lion's den, forcing us to willingly risk our lives for a vendetta they didn't have the guts to tell us about. If they can do that, what else will they do? How far will they go without consequence? Are they going to pay us to kill the next president they don't like?"

Hunter shrugged. "They did it to Kennedy in the sixties, and nothing's changed since then. The whole world may be corrupt, but get out a globe and point to a country you'd rather live in than ours."

"We're not vigilantes. We believe in the oldest, corniest lie mankind has ever told itself. We can prove our side is the right side by killing more of whoever our enemy happens to be at the moment than they kill of us."

He let out a long breath. "I know, but it's who and what we are. Thanks to you, we're a bunch of rich former action guys. Singer's gone fishing, for Pete's sake. Mongo's in New York City watching ballet. Disco's teaching kids to fly airplanes at a hundred miles per hour. And I'm living life on vacation. I mean, look at you. You're wearing sweater-vests and asking screwed-up house-wives how their husbands' drinking makes them feel. We're getting old and soft and weak."

"I don't treat screwed-up housewives," I said.

He huffed. "You get my point. Our hundred-million-dollar ship is counting fish in the Mariana Trench or some other equally meaningless craziness. Chase, how long has it been since you pulled a trigger?"

"I don't know. What do you want me to do?"

"I want you to put us back in the fight, boss. It's what we do and who we are. I mean, really. Does Mongo belong at Carnegie Hall? Does Disco get his kicks sitting in the right seat of a beat-up One-Seventy-Two teaching kids not to bounce when they hit the runway?"

I said, "We're all just trying to live normal lives. What's so bad about that?"

"Are you serious? We're the inhabitants of the island of misfit toys. There is no normal for us. We need blood in our hair, sweat in our eyes, and the smell of burnt powder in our noses. Come on, Chase. Who are we kidding? You're not a psychotherapist. You're the best natural leader I've ever seen. You're fearless, focused, and unbeatable out there past the spot where normal ends—where angels fear to tread. You know what I'm saying."

"Yeah, I know what you're saying, but I just can't do it for a bunch of crusty old men who think we're their own expendable private army. If I can't trust the people who claim the illustrious moral high ground, how am I supposed to live with myself when

I get you or Singer or any one of us killed on a mission that does nothing to make the world safer, freer, or better, huh?" I grabbed him by his shirt. "I'd rather you live to be a hundred and be bored every day than to watch you die in some godforsaken mudhole, sending bullets downrange at an enemy we don't understand."

"I get it," he said. "I do. But look up there." He pointed into the sky. "See that eagle?" I nodded, and he continued. "You could catch that eagle, put him in a cage, and feed him a ham sandwich every day for the rest of his life. He'd never encounter a predator, so he'd be completely safe. On top of that, he'd never be hungry. That'd be the perfect life for that eagle. Don't you agree?"

I deflated in my seat. "I get it, but what you don't understand is what happened inside me when I thought you, Tony, and Singer were all dead on that ship in Morocco. I'd rather die a thousand times than get any of you hurt again."

He drove a finger through the air and straight at me. "And that's exactly why you're the best leader I've ever had the honor of serving under. They don't make 'em like you anymore, Chase Fulton, and if you don't get us back in the fight, it might not be long until there's nothing left worth fighting for."

I cocked my head. "We're being a little dramatic, aren't we?"

Hunter shook his head. "I don't think so. Men like you and me have twenty years to pour everything we've got into our reason for being on Earth, and I think that reason is to keep the dream alive. We've got some real problems in this country. Nobody with any sense will deny that, but it doesn't mean we're not the greatest country that's ever existed. A handful of us are cut out of the herd by some force—maybe fate, the universe, God, whatever. It doesn't really matter who taps us on the shoulder and says, 'You're it.' What matters is that we take that torch and run with it until we can't run anymore. Then, we hand it off to somebody younger and faster and stronger, and we charge them with the same responsibility that tapped us on the shoulder."

I suddenly wished for Singer. During the times in my life when I didn't know what to say, no one rescued me like he did. "Okay, let's say, for the sake of argument, you're right. You know better than anybody what happened on our last mission."

"Let's not call it our *last* mission. Let's call it our most recent mission."

"You know what I mean," I said.

He widened his eyes. "Oh, yeah. I know exactly what you meant. You meant our *last* mission. Can you honestly say you've given everything you can to fulfill the promise you made to the men who put you in this job?"

I stuck my index finger against his shoulder, precisely where the AK-47 round entered his body. "No, but you almost did . . . and for what? How did you getting shot and almost bleeding to death make anything on Earth better?"

He didn't hesitate. "We plucked a thorn out of the side of humanity and took him off the streets."

"Okay, I'll give you that, but again, the people who sent us on that mission knew full well they deployed us under false pretenses, and they were willing to risk our lives to accomplish a personal vendetta. That's not what we are. We're not their personal army."

He subconsciously rubbed his shoulder. "I can't argue with that, but what options do we have? We've got half a billion dollars' worth of hardware and a collection of training and experience that you can't put a price tag on. If we don't use what we've been given, why do we have it? If you've decided we're through, why haven't you given everything back?"

"Back to whom?" I asked. "Who owns this house and property? Who owns that airport right over there? Who owns the airplanes and the boats?"

"How should I know?"

"I'll tell you who owns them . . . Better yet, I'll tell you how to find out. Go down to the courthouse and do a little research. It won't take you long to realize *we* own everything. Well, that's not exactly true. We don't own the *Lori Danielle*. The ship technically belongs to NOAA, but everything else is the property of the corporation we're partners in. So, who do you want me to give it back to?"

He closed his eyes and took a long breath. "Let's back up. I don't like what this conversation has become. I'm sorry I got loud. That wasn't my intention. I want you to know that I want to go back to work with you. I believe we're wasting a lot of talent, skill, and equipment. I'm not saying you're not doing good work shoving people's brains back in their heads. That's good, noble work, but there's no reason we can't still operate and you can still run the shrink business."

I tried not to smile, but I failed. "You know I love you like a brother, but—"

He threw up a hand. "Don't say that! I watched you shoot your brother in the face. I don't need that kind of love from you."

"Maybe *you* could use a dose of therapy. Have you ever thought about that?"

He threw his feet onto the cannon's carriage and pointed toward his temple. "You don't want to mess around in my head. It's dark and scary in there."

"Excellent point," I said. "But we're getting off topic. Let's say you're right and I agree. How do we ever trust the Board to dispatch us on missions with full disclosure?"

"That's above my pay grade. Stuff like that is up to you and Clark. I'm just a trigger-puller."

"You're a lot more than a trigger-puller, and you know it."

He rolled his eyes. "Who says we have to go back to work for those clowns on the Board? There's got to be somebody else. What about the Agency? Don't they farm out a bunch of stuff they don't want their fingerprints on? Why can't we contract with them?"

"You think the CIA is any cleaner than the Board? That's just two different sides of the same tarnished coin."

He gave the cannon a kick. "I don't know, Chase. I just know I'm wasting away, and so are you and the rest of the team. We're not the kind of guys who retire and draw a pension. We're the kind of men who beat back a hurricane if it threatens who and what we love, and I, for one, love this country and what it stands for. Call that corny or whatever you want, but I think you feel the same way. Figure it out. Find us somebody to go to work for. You're the team leader, so lead. Sitting still ain't leading."

He could've driven a white-hot spike through my chest, and it wouldn't have stung as badly as his admonition. After shaking off the stench, I said, "I'll talk to Clark, but it's up to you to whip the team back into shape. You said it yourself. We're getting old and soft and weak. If we're going back to work, we have to change two out of those three."

Chapter 3
Sweep Tag

As if on cue, my handler, former Green Beret Clark Johnson, appeared in the kitchen at Bonaventure the same moment I reached for my first cup of coffee. "Good morning, College Boy. It looks like you're sleeping in these days."

I dug my knuckles into my eyes, trying to force the sleep and crusties from the corners. "What are you doing here?"

He poured a cup for each of us. "Some things are better said in person."

I took my first sip. "You've been talking to Hunter, haven't you?"

"What makes you say that?"

"Just a hunch. Are you hungry?"

He bellied up to the table. "When was the last time you heard me say no to that question?"

I scrambled some eggs and made a few pieces of toast. "I know this isn't the gourmet fare you're accustomed to, but it'll have to do."

He made no objections, so we ate in relative silence until he slid back, crossed his legs, and wiped his mouth. "I've got a proposition for you."

I followed his lead and tossed my napkin onto my empty plate. "Let's hear it."

He sucked air between his teeth to either dislodge a trapped morsel or delay the conversation neither of us was looking forward to. "It's like this, Chase. If you're done, you're done, and I'm not here to talk you out of that."

"Yes, you are."

"Not really," he said. "Believe it or not, I'm here to offer you what you want."

My skepticism had to show like a neon sign as he pulled a folded slip of paper from his shirt pocket and floated it across the table.

I lifted the paper and read it carefully. "Who are these guys? I've never heard of either of them."

"Gibson Richardson and Malcolm Wainwright are the two men on the Board who dispatched us on the last mission."

I swallowed hard, sank my teeth into the flesh of my jaw, and glared at the two names on the page. The names of the men who sent my team—my brothers—and me onto the field of battle under the shroud of a lie. The two men who knew we'd discover the deception and continue the fight in spite of the deceit. The two men who are responsible for the bullet hole through Hunter's shoulder and the explosion that nearly tore Tony from this Earth.

I carefully folded the paper and slid it into my pocket as I stood from the table. "Thank you."

Clark reached up and took my wrist. "No, Chase. Not like that."

I yanked my wrist from his hand. "You knew exactly what you were doing when you gave me the names, so don't pretend like you did anything other than chisel their names on their headstones."

"Sit down," he ordered in his calm, measured tone.

My breath came hard and short as the rage inside me turned to bile and I could taste it on my tongue.

"Sit down, Chase. These aren't the kind of men you walk up to on the street and put a bullet between their eyes. These are powerful, important men who have armies around them everywhere they go."

I growled. "So, what do you expect me to do?"

"Wars aren't won with bullets and bombs. They're won in near silence behind closed doors by men in neckties and thousand-dollar loafers. The blood and sweat of men like you and me are nothing more than a play—a dance choreographed by men like Richardson and Wainwright."

I forced a finger through the air and into his face. "You know better than that, Clark. You know what we do is important. Not just important, but crucial. We sharpen our own swords, then we drive them through the hearts of men who'd destroy what we love and what we treasure."

He leaned back and sighed. "No. That's what you *used* to do."

I sent a fist that had once been calloused and hard into the table and stormed from the room. I remember the sound of the kitchen door slamming behind me as I propelled myself across the back gallery and down the stairs.

I hadn't run a step in two years, nor had I felt my prosthetic throbbing in phantom pain, but all of that changed in the next half hour of my life. I was in cargo pants, tennis shoes, and a UGA baseball sweatshirt when I took my first running stride at the bottom of the stairs, but the sweatshirt came off by the time I settled into my stride along the North River. Clark wouldn't chase me, and he couldn't have caught me if he'd tried. Although my lungs and legs weren't in battle-ready condition, the fire raging inside me fueled my body with enough adrenaline to run myself to death. Fortunately, I didn't let that happen.

I made the homeward turn north of the old paper plant and opened the throttle. It wasn't a sprint, but it was strong enough to set my lungs ablaze and send the muscles of my thighs into a screaming fit. By the time I made it back to Bonaventure, I'd covered a little over three miles and burned enough calories to justify all the desserts I wanted for the coming week.

Just as expected, I found Clark waiting in the gazebo when I collapsed into my favorite Adirondack chair. He had a glass of milk in one hand and a sandwich in the other, and he pretended I wasn't there as he devoured the second breakfast and I gasped for air. Sweat poured from my face, and my chest heaved like a machine.

With the sandwich finished and crumbs dotting his shirt, Clark asked, "Feel better?"

Through panting breaths, I said, "Not really."

He downed the milk and wiped his mouth. "Are you at least ready to talk about it?"

"Yeah."

He propped up his feet. "You've turned down every job I sent you for two years, and I understand why. I can't tell you how many sleepless nights I've spent fretting over how this was going to wash out."

"I can tell you how it's gonna wash out," I said.

He held up a hand. "Not yet, College Boy. Hear me out first."

I wiped the sweat from my face and pulled my sweatshirt back over my head. "Let's hear it."

"We've got a new president in the White House, and he's not exactly a friend. Certainly not like the last one, but in this case, that may play into our favor."

"What are you talking about?"

He leaned forward. "Never bite the hand that scratches your back."

I squeezed my eyes closed and tried forcing my brain to apply logic to whatever he just said, but it wasn't coming.

He finally said, "You know what I'm talking about. With the new administration in place, it's the perfect time for us . . . well, you. It's the perfect time for *you* to initiate a congressional hearing that just might lead to criminal prosecution. As nice as it was to have a personal friend in the big chair up in DC, sometimes we can use the opposite team to accomplish our goals."

With my breathing back to a normal rate, I asked, "Are you suggesting I contact my congressman about this whole thing?"

"Not exactly. It's actually more subtle than that. I'm suggesting you plant the seed in a few ears at Langley and then call in a few favors from a couple of high-ranking folks you rescued in Western Africa."

"You've got to be kidding. You want me to make a few phone calls and sit back and wait?"

"I can think of worse ideas. Nobody gets shot, and nobody gets blown up. You get to keep sitting in your cushy little office and listening to crybabies moan about their problems so you'll prescribe them some drug that'll make all their worries float away."

"I don't think you have any idea what I do for a living. I'm a psychologist, not a psychiatrist. I can't write prescriptions."

He scratched his head. "You went to school for a hundred years to become a doctor who can't even write a prescription? You got ripped off, College Boy."

"Let's get back to your plan. Do you really believe a congressional hearing and a criminal investigation is the right way to handle this thing? Have you ever heard of a sweep tag?"

He frowned. "A what?"

"Before I answer that question, I have another one. Have you ever seen any videos of me behind home plate?"

"You mean, like playing baseball?"

"Yes, exactly like playing baseball. Maybe you forgot, but I caught a few hundred games and ended up working for you only after a nasty train wreck at home plate in Omaha."

He said, "I didn't forget. You were mister big shot when you were a twenty-year-old kid. Big whoop-de-do."

"Give me your phone."

He tossed it over, and I typed furiously on the tiny screen. When I found what I was looking for, I tossed it back to him. "Watch that video."

He tapped the screen and squinted. Thirty seconds later, he cringed and let out a sound like a wounded animal. "My god, man! That *is* a train wreck. Is that really you?"

"Yeah, that's me. That was the last time I ever put on a catcher's mask, and that was the play that ended the life I dreamed of since the first time I ever stepped onto a baseball field."

"You were pretty good, huh?"

I chuckled. "Yeah, I was pretty good, but more than that, I was pretty fearless. I blocked the plate every time I could. A sweep tag is what catchers do when they're too soft to take the hit. They move out in front of home plate and catch the incoming throw, then they launch themselves toward the baseline, mitt first, hoping to brush some leather against a piece of the diving runner just in time to tag him out before his lead hand touches the plate. That's a sweep tag. I didn't make sweep tags. I fielded the ball on the third base line and took the shot like a man. Most of the time, I won, but even when I lost, the runner remembered how I rang his bell."

He seemed to consider my story. "What's that got to do with this?"

"It's got everything to do with this. I don't make sweep tags, and I don't call the CIA and a couple of congressmen when some piece-of-crap, self-important elitist spits in my eye and tries to get my team killed."

"You've got it all wrong, Chase. You used to block the plate and take the hit. You used to have a team. You used to fight back when somebody took shots at your teammates. But you took yourself out of the game. You quit. Remember?"

Chapter 4
A Better Psychologist

Clark Johnson would forever be a better psychologist than me. He knew exactly how to push my buttons, pull my strings, and send me over the edge.

I sat there, soaked to the skin from sweat and still red-faced. "How did I not see that coming?"

My handler—the man who taught me more about staying alive than anyone else on Earth—put on his patented crooked grin. "Just because I went to boot camp instead of fraternity rush, or whatever you college boys call it, doesn't mean I can't hold my own in the trenches with you guys who think you're smarter than the rest of us."

"I've never said I was smarter than you."

He rolled his eyes. "You didn't have to say it out loud for me to hear it."

"Then I apologize if you ever heard it from anything I did or didn't say."

"Apology accepted. Now, are you going to beat Wainwright to death with Richardson's dead body, or what?"

"The first thing I'm going to do is call Skipper."

The best intelligence analyst in the business appeared as if from nowhere. "You don't have to call me. I'm already on it. I'll have a key to their front doors by lunch."

I turned to see the woman who'd once been a spoiled brat teenager when I met her in my college baseball coach's house in Athens, Georgia. Her birth certificate labeled her Elizabeth Woodley, but because of how she skipped and danced everywhere she went, I'd always called her Skipper. The moniker stuck, and most of the people in our world wouldn't have any clue who Elizabeth Woodley was. Skipper, on the other hand, was the Diana Ross of the intel world. Everybody knew her name.

Clark and I stood, as Southern gentlemen should when a lady arrives.

I said, "Where'd you come from?"

She planted hands on her hips. "Sit down, boys. Don't you know I'm always lurking in the shadows anytime the two of you have one of your secret-squirrel meetings?" She took a seat inside the gazebo and turned to Clark. "Did it work?"

He nodded. "Yep. You were right. He walked right into it."

"Wait a minute," I said. "You were in on this?"

She laughed. "Everyone was, except you."

"Why do you people do this kind of stuff to me?"

Skipper said, "Because, according to Hunter, you're too stubborn to listen to reason."

I palmed my forehead. "How did I not see this coming?"

"That's an easy one, even for me," Clark said. "You were too busy focusing on everything except doing what you were put on Earth to do. Remember, College Boy, life is like soccer. It doesn't matter how fast you run, if you step out of bounds, the touchdown doesn't count."

I shivered involuntarily. "Do you even know what that's supposed to mean?"

He cocked his head. "Sure I do. It means stay on the field where you belong, and in this case, that field is a battlefield."

"It's all an act, isn't it? Screwing up common phrases and pretending to be a window licker is a big game for you."

The crooked grin remained, and he gave me a wink.

"So, what's next?" I asked.

"What do you mean, what's next?"

I furrowed my brow. "It means, what do you want me to do next? Is this an official op, or are we going rogue?"

Clark threw up his hands. "I have no idea what you're talking about, man. You don't work for me anymore. Besides, what you're talking about sounds like treason to me. I can't have any part of something like that. In fact, I'm late for lunch in Miami. I'm outta here."

Coincidently with Clark's departure, Singer and Sergeant Grimley motored up to the Bonaventure dock.

I yelled from the gazebo. "Did you catch anything?"

Singer looked up. "No, did you?"

It was my turn to wear Clark's crooked grin. "It looks like I caught a dose of my own medicine . . . and maybe a job."

Our sniper shook Grimley's hand, and the looks on their faces said both had been returned to a world that had no idea what to do with old warriors like them. Singer continued up the slope and into my fortress of solitude. Okay, maybe the gazebo didn't provide any solitude, but it was where I did my best thinking, and in the previous two years, some of my best drinking.

By the time Singer was nestled in, Hunter showed up and pulled off his hat. "I heard Clark stopped in for a powwow."

"I guess good news travels fast," I said.

Hunter claimed his seat. "Yep, it sure does. So, when are you going to brief us on the new operation?"

I turned to Skipper. "How long will it take you to dust the cobwebs out of the ops center?"

She grinned beneath her few freckles. "There's never been any cobwebs in my ops center. In fact, Disco and Tony are up there right now, just waiting for the rest of us."

"Of course they are."

We climbed the stairs to the third floor of the house that looked, at least from the outside, a lot like the original brick structure my great-grandfather built a couple hundred years before, exactly on the same piece of earth. The exterior of the house and the library were the only remnants of the original look. Everything about the house, especially the addition of a third floor, was ultramodern. That floor existed for only one reason: to house the state-of-the-art operations center that had become Skipper's lair.

She keyed in her access code, stared into the retinal scanner, and the magnetic locks retracted into their housings. I walked through the doors and into the room that would be perfectly at home in the basement of the White House or across the river at the Pentagon. It was truly a marvel of modern electronics. From inside that sealed room, communication with any friendly government—and a few unfriendly ones—was possible. Buried behind the walls in climate-controlled perfection rested a supercomputer of magnificent design and function. I had no way to know for sure, but according to Skipper, our ops center's computing capability was superior to any intelligence agency in the world, except maybe the CIA, Mossad, and the Russian SVR.

When the doors closed and latched behind us, the room became a sensitive compartmented information facility, commonly referred to as a SCIF—a secure facility where sensitive information could be viewed and discussed without fear of outside surveillance or spying. When used as a SCIF, there were no cell phones or electronic devices of any kind inside the room, with one exception. The electronics of my prosthetic foot weren't considered to be a potential portal for spying, so I got to keep my robotic body parts in place, even when inside the ops center.

The room was Skipper's domain, so I deferred to her once inside.

"May I?"

She swept an open hand toward the chair that had once been mine at the head of the table, and I took a seat.

I said, "Since I seem to be the last one to know anything that's going on around here, I guess you guys should stop me if you've heard any of this before. We have an unsanctioned, unsupported, and likely illegal mission. Our target package is a pair of Americans named Gibson Richardson and Malcolm Wainwright." I pointed toward the overhead display. "Bring up their headshots, Skipper."

The two men's faces filled the side-by-side screens, and I continued. "These are two members of the Board. The same Board that's been handing down our assignments since the dawn of time."

I paused long enough to down the bottle of water Skipper placed in front of me. Perhaps it was an attempt to quench the fire burning in my soul. "These are the two jackasses who unleashed us on Marcus Astor and Ilya Mikhailovich Semenov as their personal mercenaries. As you know, the mission was not an official assignment from the full Board. It was an under-the-table deal with these guys because Mikhail's father was responsible for the death of two little girls who just happened to be Wainwright's and Richardson's granddaughters. One of their sons married the other's daughter, or something like that, but I don't care. They got Hunter shot and Tony blown up for an unsanctioned, unauthorized, personal mission."

Singer leaned forward and spoke in his trademark gentle voice. "You mean an unsanctioned, unauthorized, *person* mission, just like the one we're about to embark on?"

Our sniper had a long history of stumping me with his wisdom, but that time, I was ready for him. "There's one huge difference, my friend. Nobody is dispatching you on this one. I'm briefing you on the mission *I'm* undertaking. Just like every other mission I've ever done, none of you are under any obligation to come with me."

Singer tipped his imaginary cap. "Well played, sir. And for the record, I'm in, sanctioned or not."

Hunter said, "You know I'm in. I've been in, and that ain't gonna change. I'd chase you through a field of pigmy goats just for a chance to butt heads with the big billy."

"I feel like I'm talking to Clark. What on Earth does that mean?"

"Get Clark to explain it to your big brain."

I scanned the remaining members of the team until my eyes fell on Mongo, and he looked away. I tried to ease his mind. "Don't worry, big man. I understand if staying home is what you need to do. Irina is too important to—"

"Oh, no," Mongo said. "You've got it all wrong. I'm not staying home. You guys might need me to leap a tall building or something. I just need you to know that I've gotten fat and lazy, and before I get back in the game, I need some serious time to get back in shape."

Everyone except Skipper chuckled, and Disco said, "You? Look at me. I'm fifteen years older than you and way fatter than you've ever been."

Hunter tapped on the table. "Don't worry, guys. I've got a plan to whip us back into shape in no time, but you're not going to enjoy it."

Skipper cleared her throat. "I don't know if you're including me under the umbrella of 'guys,' but I'll have you know that I've not gained a pound in the past two years, and I've still got an eighteen-minute five-k."

Hunter said, "We'll get that five-k time down under seventeen if you think you can hang with the boys."

She pulled off her glasses and stared at him. "I'll make a bet with you. I'll sit on my butt for two months while you train, and I'll still outrun whoever is brave enough to take the challenge."

"What's the wager?"

"You name it," she said.

Tony smiled as if he were sitting on a secret that only he knew. "I'll take that bet."

Skipper raised an eyebrow. "Go ahead, big boy. Show off in front of your friends, but just wait 'til I get you home."

He ducked his head, and we were tempted to laugh, but no one had the courage.

Singer pulled us back from the edge of frivolity and hit me like a truck. "So, what's the plan? You're not thinking of killing these guys, are you?"

Shocked, I sat silent for a long moment. "I haven't thought that far ahead. I guess I want them to pay for what they did to Hunter and Tony."

Without consulting either of our wounded, Singer asked, "What are you going to do, shoot Wainwright in the shoulder and make Richardson sit on a block of C-four?"

I shrank in my seat. "I guess I want them to go to prison."

Singer frowned and lowered his chin. "Come on, Chase. You know neither of them is going to prison, but if you stir up an investigation, we might find ourselves in handcuffs and striped jumpsuits. If we're going to do this, we need a clearly defined objective, and it has to come from you."

Hunter made his serious face. "Have you ever thought about asking me and Tony what we want? I appreciate you being pissed off on our behalf, but we were the ones who got hurt, after all."

"You're right," I admitted. "And I'm sorry. I should've come to both of you two years ago and asked that question. Please forgive my timing and selfishness. What do you want?"

After a glance at Tony, who didn't seem to have anything to say, Hunter said, "I can't speak for our Coast Guard contingent, but as for me, I don't want anything. I knew I'd probably get shot the day I signed on with this crew. Don't get me wrong. It sucked, but it's part of the game. It's like some philosopher said . . . 'If you're going to grab a tiger by the tail, you'd better have a plan to deal with his teeth.' I knew I'd get bitten, and to be honest, I figured it would kill me, but I was wrong. I survived. Your intentions are noble, Chase, but it's not going to make my shoulder hurt any less knowing those guys are in some country club federal prison somewhere sunny and warm."

I gave Tony a chance to spit out whatever was twirling around in his head, and he didn't disappoint. "I look at it this way. Hunter's right. His shoulder is going to hurt for the rest of his life, and there's nothing we can do about that. I'm going to have these headaches and seizures as long as I'm on the planet, but I'm alive, and I have Skipper. What more could a guy want?"

I said, "To not have the headaches and seizures would be one thing. So, does that mean you don't want to make these guys pay for what they did to you?"

Tony gave Hunter a look and said, "No, Hunter's right. We don't want to make 'em pay for what they did to us, but what we do want is to make sure they never do it to anybody else."

I said, "In that case, it sounds like we've reached an objective we can all agree on. Let's rattle their cage and see if we can get their attention."

Skipper said, "Maybe we should take a look at those cages before we rush in to do any rattling."

I spun in my chair to face her station at the console. "You make it sound like you know a few things about their cages. Let's hear it."

Her fingers flew across her keyboard, and soon, images filled the overhead screens. She hovered her mouse over a picture that was clearly taken on the street in DC. "Take a look at this one. It's Richardson and his ex-wife in Georgetown. How many bodyguards can you pick out?"

We squinted and studied the picture.

Hunter said, "I've got three and a possible. The two guys wearing Danners six feet behind him are obvious, and the third is Mr. Cell Phone over there."

"Good eyes," she said. "Now tell me about your possible."

"The jogger. He's not sweating, and his hair is perfect. He may just have begun his run, or maybe he's pretending to be a runner, when in fact, he's a shooter."

"Not bad," Skipper said. "Anybody else?"

I closed one eye and leaned toward the screen. "That's not his ex-wife."

Skipper asked, "How do you know? Until today, you didn't even know his name, and now you sound like you know his ex-wife."

I shook my head. "No, I don't know his ex, but look at *his* left hand. He's wearing a wedding ring, but she's not. No remarried guy would walk that close to his ex-wife. She's half a stride ahead of him, and look at her eyes. She's checking across him. She's leading the security detail, and he's the primary."

Skipper caused the speakers to ring like a slot machine's bell. "Congratulations! We have a winner. I guess that's why you're the boss."

"Used to be the boss," Hunter said.

Skipper smiled and gave him a wink. "You're the one who missed the most obvious bodyguard in the picture, so I think it's safe to say Chase is still the boss."

Chapter 5
Leading the Charge

I'd never been fat before. Having played baseball since I was four years old, and having fought the enemies of freedom for over a decade, fitness had always been an unconscious part of my life. In the previous two years, however, the only weights I lifted were heavily laden forks on their way to my mouth. Ten minutes into day one of Stone W. Hunter's boot camp, it was obvious that was about to change.

The first two hours consisted of alternating wind sprints and swimming laps in the water of the North River that was twenty-five degrees colder than our bodies. Tony never missed a beat, and he thrived in the water, but by the time those hundred twenty minutes were behind us, our rescue swimmer took a knee and crushed his temples beneath the heels of both hands. Everyone noticed.

The instant I knelt beside him, he melted into my arms, so I cupped the back of his neck and laid him on the grass. Singer scooped Hunter's med kit from the dock and sprinted to my side. He had an IV started and an oxygen mask in place in seconds, and I slid the bell of the stethoscope over Tony's chest.

"Breath and heart sounds are normal."

Singer peeled open Tony's eyelids. "Pupils dilated and unresponsive."

I yelled over my shoulder, "Hunter, get an ambulance . . . "

Before I could finish my sentence, Mongo scooped up Tony's limp body and ran for the front of the house. "Somebody get a truck door open!"

Fifteen minutes before an ambulance could've arrived, the whole team was inside Hunter's Suburban and making ninety miles per hour toward the medical center.

Singer pressed his phone between his shoulder and ear. "We're inbound with a twenty-eight-year-old white male with a history of severe concussions. Post-physical exertion, he's nonresponsive, pupils dilated, respiration twelve, and heartrate one oh five. Suspect possible stroke or aneurysm. Large-bore normal saline IV started three minutes ago. Transport is a black Chevy Suburban, and we'll be at the ER in less than five minutes."

A pair of medics in green scrubs met us beneath the portico with a gurney. When they leaned into the back seat of the Suburban to slide Tony onto the waiting bed, Mongo shoved them aside and pulled our unconscious rescue swimmer from the vehicle. I tried to keep pace with the giant while juggling the oxygen bottle and IV bag, but slowing Mongo down isn't an easy task.

"Sir! Put him on the gurney. We'll take it from here."

I'll always believe Mongo heard the medic, but he wasn't interested in wasting another second getting Tony in front of an ER doctor. Inside the hospital, Mongo's size sixteen boot added two oak doors to the bill I'd later pay, but not even magnetic locks and two hundred pounds of wood could stop him.

Our entire team, still dripping wet from the North River swim, stormed through the treatment area of the ER and into a curtained exam room.

As our behemoth of a man gently laid Tony on the bed, he yelled, "Hunter, find a doctor!"

Disco took the IV bag from my shoulder and suspended it on

the curved hook above Tony's head while I pulled the oxygen hose from our bottle and plugged it into the nozzle protruding from the wall behind the bed. I adjusted the flow and repositioned the mask over Tony's mouth and nose.

Hunter slung the curtain back and barged into the exam room with a man in a lab coat thrown across his shoulder. He deposited him beside the bed. "This guy looked like a doctor to me."

The man scanned the room with terror in his eyes. "Who are you people, and what's the meaning of this?"

Mongo, the gentlest man I've ever known, grabbed the doctor by his lapels. "If our friend dies, you're going to wish you had, too."

Apparently, the man didn't need any further encouragement. His stethoscope went into his ears, and his flashlight came out of his pocket. Thirty seconds into the exam, as Mongo briefed the scenario, the doctor peered between us at a nurse and ordered, "Get a head CT and MRI now, and kick anyone who's waiting in line out of the way."

The nurse took command of the scene. "You gentlemen need to wait outside. We'll take care of your friend, but you can't be in here dripping water all over the place."

The doctor stepped around Mongo and headed for the nurses' station, but the big man caught him by the arm. To my surprise, the doctor yanked his arm free from Mongo's vise-like paw and said, "If you want your friend to live, you'll get out of our way and let us do our job." He stormed away and pounded on the counter. "Page Dr. Wilkins, and get him down here now."

Undaunted, Mongo pinned the man to the counter. "Who's Wilkins?"

The doctor squirmed away and shook off the layer of filthy water on his lab coat. "Dr. Wilkins is the on-duty neurosurgeon. If my suspicions are correct, your friend is going to need him inside his head in the next few minutes. The O2 and IV were good ideas, whoever did that, and it's obvious this isn't the first time you guys have dealt with an injury. Are you military?"

Every eye turned to me, and I said, "Something like that. Just keep him alive, and don't worry about the bill."

As if the five of us weren't enough chaos for the young doctor already, Skipper stormed through the broken double doors. "Where is he?"

I turned to intercept her, but she juked around me and sprinted down the corridor behind a pair of orderlies pushing Tony on the gurney.

The doctor yelled, "Ma'am. You can't go with him. You have to wait outside."

She spun on a heel, looking like a furious momma bear, and pointed at Mongo. "You send anybody who wants to stop me to him."

Our monster stepped to the center of the corridor and crossed his arms as the doctor sighed and slowly shook his head. Finally, he looked up and said, "Gentlemen, we can't have this type of behavior inside the ER. Please wait outside, and we'll let you know as soon as we have some test results. Please don't make us call the police."

I pulled out my phone and shoved it toward the doctor. "The chief of police is speed dial three. Give him a call. We'll wait right here."

Suddenly, Tony wasn't the only person in the ER with a massive headache.

The doctor leaned across the counter. "Have someone find some dry clothes for these gentlemen, and make sure radiology knows that lady—whoever she is—is going with the patient. What's his name anyway?"

I spent five minutes filling out the paperwork and providing Tony's identification. When I reached the line asking for next of kin, my heart sank into my gut, and I pulled out my phone.

I dialed, and he answered on the second ring. "What is it, College Boy? Are you calling to quit again?"

"Clark, your brother was working out with us, and he went down. We're in the ER at the medical center now, and they're doing a CT and an MRI. It may be a stroke or an aneurysm. He's unconscious, but his vitals are good. That's all we know right now, but I'll call you back as soon as we know more."

Without a moment's hesitation, Clark said, "I'll be there in an hour. Call the sat-phone as soon as you know anything."

With that, the line went dead.

When I sloshed out of the ER, I found my team changing clothes behind the Suburban. Hunter threw me a pair of jeans and a T-shirt, so I joined the party. Mongo emerged from behind the truck wearing a pair of orange scrub pants that almost fit and a bright yellow T-shirt with a pink heart and "Virginia is for Lovers" stenciled across the chest. The shirt might have fit him when he was twelve, but definitely not twenty-five years later.

He held up a fist. "Don't you say a word . . . Not one word. Irina is on her way down here with some man-size clothes, and until then, you keep your mouth shut."

I choked back the laughter. "I talked to Clark, and he's on his way. Let's get back inside."

Everyone turned to head for the doors except Mongo. He said, "I'll just wait here for Irina, and we'll be in when I get dressed."

I couldn't resist. "Whatever you say, Virginia Slim."

Part of me expected him to lift the Suburban and hurl it at me, but instead, he just turned away.

It had probably only been ten minutes, but it felt like hours by the time a fireplug of a man in University of Alabama scrubs took a knee in front of us. "I'm Dr. Wilkins, the neurosurgeon. They're prepping your friend for surgery. He experienced multiple hemorrhagic aneurysms, and the bleeding is quite severe, but I'll do my best to relieve the pressure and take care of the bleeding. I get the feeling you're not going to leave, so I'm having someone sent down to get you settled in. We have a private waiting room for you. It's going to be a long day."

I asked, "You know about the previous concussion, right?" He nodded. "Yes. A Dr. Shadrack emailed Mr. Johnson's medical records. Don't worry. We'll take good care of him."

His quiet confidence instilled a sense of relief, but that didn't stop me from closing my eyes and talking with God about the coming hours of Tony's life. When I looked up, Singer gave me a knowing smile and a barely perceptible nod.

A young lady appeared minutes later and installed us into a private waiting room outside the surgical suite. By the time we settled in and started our first pot of coffee, Skipper, Mongo, and Irina pushed through the door. I stood and briefed what we knew, and Singer, in his typical style, laced an arm around Skipper and led her outside.

I checked my watch. "I guess I should call Clark, huh?"

Everyone agreed, so I dialed his sat-phone. "They've taken him into surgery. The surgeon said there's bleeding inside his skull, and they have to relieve the pressure and get the bleeding under control. They say it'll be a long surgery, but they put us in a private waiting room, so let me know when you land, and I'll come get you."

He said, "I'll be on the ground in ten minutes."

I put my phone away. "I'm going to pick Clark up from the airport. Does anybody want to come?"

Hunter pulled his keys from his pocket and tossed them to me.

"I guess that's a no, so I'll be back shortly. Does anyone need anything?"

No one spoke up, so I headed for the parking lot. The conversation with God continued on the way to the airport, where I was rewarded with getting to watch Clark make one of the most beautiful landings I've ever seen.

He bounded down the stairs of the King Air. "Anything new?"

"Nothing yet. He's still in surgery."

We tugged the airplane into the hangar and broke every traffic law we could on the way back to the hospital. Skipper and Clark spent a long moment in a hug they both needed.

When they separated, Skipper said, "I called Wanda, and she's on her way."

Clark said, "Yeah, I talked to Mom on the way up. She's worried, but she's tough. You know she'll come in here like a bull in a china shop."

Skipper almost laughed. "Oh, I know. She does everything at full speed."

They stood holding hands in silence until a tear slowly rolled across her cheek. She swallowed hard and whispered, "He's going to be all right, isn't he? I told him not to do it, but he wouldn't listen. It was too much too soon, and he's so stubborn."

Clark wound an arm around her. "All we can do is pray and have faith that everything is going to be all right."

Several pots of coffee and five pizzas later, Dr. Wilkins came into the waiting room looking as if he'd wrestled a gorilla all afternoon, and he immediately had everyone's attention. "It went as well as anyone could hope. There was a lot of bleeding and swelling. He's alive but still in critical condition. We'll keep him in a medically induced coma for a while and keep an eye on the swelling. He's a long way from walking out of here, but somebody saved his life by getting him in here as quickly as they did."

"What does that mean?" Skipper asked. "A medically induced coma? Will he wake up? Is he going to be okay?"

Dr. Wilkins laid a rock-steady hand on her forearm. "We just don't know yet. There was a lot of damage, and it's too early to make predictions. But we're going to watch him very closely, and if anything doesn't look positive, we'll move him to Atlanta or Birmingham."

"Why don't you move him now, just in case it gets worse?" she asked.

"It's not worth the risk associated with transporting him. If he takes a turn for the worse in a helicopter, there's not much we can do. He's much safer here under our observation. Now, if you'll excuse me, I'm going to lie down and get some rest, but I'm not going home. I'll be here until we see how he's doing tomorrow morning. If anything happens, they'll wake me up."

Skipper wilted into a chair, and the tears consumed her.

Clark set his jaw and stared into my soul. "You're down a man. I'm in. We're going to turn those bastards inside out, and I'm leading the charge."

Chapter 6
Standing Vigil

Exactly as everyone expected, Wanda Johnson burst through the waiting room door like the grande dame she was and made a beeline for Clark. He threw out his arms to embrace his mother, but she put a move on him like a Hall of Fame running back and plunged herself into Skipper's waiting embrace. "Where's my baby boy?"

Clark shot me a look, and I shrugged.

Skipper encouraged Wanda onto an oversized seat and nestled beside her. "He's out of surgery, and they're moving him to ICU in a few minutes. The surgeon, Dr. Wilkins, said it went well, but they're going to keep him in a coma while they watch for the swelling to go down."

"When can I see him?"

Skipper patted Wanda's leg. "They may let us see him later, but they're still getting him settled into the ICU. I'm sure they won't let all of us go back there."

"That doesn't matter," Wanda said. "As long as you and I get to see him. He needs to know you and his momma are here."

The perfectly quaffed Southern belle glared up at Clark. "Get over here, Mud Pie, and tell me what happened."

I couldn't believe I'd forgotten Wanda's nickname for her first-born, and it was no time for laughter, but I couldn't contain it.

Disco leaned toward me and whispered, "Did she just call Clark Mud Pie?"

I turned away from the scene to hide my amusement. "I should've briefed you guys, but there's no way to prepare for Wanda Johnson's arrival."

With my composure back in place, I turned to see one of the strongest-willed men on Earth almost cowering beside his mother. "Yes, ma'am. He was working out with the rest of the guys, and he passed out. But they got him here within minutes, and Dr. Wilkins said they probably saved his life."

She huffed and turned back to Skipper. "Now, you listen to me, Elizabeth. It's time for you to get that man under control. You're old enough to know men don't have the good sense to take care of themselves, and they need a good woman to keep them on the straight and narrow. Give me your hand."

Obviously baffled, Skipper offered her right hand, and Wanda slapped it away. "No, girl, not that one. Your left hand."

She took Skipper's hand in hers and raised an eyebrow. "When Little Bit gets out of this mess he's in, we're getting a ring on that finger of yours, and you're gonna put that boy in a harness. He's just like Mud Pie—too stubborn to know what's good for him. And that boy's not long for this world if you don't glue him to the floor."

For the first time in my life, I saw Skipper completely lost for words. I wanted to help, but I was smart enough, even back then, to stay out of that particular china shop.

Clark pushed himself from the chair, but Wanda dug five perfectly manicured nails into his thigh. "Oh, no, you don't. You stay right here with your momma. And speaking of men without good sense, where's your sorry daddy? He's probably laid up in some house of ill repute with girls dancing around him and feeding him grapes. I swear to my soul, that man is gonna be the death of me yet."

Clark resettled on the chair. "I called him, and he's on his way, Momma. Please don't make a scene when he gets here."

She smacked his hand. "When did you get big enough to tell your momma when she can and can't make a scene?"

"You're right, Momma. I'm sorry, but . . ."

She pinched his cheek. "Don't be sorry. Just get your momma a martini from somewhere. Surely this place has a bar."

Wanda turned from her son and leaned toward Skipper. "How's my makeup, Sugar? Do I look all right? You know I can't have that man seeing me not put together."

Skipper smiled. "Wanda, you look like a goddess, and you know it."

"I may need to touch up a little before he gets here. That's all."

A young lady in Winnie the Pooh scrubs pushed through the rear door into the waiting room and scanned our faces. "Hi, I'm Monica, one of the ICU nurses. He's resting, and I can take two of you back to see him, but just for a couple of minutes."

Wanda leapt to her feet with Skipper's hand clenched in hers. "We'll go. I'm his momma, and she's his . . . Well, sweet Tony knows her voice better than anyone else's."

Monica said, "Okay, come with me, but I have to prepare you. His vitals are strong, but he looks worse than he is. He's, of course, on oxygen and a heart monitor, but his head is bandaged, and there's some bruising. Just remember, he's been through a lot. The doctor told you he's in a medically induced coma, right?"

Wanda stepped toward the nurse. "Yes, of course, honey. We've been through it all before. Those boys of mine just can't keep themselves out of the hospital. Now, scoot along and take us to see my Little Bit."

I made another pot of coffee and flipped open a few pizza boxes, but there wasn't a morsel left. By the time Wanda and Skipper returned, the pot was empty, and we were anxious to hear anything.

Skipper pressed her lips into a thin horizontal line, and Wanda dabbed at the corners of her eyes with a tissue.

She cleared her throat and said, "He's a mess, y'all. They've got hoses and pipes stuck all in my baby boy. It's like he's not in there at all. He just looks like a machine. And that smell. Oh my god, it's all just too much."

She collapsed onto a seat, and Clark nestled beside her.

I moved toward Skipper. "What smell is she talking about?"

She shook her head and led me to the other side of the room. "It's just antiseptic. It's that hospital smell. But he does look bad, Chase. I've never seen anybody look so bad."

Her chin fluttered as the tears came, and she pressed herself against me. I wrapped her in my arms and held her.

Through tears and sniffling, she breathed, "Tell me he's gonna live, Chase. Just tell me, even if it's not true."

I helped her to a sofa and held her hands. "I've never seen anybody tougher than Tony. What happened to him in Morocco would've killed any of us, but he held on, Skipper. He's stronger than the rest of us combined. If anybody can survive this, it's Tony Johnson, and you know that as well as I do."

She swallowed and tried to stop the tears. "I know, but it's just . . ."

I slid my hand behind her ear and pulled her against my chest. "He's going to come through this. He's got a thousand prayers going up every minute, and he's in good hands with Dr. Wilkins."

She sobbed, and her body jerked against me. "I love him, Chase. I love him so much."

"And he loves you," I said. "I'm sure he can't wait to wake up so he can see you again."

"I just feel so helpless."

"We all feel that way. But I promise you we'll get the men who are responsible for this, and they'll never hurt anyone else again."

She coughed and choked out the words. "I know we will."

After half an hour of talking and crying with Skipper, I stood from the sofa. "I know everyone wants to stay here and stand vigil, but there's nothing we can do for Tony in this room. We have plenty of space at Bonaventure, so anybody who wants to get some rest is welcome there."

Mongo's Russian wife, Irina, spoke for the first time. "We have also room for anyone to sleep. I do not know what to do in times like this, but I love all of you, and I will do anything you tell to me."

Mongo smiled down at her. "You're gonna make a fine Southern lady."

Irina looked toward Wanda. "Maybe like her?"

"Maybe not exactly like her, but you never know."

She laid her head against his massive chest. "We have Tatiana, but maybe we could have also more babies to call sweet names like Mud Pie. This to me is funny."

Mongo's eyes turned to beach balls. "Uh, I don't. I mean . . ."

Irina kissed his cheek. "I am only playing funny with you. Do not worry. Tatiana is enough."

It wasn't possible to get Skipper, Wanda, and Clark out of the hospital, but the rest of us headed home for some much-needed rest.

* * *

Days ticked by, and Tony showed gradual, consistent improvement. Our renewed determination drove the team into the water every morning for long-distance swims against the tide, and every day, we grew stronger and more driven. Afternoons were consumed by hours upon hours on the firing range and inside the shoot house. We practiced close-quarters battle, room-clearing, and hostage-taking, and we sent tens of thousands of rounds of ammunition downrange.

The training regimen pushed our bodies to their limits and kept our minds from devolving into thoughts of Tony taking a turn for the worse. After every day's dinner, we spent hours in the hospital rotating through our turn to spend a couple of minutes beside our brother's bed, listening to his rhythmic breathing and praying for him to open his eyes.

Dominic Fontana, my first handler and Tony's father, arrived and wouldn't leave the hospital or Wanda's side except to eat and shower. Thankfully, he didn't bring any twenty-year-old Cuban goddesses with him. I feared Wanda may have gone to prison for murder if he had.

* * *

With thirty-four days logged in the river and on the range, the team and I fell into our chairs around the Bonaventure dinner table, and we shoved calories down our throats as if we hadn't eaten in weeks. Our bodies were stronger and faster, and our pants didn't fit anymore.

Hunter downed a glass of tea and said, "I think we're almost ready. Is there anything else you guys want to work on before we mount up?"

I leaned back in my chair. "I agree. We're physically ready, but we have a lot of groundwork to do. We really need Skipper, but I don't know how to ask her to trade the waiting room for the ops center."

Almost before I finished the sentence, my phone chirped. "Speak of the devil." I stuck it to my ear. "Hey, Skipper. We were just talking about—"

She screamed into the phone, "He's awake!"

The table was left uncleared, and we slid into the medical center parking lot on two wheels.

Ignoring the hospital policy, the whole team surrounded Tony's bed as he slowly drew himself from his month-long siesta.

He licked his lips and spoke in a hoarse tone. "I know this isn't Hell 'cause Singer's here. And it can't be Heaven 'cause Mr. Hunter's here. So, I must still be alive."

Skipper grabbed his hand, and the tears poured. "I love you! I love you a thousand times!"

Tony tried to smile. "I know. You've been telling me that every day, but I couldn't make my lips move to say it back. But I love you, too, and I think we should get married."

"What took you so long?" Wanda belted.

He turned his head ever so slightly. "Hey, Momma. Thanks for coming."

"Your daddy's here, too, Little Bit."

Tony took a long breath as if exhausted. "What happened?"

Mongo said, "Hunter tried to kill you."

"Don't make me laugh, big guy. I'm not sure I could handle it."

Skipper said, "You retired. That's what happened. You had a bunch of strokes from running and swimming and doing everything I told you not to do."

"What day is it?"

"It's Wednesday," Skipper said, and Tony squeezed his eyes closed. "So, I've been out for three or four days?"

Skipper giggled. "You've been out for thirty-five days, silly boy. It's April."

"Thirty-five days?" He groaned. "Are you serious?"

Clark reached down for his brother's hand. "Yes, she's serious. You had us all scared to death."

Tony looked up into his brother's eyes and then turned to me. "Did you go without me?"

I shook my head. "Not yet, but now that you're back, you've got some catching up to do."

Skipper slapped my arm. "Oh, no, you don't. You're not getting back in that river ever again."

Tony's eyelids fluttered. "I'm pretty tired, but I love all of you guys." He squeezed Skipper's hand. "Especially you, pretty girl."

Chapter 7
Powdermen

Thankful to have my big-time Hollywood screenwriter wife back home, we spent the day being lazy and enjoying a little quiet time together.

I shucked off my shirt and headed upstairs. "I'm going to get a shower, and then we'll go grab a bite to eat if you'd like."

Penny slid her glasses down her nose and gave me *the look*. "I know Hunter's killing you with his little boot camp program, but I'm liking the results. You're starting to look like that hard-body hottie I fell in love with again."

I shook my head and gave her a flex. "It's hard to hide this much sexy, and you're right—Hunter is determined to kill every one of us. Especially Disco."

She poked out her lip. "Aww . . . poor baby."

My phone chirped before I could retaliate, and I thumbed the button. "This is Chase."

"It's Skipper. You need to get over here."

"Is Tony all right? What's going on?"

"Yes, he's fine. In fact, he may be better than fine, but you've got to see this."

"What is it?"

"Just get over here. I can't describe it."

I said, "I'll be right there, and I'm bringing Penny."

Back on went my shirt, and Penny took my hand as we bounded down the back stairs. Walking hand in hand with Penny along the river had become one of my favorite things, and although that trip was a little faster than most, I enjoyed it just as much.

Skipper met us on the front porch of her new home on the northwest corner of the Bonaventure property. She was watering a collection of hanging ferns. "There you are. What took you so long?"

Penny said, "We decided to walk instead of drive. Your ferns look great."

Skipper pointed with the spout of her watering can. "There's a bird's nest in that one, and it has five or six eggs. I can't wait to see them hatch."

I peered through the partially open door. "You didn't call us over here to show us bird's eggs, did you?"

She set her can on the porch and pushed the door to its stop. "No, and you're never going to believe this. Come with me."

We followed her through the house and into the sunroom, where Tony sat with a blanket over his legs. He pushed himself from his chair when we walked in.

"Don't get up," I said. "We're family."

He continued to rise. "No, I was getting up anyway. The doctors say I need to walk as much as possible. What brings the two of you all the way across the prairie?"

I laughed. "I'm not sure I'd call it a prairie, but Skipper called and said there was something we just had to see."

He rolled his eyes. "She's making a big deal out of nothing. She does that sometimes."

Skipper huffed. "We'll let Chase decide if it's a big deal, and you'll see."

She led us through the house to the corner that had been desig-nated as a breakfast nook. Nobody ever ate breakfast there, so it seemed like a misnomer to me. To my surprise, an artist's easel stood by the window holding a canvas with one of the most beau-tiful paintings I'd ever seen. A pair of massive seventeenth-century warships lay abeam with white smoke roiling from their gunports. Enormous rigging stood on their decks with splinters flying and yardarms crashing down. The orange fire belching from the muz-zles of the cannons looked realistic enough to burn a hole through the canvas.

I stood in awe of the creation, studying its every detail. "Where did you get this? It's magnificent. Who's the artist?"

Skipper was silent, so I turned, expecting an answer. Instead of opening her mouth, she pointed at Tony.

I said, "You bought it?"

Tony reddened in obvious embarrassment. "No, I didn't buy it—"

Skipper cut him off. "No, he didn't buy it. He painted it!"

I gasped. "What? You did this? I didn't know you could paint."

Tony stared at the picture for a moment and shrugged. "Nei-ther did I."

"What do you mean?" I asked.

He pointed at the canvas. "This is the first thing I've ever painted, and to be honest, I don't really remember doing it."

"I'm not tracking," I said. "You've never painted anything be-fore this?"

He shook his head. "No. Well, I mean, we painted the ship con-stantly when I was in the Coast Guard, but I've never painted pic-tures before this one. The doctor told me I should take up a hobby, so I guess this is it."

Penny was speechless and stepped toward the painting. She studied every stroke and whispered, "Wow."

"Yeah, wow is right," I said. "How do you know so much detail about three-hundred-year-old warships?"

"I seriously don't know. It just came out of me. It's kind of freaky when you think about it. I've read a few of Patrick O'Brian's books about Captain Aubrey and Dr. Maturin, but I've never researched old ships. I guess the books just stuck in my head somewhere, and now they're coming out of my hand through a paintbrush."

Penny sighed. "Tony, this is a masterpiece. I mean it. Most painters spend their whole lives dreaming of painting like this. I'm amazed."

Skipper said, "See? I told you." She turned to Penny. "He says he's not going to paint another one because it freaks him out."

Penny's eyes went wide. "Oh, no! That's crazy. You have to keep painting. You've got a real talent, and the world needs to see it."

Skipper stuck her hands to her hips. "I told you. I'm going to the art store in Jacksonville this afternoon, and I'm going to buy every blank canvas they have."

As the women berated Tony for his lack of interest in painting another picture, I pointed toward the corner of his work of art. "What's that little boat supposed to be?"

Tony said, "That's the one thing I do know. That's called a powderman. Apparently, when ships of the line were battling it out, beam to beam, they'd run out of gunpowder if the battle raged on for a long time. These little boats called powdermen would row upwind and take on loads of powder from another ship that wasn't involved in the fight. Then they'd hoist that small sail and run back downwind to deliver the powder."

I studied the small craft. "I had no idea they did that."

Tony chuckled. "Neither do I. I don't know if it's true. I think I mostly made it up, but that's my favorite part of the painting. That little tiny boat with four men aboard can mean the difference between running out of gunpowder or staying in the fight to win it all."

Staying in the fight to win it all. I had no idea that those words would echo through my mind for years to come.

"I want it," I said.

A silence fell over the room.

Penny said, "I don't think I've ever heard you say that before."

Tony smiled. "You want the painting?"

"Yeah, I do. I'll buy it. I don't want you to give it to me, but there's something about that powderman that I love."

He said, "You can have the painting, but remember, I don't think the powderman is real. I don't think they ever really existed. I just made it up."

"That's why I love it. Maybe they're not real, but maybe they were. Maybe the powderman crews were a handful of brave men willing to do whatever was required to win the ultimate battle. Maybe without them, Napoleon would've won."

Tony stared at his masterpiece. "Kinda sounds like some people I know. Maybe we're a powderman crew, Chase. Have you ever thought about that?"

His words washed over me, leaving me ashamed to have stepped off the battlefield some twenty-seven months before. "No, I've never thought about that until this moment, my friend, but you're exactly right. I'll give you a million dollars for the painting."

He laughed. "You're a funny guy, you know that?"

"I'm serious," I said. "You followed me into a hell of our own making, and you came as close to losing your life as any man can. Instead of lying down and quitting like I did, you jumped in that river with us, and you didn't give up. You'll always be part of our team, even though your days in the trenches are over. The million bucks isn't just for the painting. Think of it as a severance package."

"You're firing me?"

I chuckled. "No, you're not fired, but we have to put you on the injured reserve list. You keep painting, and the rest of us powdermen will keep rowing."

I carried Tony's masterpiece back across the path to Bonaventure. Pecan, the nosey quarter horse, ambled along beside us and seemed to stare at the painting with every step.

Penny ran her hand across Pecan's mane. "Give me a leg up. I want to ride."

"You're going to ride that horse without a saddle?"

She giggled. "Yes. I do it all the time. Pecan is the gentlest animal on Earth."

"No, she's not. She's a demon-possessed wild mustang."

"Only when *you* try to ride her. With everybody else, she's a sweetheart. Isn't that right, Pecan? You're a sweetheart."

Careful to keep the painting away from the beast, I offered a cupped hand, and Penny stepped up onto Pecan's bare back. We continued our stroll along the riverside, and the horse never seemed to notice—or care—that Penny was on her back.

* * *

Bud at the framing shop had Tony's painting ensconced in a gorgeous, gilded frame in no time, and the masterpiece found its home above the fireplace in the Bonaventure library. It looked as if the house had been built around it.

As I sat behind my desk, staring into the hypnotic scene inside the frame, a gentle knock at the door yanked me from my trance.

Clark stepped through the door and followed my line of sight to the painting. "Where'd you get that?"

"You wouldn't believe me if I told you."

"Try me."

"Little Bit painted it."

He scoffed. "Seriously, where'd you get it? I like it."

"No kidding. Tony painted it. It's one of those weird things, like when a person can all of a sudden speak a foreign language after getting struck by lightning. Apparently, Tony's a painter now."

Clark studied the work of art and then plopped down into a wingback. "I'm gonna tell you something, but you have to swear it'll never leave this room."

"Sure. What is it?"

"When Mom and Dad got divorced, I was seven or eight. Dad had been gone for a year or more before they officially divorced. During the time Dad was gone, Mom had a really good friend who used to paint, nonstop. He was pretty good, and I think he runs a gallery in New York now. At least he did. Anyway, Tony was born a few months after the divorce was final. I'm not saying Dominic isn't Tony's dad, too, but me and him don't look much alike if you ask me."

I locked his story away, swearing never to let it out. "Have you ever heard of a powderman?"

"No, what's that?"

I knocked my knuckles on the desk. "Let's go to work, and I'll show you."

Chapter 8
Remember That Time . . .

I asked, "Remember that time in Moscow when I almost froze to death?"

Clark pulled up his shirt, exposing the nastiest of his collection of scarred bullet wounds. "Are you talking about the time you got me shot in Comrade Norikov's bedroom on the Moscow River?"

"Yeah, that would be the time. Remember the look in his eyes?"

Clark smiled. "I'd call it terrified disbelief."

I pointed to him. "That would make you correct, my friend. Let's do that again."

He frowned. "You want to fall in the frozen Moscow River in front of the Kremlin again?"

"We weren't in front of the Kremlin. We were miles away from Red Square when I took the plunge. But no, that's not what I want to do ever again. I want to show Wainwright and Richardson exactly what it means to be afraid, just like we did to our old buddy Norikov."

Clark put on the grin only he could do. "Just like your buddy Captain Sprayberry on the *Lori Danielle* says, 'That's a terrible idea . . . What time?'"

* * *

We found Skipper in the ops center with her head and shoulders buried in a wall panel.

I said, "Is everything okay in there?"

She growled and pushed herself from the compartment. "There's a cooling fan that chirps every three seconds, and it's driving me insane."

"Did you fix it?"

She dusted herself off. "We'll see. What do you two want?"

I threw up my hands. "Whoa! Grouchy much?"

"Sorry. I didn't get much sleep, and then the whole squeaking fan thing. Now, what can your analyst do for you today?"

"Much better," I said. "We want to sneak into Richardson's and Wainwright's bedrooms and scare the crap out of them, and we want you to help us pull it off."

Her mood turned on a dime. "Oh, yeah, baby. I'm in. When do you want to do it?"

"As soon as you can get us inside," Clark said.

Skipper pulled latex gloves from her hands and lifted the wall panel back in place. "If that thing squeaks again, I'm putting a bullet through it, so get ready to write a check."

I said, "Hey, I just wrote your boyfriend a check for a million bucks. Take it easy on a guy."

Skipper ducked her chin. "That was really cool of you, Chase. Thank you."

"It wasn't charity. It was an investment. I'll bet I can double my money on that painting in eighteen months."

She laughed. "Yeah, right. Something tells me you'll never part with that painting. It is pretty amazing, right?"

"Definitely. When is he going to start the next one?"

She pulled out her phone, scrolled through her pictures, and handed it to me. "He's done with number two already, and he's starting number three today."

"You've created a monster," I said.

She huffed. "Me? I don't think so. You're the one who convinced him they're worth a million bucks apiece."

Clark cleared his throat. "This is all great and stuff, but we're here to talk about making Wainwright and Richardson wet their beds."

Skipper rolled her seat to her workstation and set the keyboard on fire. Without looking up, she said, "Wainwright is on the left overhead, and Richardson is on the right. Let's start with Wainwright."

She zoomed in on a sprawling mansion surrounded by lush trees on the bend of a river. "He's on the Potomac in McLean, Virginia. Get this. The main house is eighteen thousand square feet and sits on five acres."

"It's no Bonaventure," I said, "but it looks like a nice place. What about security?"

"It's around the clock with a gatekeeper, two roving patrols, a bunch of really nasty-looking dogs, and every inch of the place is covered by monitored cameras. Grand Star Security has the contract, and I'll bet you can't guess who owns Grand Star Security."

"Wainwright?"

"He's one of the major shareholders," she said. "And Richardson is another."

"How convenient," I said. "I'd bet dollars to donuts the Board picks up the tab for the security services."

"And you'd win that bet. To the tune of nine hundred grand a year."

Clark let out a low whistle. "We're in the wrong business."

"Don't wander off," she said. "Stay focused. We've got a lot to go over, and I don't want to lose you."

"Can you get into the camera system?" I asked.

"Probably, but I want to make sure I don't spook them by probing around and setting off alarms. We don't need them beefing up security before we get there."

I said, "I agree. Be gentle, but see what you can do. We'll need to control the cameras, at least, and you're not going to like my next idea."

"You never know," she said. "Let's hear it."

"I want to hit both properties simultaneously."

It was Skipper's turn to whistle. "You don't want much, do you?"

"It's the only way. If we hit either of them first, the other will pile on security and maybe even leave the country."

"What are you planning to do when you get in there?"

"I don't know yet, but I'm leaning toward making them believe in ghosts."

"You're not going to kill them, are you?"

"No. If we do that, we're no better than they are, but I *am* planning to make them *wish* they were dead."

She panned around the property so Clark and I could get an idea of what we'd be facing when we went in. I studied every inch of the satellite imagery.

Skipper said, "Look at that. I just found their soft spot. It looks like good ol' Malcolm Wainwright doesn't believe the river is a vulnerability."

I leaned in close to the screen and smiled. "He spent all that money to build a three-sided wall. Of all people, he should've known the waterline was his weakest link even before building the fence."

Clark played with his toothpick. "What was it that Sunny-Side-Up guy said? Never interrupt your enemy when he's screwing up?"

I shook my head. "I'm pretty sure you mean Sun Tzu, and I'm definitely not planning to talk Wainwright into building a fourth wall."

Clark snapped his fingers. "Yeah, that's the guy. Smart dude. Do you think he's still alive?"

I palmed my forehead. "He was born in five-forty-four B.C."

Clark closed one eye and shot the other toward the ceiling. "So . . . probably not still alive, huh?"

"No. Probably not."

Skipper clapped her hands. "Boys! Focus! You two are the experts, but based on the fencing and layout, it looks like an amphibious assault from the Potomac is the way in. Do you agree?"

"Maybe," I said. "It depends on how deeply you can get inside the camera and alarm network."

She sighed. "Ah, the alarms. I'm glad you brought that up. Unless the plans for the system magically fall from the sky and land on my lap, there's no way to know what kind of alarm system is installed. With the number of full-time guards on the property, it's possible the alarm system is a LAN."

I held up a hand. "A LAN?"

"Yeah, a local area network. It may not leave the property. That's the best option. If the signal isn't monitored off-site, that makes my job a breeze. I'm sure I can cripple the cameras long enough for you to get in, but the egress might be tricky."

I ran a hand through my hair. "I agree. As soon as we wake up our sleeping beauties, we're blown. We'll have the upper hand the whole time, right up to the moment we run. After that, it's a footrace, and we'll need a better plan than a pair of rubber boats."

"How about the RHIB from *Aegis*?"

"That could work, but we need two of them. Each infiltration has to be independent of the other. If we only have one boat as an exfil plan, there's too much that can go wrong."

Clark clicked his tongue against his teeth. "Do we have to hit both houses at exactly the same time?"

I spun to face him. "What's going on in that head of yours?"

"I'm just thinking, but we might be able to share a ride out of there. How far apart are the properties?"

Skipper combined the two maps into one and brought up a measuring tool. "It's just a few miles, and of course the current flows south, but it's a slow current, usually less than two knots, unless it's one of those freaky times when the moon pulls harder than usual."

"Lay it out for us, Clark."

He slid a pad of paper in front of him and drew the course of the Potomac River. "If we hit the upstream house first and it takes us twenty minutes to get in, do our dirty work, and get out, we could hit the waiting RHIB and run downstream to drop off the second team to assault the McLean house."

"That's still just one boat," Skipper said. "And remember, one is none, and two is one."

I leaned back in my chair. "We've got two RHIBs. Remember, we commandeered the SEALs' boat from the Moroccan mission."

Clark grinned. "Where is it?"

I motioned with my chin toward the river. "It's in the boathouse, but it needs some love before we throw it into a fight. I'll get Earl on it."

"If we do this thing right," Clark said, "it won't be a fight. We'll get in, get nasty, and get out."

Skipper cleared her throat. "Excuse me, boys. While you two are having your little pep rally, we've—let me rephrase that—I've got a lot of work to do to get you through the wall."

I glanced back up at the map overlays. "How deep is the river at the Great Falls property?"

Skipper let her fingers dance across the keys. "It's a rocky shoreline, and it looks like it's ten to fifteen feet deep a few feet off the rocks. What are you thinking?"

I tapped Clark's shin with my prosthetic. "Remember that time in Panama—"

He raised a finger. "Do you mean that time we sank a Chinese spy ship in the Miraflores Locks?"

"Oh, yeah. That's the one. We need to make a sacrifice."

"Not the RHIB," he said.

"No, not the RHIB. We'll find something a little less valuable to send onto the rocks."

Skipper nodded slowly. "I like it. I can put a drone over the river and watch the commotion."

I said, "I've got some ideas for harassing them a little over the next few days. With any luck, we can make them question the authenticity of an alarm from the river."

"Perfect," Skipper said. "While you're messing with that, I'll find a way into their network so we can see what they see."

I played with an ink pen, and Clark said, "There's something you don't like. What is it, College Boy?"

I took a long, full breath and let it escape. "I don't know if I want you on the ground for this one."

He immediately dropped his chin and raised both eyebrows. "Come again?"

I let my eyes meet his. "No disrespect, but you're busted up, and I think it's a little too close—Tony being your brother, I mean."

He leaned back and seemed to be doing everything in his power to avoid exploding. "I'm too close? Really? You shot your own brother in the face. Were you too close? Should I have kept you away from that mission?"

"No, and here's why. I wasn't embarking on a mission with ten pounds of screws and steel rods in my back. There's a better-than-good chance that we're going to end up in a fistfight, if not a gun-fight, and I don't want the wounds that nearly killed you on the Khyber Pass to come back to haunt you."

He huffed. "I've been working my butt off right beside you for a month, doing everything you've done—every step, every swim, every shot, everything—and you still doubt my ability to stay in the fight. Is that what you're saying?"

There was never a good time for the conversation, but I had jumped into the shark-infested pool, so swimming to the other side was my only option. I just hoped I could do it without turning into chum.

"No, Clark. That's not what I'm saying. We are going to be armed trespassers breaking into the house of not one, but two extremely wealthy and powerful men. There will be a fight, and it might be a gunfight. If you go down, I'll carry you out of there no matter what the cost."

"And I'll do the same for you. So, what's the difference?"

I stilled myself. "The difference is simple. I'm going in there to hopefully stop a man from putting any more teams like ours in jeopardy for a personal vendetta. And you'd be going in there to make a man pay for what he did to your brother. You know what they say about digging two graves before setting out on a quest for revenge."

"No, I don't know what they say about that, but I want you to be wrong."

I leaned toward him and laid a hand on his forearm. "Listen to me, my old friend. I'll make them pay. I promise you that, but my first priority has to be protecting the other operators under their thumb. That's gotta come first."

He threw his feet onto the conference table. "It sucks, doesn't it?"

"What does?"

Clark examined his wilted toothpick. "Being in charge."

I added one real foot and one robot to the table beside Clark's boots. "Yeah, it sucks. But not as bad as being fired by your subordinate, huh?"

Chapter 9
How We Did It in the Coast Guard

"Let's get 'em up here," I said.

With the behind-the-scenes groundwork laid between Skipper, Clark, and me, it was time to call the team into the huddle and brief the plan. There was only one thing missing . . . our new guy.

Since we'd been out of the game of taking fire and shooting back for over two years, the team was still a little rough around the edges and not the polished, tier-one team of operators we'd once been. It took twenty minutes to assemble the team in the ops center—a task that should've taken less than a third of that time.

"Now that everybody's finally here, let me start by saying the mission we discussed earlier is now a definite go."

Although our table wasn't round, the warriors in the seats were knights of the highest caliber. Just like at King Arthur's table, every swordsman's opinion carried weight, but when the sun set on a mission, I carried the full weight of our failures and credited the team for our victories.

I laid a pen on a legal pad and slid it down the table to our Coast Guard contingent. "Since you decided to call in sick, you don't get to vote, but you do get to make a list of things I forget to brief, so let us know if you need more paper."

He rolled his eyes. "Yep, that's me, ole Sick Day Johnson. How many of you guys would come back to work after getting blown up, nearly drowned, and spending a month in a coma?"

I eyed my team, and one by one, every man except me raised his hand. Instead, I shucked off my boot and held up my prosthetic foot.

Tony sighed. "Okay, I get it. Thanks for still letting me sit at the grown-ups' table."

"That's enough nonsense," I said. "Let's get to work. Our boys, Wainwright and Richardson, live only a few miles apart in matching palatial estates on the Potomac. Both have a three-sided perimeter fence facing the water. They both have roving guards and . . ."

Skipper slapped her console and declared, "I did it. I'm in."

The attention that had been focused on my briefing shifted instantly to the analyst, and she said, "Check out monitors one, two, and three."

The screens filled with live video feeds from one of the two compounds.

"Which one is that?" I asked.

Skipper checked her watch and made a couple of handwritten notes on her pad. "It's Wainwrights, but I'm in Richardson's as well. They were nice enough to give me a piggyback ride right into their camera system."

I said, "Break that down for the rest of us who aren't smart enough to understand what a piggyback ride means."

"It's simple," she said. "The camera system conducts a self-test every twelve minutes. The system is programmed to allow the test to run unimpeded. That means it doesn't do anything to stop the automatic test from taking full control of the network five times every hour. So, here's the cool part, I attached a bot to the self-test algorithm, giving us unrestricted access to the cameras for about ninety seconds every twelve minutes. Simple math tells us that I have full access to everything those cameras see for seven and a half minutes of every hour."

"That does sound cool," I said. "But what good does seven and a half minutes do us?"

Skipper huffed, and Mongo came to her rescue. "It's brilliant and simple, Chase. Skipper can grab that four hundred fifty seconds of video every hour of every day until we hit the compound. By then, she'll have a nice collection of exactly how the property should look every twelve minutes around the clock. With a little video splicing and editing, she can feed that video back to the cameras and make the guards monitoring the video believe they're seeing real-time video when, in fact, they're watching pieced-together reruns."

I frowned at our giant. "How do you know this stuff?"

He glared back at me. "How do you *not* know this stuff?"

Skipper said, "That's enough, boys. Mongo is partially right. Replaying video back to the cameras might work, but there's a lot that can go wrong with it. The most valuable thing those seven minutes of access every hour gives me is the ability to roam around inside the software until I find the source code that turns off the camera system's self-defense mode. With enough time, I'll find the code, write a virus that will leave the camera system open any time I want, and just like that, I'll have twenty-four-three-sixty-five access to the cameras."

Hunter scratched his temple. "What good does it do for us to have control of the cameras? It's not like you can turn them off when we hit the property. If you do that, the guards will lose their minds."

Skipper nodded. "You're right, of course, but fortunately for us, we'll run this operation in the dark."

Hunter frowned. "Darkness doesn't matter if the cameras are

infrared or thermal imaging. We'll be on night-vision nods, so surely their cameras have at least some low-light capabilities."

Skipper said, "Good. You're thinking and paying attention. The difference between you and me is a matter of perspective. You see nods as a way to see in the dark, but I see night vision as an opportunity for exploitation. Every night-vision system has its own unique set of strengths and weaknesses. Those cameras absolutely have the ability to see in the dark. I'm already collecting data from the cameras, and once it gets dark, I'll be able to tell if they're using active infrared or passive."

I stuck a finger in the air. "Do we really need to understand the science of how the cameras see in the dark? It feels like we're getting pretty deep in the weeds."

Skipper spun from her console. "Yes, you absolutely need to understand the science. Your night-vision goggles are active infrared. They shine a short-wavelength IR light ahead of you, capture the energy that returns, and digitally create an image inside the nods. That happens about a thousand times every second, so it's seamless from your perspective, but not to the microprocessors that are working their butts off to turn the reflected energy into something the human eye can identify."

"I get that part," Hunter said. "Obviously, the cameras are going to be able to see the IR light emitted by our nods, so that'll make us light up like Christmas trees. What do we do about that?"

Skipper said, "Hold on to your shorts. I wasn't finished. True thermal imaging is an entirely passive system, meaning it does not emit an IR beam of any kind. It simply receives infrared energy, but only in mid or long wavelengths. They do not detect reflected light. All they can see is heat energy. Obviously, the images produced from the passive systems have very little detail. The guard dogs will appear as bouncing white blobs of heat, while a snake would blend into the ground temperature and be invisible to the cameras."

Hunter said, "Got it. So, all we need to do is crawl in on our bellies like snakes."

I ignored him and asked, "What if they've got both?"

Skipper lowered her head. "That's what I'm afraid of."

Clark spoke up. "We'll burn that bridge when we come to it. For now, let's assume we can get past the cameras and make entry without getting ourselves shot or arrested. Brief the contact, Chase."

Skipper jumped in. "Wait. Before you do that, don't worry about getting past the cameras. I'll make that happen, no matter what it takes."

I gave her a nod. "We know you will, and we're glad you're on our team."

Tony said, "I can tell you how we did it in the Coast Guard."

Almost before he could finish his sentence, everyone in the room—except Skipper—called out, "We don't care!"

Our Coastie threw up his hands. "It's nice to know you still love me."

I gave the table a knuckle rap. "Seriously, Tony. Get with Skipper when we're done here and see what the two of you can come up with."

I turned to our analyst. "If Tony bothers you, you have my permission to kick him out."

Skipper giggled. "That's cute, but I don't need your permission to kick him out of *my* ops center."

Well scolded, I turned back to the team. "We're getting ahead of ourselves, so let's talk about the overall big picture. Our goal is to get Wainwright and Richardson to tremble in their thousand-dollar loafers. When we get in—and we will get in—we're going to flood their brains with speed and violence of action. Make it dynamic—loud, hard, and fast. What we say isn't as important as how we say it, but the last thing they hear has to be crystal clear: You screwed up, and you're going to pay."

I paused as my message sank into the rock-hard heads around the table. "Forty-five seconds or less. From the time you yank them from their sleep until you're out the door has to be less than forty-five seconds. No exceptions!"

Disco asked, "How far is it from the house to the waterline?"

Skipper shot a look across her shoulder. "One hundred forty-five feet at Wainwright's place and two hundred feet at Richardson's."

Our pilot nodded. "Even in full battle rattle, we can cover those distances in less than thirty seconds."

"You're right," I said. "But we're not going in kitted up. We'll be as slick as possible. No rifles. Small arms only, a pair of flashbangs on each man, and face coverings."

"No body armor?" Singer asked.

"That's yet to be determined. When we get a peek at how the guards operate, we'll know if they're a ballistic threat. I'm sure at least some of them are well-armed, but we'll make that determination as soon as we have some good footage."

With every glance, our Southern Baptist sniper exuded wisdom, and that moment was no exception. He bit his lower lip. "Why wouldn't we armor up?"

"Speed and freedom of movement," I said.

He never looked away. "Guys with bullets stuck in their body armor are still free to move with speed, but bullet holes in our chests make it challenging."

I silently wondered if the day would ever come when I didn't learn something from Singer.

I gave him the deferential nod I only use with him. "Body armor is available for anyone who wants it. Kit up as you see fit. Hunter and I will hit Richardson, and Singer and Mongo get Wainwright."

Tony looked up. "I thought Clark was . . ."

His brother said, "You're the one with a traumatic brain injury. What you think has very little to do with reality."

The Coastie shrugged. "Okay, I guess that's fair."

I continued. "We'll kayak in from upstream, hit the property, and get out. Mongo, Singer, and a player to be named later, will scoop us up in a RHIB and head downstream toward Wainwright's property. Along the way, we'll recover the kayak and repeat the performance downstream. We'll be wet and cold, so we'll change roles south of Great Falls and get into some dry gear aboard the RHIB. Any questions so far?"

Disco looked up. "Just one RHIB?"

I shot him with my thumb and forefinger pistol. "Look at you, thinking like a commando. I'm so proud, and the answer is no. Remember, when it comes to gear in combat, two is one and one is none. If the RHIB wets the bed in the middle of the mission, we're dead in the water, and I'm not willing to take that risk. You and Clark will loiter upstream in a distant trail with the second RHIB. If everything goes perfectly, we'll never need you, but when was the last time an operation went perfectly?"

Tony said, "What about me? Just because I can't fight doesn't mean I can't run a boat."

Skipper dug a heel into the carpet beneath her chair and spun to face the man she loved. She pulled her cell phone from her pocket and threw it onto the table in front of him. "Get your mother on the phone. When you talk her into saying yes, I'll say yes."

He flicked the phone back across the table and shrank into his chair.

As much as I wanted to feel sorry for Tony, my desire to laugh was stronger. "Okay, so that means Tony is out, unless somebody else wants to call Wanda."

No one volunteered, especially not Clark, and I continued. "Final exfil point to be determined. We'll study some terrain and find a nice, lonely boat ramp where we can recover the RHIBs and hit the road. If it becomes necessary to scuttle the boat and swim out, we have to be willing to sacrifice the machine to get us out of the fire. We can't let the Board know we're in DC. That brings up another good point. Just how embedded is the Board in our lives, Clark?"

Our handler swallowed hard. "We have to go shopping."

Chapter 10
Eight-Hundred-Pound Ugly Duckling

The meeting broke, and I took Clark by the arm. "Follow me."

I suspect he knew what was coming, but instead of putting up a fight, he dutifully fell in line behind me. Strolling along the riverside with Clark wasn't as much fun as it was with Penny, but conversing without prying ears was the order of the day.

"You didn't directly answer my question up there."

He nodded. "I know, and you'll soon understand why."

"I think I already know, and I don't like it. Is our ops center bugged?"

He picked up a smooth stone and skipped it across the surface of the water. "No, but some other assets are."

"Which assets?"

He pointed downstream toward the Bonaventure dock. "The boats, for starters."

I stopped in my tracks. "Are they wired for sound or just GPS location?"

"Just location."

"How about the airplanes?" I asked.

"The Citation is clean, but it's easy enough to track just by the tail number. It's likely the Caravan is tracked because it was a company asset before you bought it from my dad."

"I thought so. How about our satellite comms?"

He sighed. "They're likely tracked and recorded. Short of buying our own, there's no way around that."

"Why didn't you tell me any of this before today?"

He spat into the edge of the river and kicked a clump of dirt down the slope. "Because I believed we could trust the Board."

I took a seat in the grass, and he did the same. "Is there any oversight for those guys?"

Clark pulled out his pocketknife and carved smooth shavings from a stick. "Yes, but neither of us has the clearance to know who they are. I suspect it's the chairman of the Joint Chiefs, the national security advisor, maybe the director of Central Intelligence, and the president. I could be wrong about all of them. Maybe it's just the president."

I considered his honesty. "How long has the Board existed?"

He pointed the tip of his blade toward me. "You always know the right questions to ask. Do they teach you that sort of thing in college?"

I shook my head. "Nah. They didn't teach me much of anything in college. The things that really seem to matter are the things I learn from Singer, Penny, and you."

He stuck the carved piece of wood into the corner of his mouth. "I ran out of stuff to teach you years ago, kid. We've come a long way together, haven't we?"

"How does it all end?"

He examined the stick. "Who knows? I thought I'd end up in a pine box a long time ago with a green beret carved on a chunk of marble above my decaying corpse."

"Subtlety's not your thing, is it?"

"We had this chat a hundred years ago. You're the surgeon. I'm the freight train on Main Street. If you can find a door I've not kicked down, let me know, and I'll add it to my to-do list."

"Is this going to work?" I asked.

"I'm not going dance around the eight-hundred-pound ugly duckling in the room."

I threw up a hand. "Wait! Please promise me that if I can find an eight-hundred-pound ugly duckling, you'll dance with it."

He furrowed his brow. "Come to think of it, that saying has never made much sense to me, either. Anyway, guys like us don't get our pictures on Wilford Brimley's weather report."

I clamped my eyes closed and begged the universe for help with that one. "Please tell me what that's supposed to mean."

He gave me a shove. "Come on, College Boy. You know what I'm talking about. That Wilford Brimley cat on TV every morning who shows pictures of folks who are a hundred years old. And then he does the jelly commercials."

"I'm starting to believe you're the brother with the traumatic brain injury. You obviously meant Willard Scott. Wilford Brimley was the Quaker Oats guy with the paintbrush mustache. I'll admit I have no idea what you're talking about, but you must be trying to make some sort of point about none of us living to see a hundred years old."

He snapped his fingers. "I knew you'd catch up. We die young, and somebody even younger steps into our boots. It's the way of our world. We're picking a fight with a pair of mighty big ugly ducklings, my friend. It's probably not going to work, and we'll end up with bullets in our heads, but that's the difference between men of honor and those cake-eaters in DC. We do the right thing because it's the right thing to do, no matter what it costs us. We're a rare breed, Chase Fulton, and there's fewer and fewer of us every day."

I watched the lines around his eyes deepen with every word. "I didn't mean for this to turn into whatever it's become. I brought you out here so I could yell at you for not telling me that our gear and facilities are bugged."

"You can yell at me if it'll make you feel better," he said. "But it's not going to fix anything. By the way, Thomas Jefferson was a founding father."

I shook my head. "Thanks for that tidbit, but everybody knows Jefferson was a founding father. He signed the Declaration of Independence."

Clark stood and dusted off his pants. "Not a founding father of the country . . . A founding father of the Board."

I looked up at my old friend. "I'm about to start a pissing match with a two-hundred-fifty-year-old, eight-hundred-pound ugly duckling."

"Yep, you sure are. And I'm gonna help." He offered me a hand and pulled me to my feet. "We've got some shopping to do."

Over the next six hours, we spent more money than most people earn in a lifetime, and our asset list grew accordingly. We bought two F-350 dually trucks, a pair of matching enclosed trailers, a satellite communication system with encryption that would make the Navy SEALs envious, an armada of drones, and fifty-thousand dollars' worth of stainless steel. We added a pair of Glock 17s for every teammate, including Tony, and a nice stack of towels to dry the Potomac River from our skin just in case we survived our little adventure in one of the most corrupt cities on the planet.

Cajun Kenny LePine answered the phone instead of the world's best diesel mechanic. "You-whee! Dis here be Kenny. Who dis be?"

Kenny was the only person in my life who was harder to understand than Clark. "Hey, Kenny. It's Chase."

"Howdy, you. How you been, you? Is dat 'lectric foot of your'n still ticking like da ol' clock, her?"

"The foot's just fine, Kenny. Thanks for asking. Could I speak with—"

He made a sound that had never been a word in any language then asked, "How 'bout dat dere boy? How he be? Da one with all dem smarts and got knocked clean out. Ol' Kenny used to mess 'round wiff one o' dem nursing girls up dere at da medical center. You know da one. Dat great big-un wiff dem toofers. And she told ol' Kenny, me, said one dem boys from out at dat dere pecan plantation done got all busted up and his head turned all inside up, she did. How dat boy is?"

I'm almost certain part of my left eye melted and dripped from its socket. "Kenny, I don't understand the question . . . if there was a question somewhere in that mess."

He laughed like a hyena. "You sho-nuff is one funny fella, you. You knows I be talkin' 'bout dat boy what use be in da Cose Guard. Timmy or Tommy or sompin' wiff some tees and some kinda soft letter at da back of his front name, him."

I found part of a second when he wasn't making mouth noises, so I jumped in. "That's Tony, and he's doing fine. I'll tell him you asked about him. It's been great talking with you, Kenny, but I really need to talk to Earl."

"Fo' you go talkin' wiff my fine girl, her, you got any work need doin'? I gots me a whole crew o' men needin' some dirt to scratch at and move 'round."

I suddenly wanted Skipper's supercomputer to help translate that for me, but I pieced it together. "Come to think of it, I do need a little earthwork done. Penny wants a corral where she can train her horses. Do you know anything about building corrals?"

Almost before I finished asking, Kenny said, "Whooh! You be knowin' ol' Kenny know e'reting dey is to be knowin' 'bout scratchin' out dem places for dem big ol' animals to be playin', me."

Believing all of that meant yes, I said, "Give Penny a call, and she'll tell you what she wants. It doesn't matter what it costs. Just make her happy."

"Ol' Kenny be doin' dat right now, me garohntees, me. Bye now."

And with that, the line went dead.

I stood staring down at my phone, and Clark said, "What was that all about?"

"I think I just gave Kenny a job, but I'm not sure."

"I thought you were calling Earl."

"I was, but Kenny answered, and my brain lost everything it knows about language."

Clark laughed. "Maybe you should call her back."

I sent my thumb toward the redial button the same instant the phone chirped. "Hello, this is Chase."

One of my favorite humans and the best diesel mechanic alive was on the other end of the line. "Hey there, Baby Boy. My sexy Cajun king told me you need me. What did you break now?"

"Hey, Earl. I'm still learning how to communicate with your man, so he and I may have some sort of verbal contract right now, but I'm not sure."

She said, "If you think he's hard to understand, you should hear me try to make a sentence when that man of mine does that thing with his . . ."

"No, Earl! Stop! I don't need that in my head. What I do need is for you to build me a pair of enclosed boat trailers. I bought the two trailers and a bunch of stainless steel. Do you think you could work me into your schedule?"

"Sure, I can, Stud Muffin. All I need is a tape measure, the boat, and a torch."

"Fortunately, I have all three of those things. In fact, it's two boats. And that reminds me. While you're at it, I need you to get the RHIB that we got from the SEALs in tip-top condition."

She said, "I'll be there as soon as I get enough feeling back in my legs to walk. You see, me and Kenny were—"

I crushed the end button before she could finish whatever she was about to describe.

Clark said, "That sounded weirder than the conversation with Kenny. Is she going to build the trailers for us?"

"She said she'd be over soon."

Earl kept her word and arrived half an hour later. She studied the enclosed trailers and scratched her chin. "Tell me again what it is you want me to build."

"I want to use these two enclosed trailers as boat trailers for the two RHIBs, but I don't want them to look like boat trailers from the outside."

She lowered her chin. "You're going back to work, ain't you, Baby Boy?"

"We are," I admitted. "And we need to deliver and recover the RHIBs without anyone knowing we're hauling boats."

She closed one eye and studied the trailers. "Yeah, I can do that, but I'll need to rewire and seal the light and brake circuits. They're not built to be underwater. It'll probably take me three or four days for the first one, but the second one will be pretty quick after I learn on the first one."

"Great," I said. "Get to work, and let me know what I owe you."

She grinned. "If all you boys will take off your shirts and go running by the shop all hot and sweaty every thirty minutes so Momma can look up and watch the show, that'll be plenty of payment for me."

I put on my offended look. "We're a lot more than pieces of meat, Earl. We do have minds and feelings, you know."

She cackled like a witch stirring her brew. "Yeah, you just keep thinking that, but wear them tight little shorts when you run by, will you?"

An hour later, a bulldozer, a motor grader, and a survey crew were hard at work near Penny's horse barn, and Earl had the torch spitting fire like a furious dragon.

Chapter 11
The House That Built Us

Just for laughs, we tugged on the smallest, tightest shorts we could find and gave Earl a show, but not exactly the one she requested. Instead of a run by the shop door, the whole team climbed atop the trailer she had positioned inside the garage and waited for her to return from lunch. When she came through the door and flipped on the lights, the six of us leapt to our feet and broke into our rendition of YMCA. She watched, laughed, and fanned herself with her welding helmet. When the show was over, she pulled out half a dozen bills from her pocket and threw them toward us. "You boys sure know how to make a girl swoon. I think I need a cigarette and a nap after a show like that."

We climbed down, gave Earl a hug, and I said, "Don't you tell our boss about this. We need our day jobs, so we can't afford to get fired for sexual harassment in the workplace."

She slipped her helmet on and adjusted the strap. "Don't worry, boys. Momma won't be reporting no sexual harassment. But I will be grading it, and you boys get the highest marks I can give out."

We hit the trail for another five-mile run. Our times were improving nicely, and our lungs were back in fighting shape. Confident in our conditioning, we gave our bodies a couple of days off from the torture of running, swimming, lifting, and hand-to-hand combat drills. In place of the strength and fitness training regimen, we doubled our firearms, close-quarters battle, and breaching training. I hoped we wouldn't have to pull a single trigger on the coming mission, but hope is not a plan, and luck is not a strategy. Being prepared for the worst was our only option.

* * *

With less than thirty-six hours to go before our planned launch, Mother Nature handed us an unexpected—and in my opinion—terrible surprise.

Mongo strolled into the kitchen with his phone in hand. "Have you seen the weather prophecy?"

"Yeah, I saw it, and as much as I hate to do it, it looks like we'll have to move the mission back until the storms pass."

He looked confused. "What are you talking about?"

"The storms," I said. "They're going to be nasty in DC. We can't pull off an operation this complex in weather like that."

He leaned forward and stared into my head. "Are you insane?"

I leaned back. "Sometimes, but what am I missing?"

He held up his phone and shook it. "This is perfect weather for our op. It couldn't be any better. Everything in the environment will be rain-soaked and exactly the same temperature . . . including our clothes and gear."

I palmed my forehead. "Why didn't I think about that? You're right. Where's Skipper?"

He motioned upward with his head. "She's in her lair. Where else?"

He and I pushed through the ops center door to find Skipper with Doppler weather radar on every screen.

Her eyes lit up as soon as the door closed behind us. "Have you seen this?"

I said, "Oh, yeah. We were just talking about it downstairs."

She grinned. "It's like God is on our team all of a sudden. This is perfect. I've got full control of the cameras at both properties, and a liquid environment solves all our problems. You guys *are* ready to roll, right?"

"We are. Earl finished the second trailer this morning, and both RHIBs are nestled in their first-class seats for the trip to DC."

She pulled a pencil from the pile of hair stacked on top of her head and turned back to her console. Mongo and I stood there watching as if she were about to produce some morsel of analytical brilliance, but instead, she shot a glaring look across her shoulder. "So, why are you still here? Go to work!"

Forty-five minutes later, the new trucks, trailers, RHIBs, gear, and commandos were headed north on Interstate 95. Our first fuel stop near Fayetteville, North Carolina, turned into more than just a gas-and-go. After spending a hundred bucks on snacks and drinks to feed the troops, I pushed through the door of the gas station to find my team standing shoulder to shoulder and peering to the northwest.

I deposited my loot into both trucks and ambled over to see what had their attention. "What's going on, guys?"

Singer pointed across the interstate. "Clark, Mongo, and I were just paying a little homage to the house that built us."

I followed his finger, but nothing jumped out at me. "Forgive me, but I don't know what you're talking about."

Clark slapped me on the back. "That's because you were a draft dodger, College Boy. If you took off walking that way for about ten miles, you'd stumble onto Fort Bragg, home of the Eighteenth Airborne Corps and First Special Forces Command Airborne. That's where we first donned our green berets while you were chasing cheerleaders and playing with your little bats and balls."

The good-natured ribbing was part of the relationship we shared, but for the entirety of my life, I would always feel a thin green line between myself and the men who stepped out of their uniforms to fall in beside me in serving what we believed to be the greater good.

I gave Clark's shoulder a squeeze. "You've got it all wrong. Baseball players don't chase cheerleaders. Cheerleaders chase us."

We moved to remount our vehicles, and Clark stopped short of his truck. "Hey, Chase. Look back there."

I stepped beside him and followed his line of sight. "What is it? It looks like an abandoned parking lot to me."

"Me, too," he said. "And that's exactly what we need for a few minutes. Let's take advantage of the solitude and make our trailers invisible."

We pulled behind the station to the back of an enormous gravel parking area spotted with a few abandoned cargo trailers and the remains of a truck or two. Fifteen minutes later, our cloaking devices were solidly in place, and we stood back to examine our work.

The four-foot-tall U.S. Environmental Protection Agency seals on each side of our trailers stood out like flashing beacons in the rest of the world, but once we crossed the Potomac into our nation's capital, the government placards would make the trailers virtually invisible. Nobody would give a pair of EPA trailers a second look inside the beltway, and that's exactly the camouflage we needed.

Our little convoy pulled into the driveway of the house Skipper rented for us, and the place couldn't have been more perfect. Hundred-year-old oaks stood as a natural barrier between the house and the rest of the world. The Sycamore Island property was nestled beautifully on the banks of the Potomac, directly across the river from the Central Intelligence Agency compound in Langley. Something about that made me smile. My team and I were thirty-six hours away from conducting a pair of clandestine midnight raids against a duo of men whose egos had outgrown their respect for freedom, and we'd pull off the whole operation, quite literally, under the nose of the premier intelligence service on Earth.

The team explored the property for telltale signs of surveillance and discovered nothing nefarious. The house proved to be comfortable and roomy, but we wouldn't be there long enough to enjoy the stay.

With our bladders empty and our coffee cups filled, I said, "This is it, guys. If you're having second thoughts, now's the time to speak up."

The ridiculous notion of one of my teammates backing out at the last minute made everyone chuckle.

"Okay. Don't say I didn't give you a chance to be a coward. Let's make a recon run."

Earl's craftsmanship with the enclosed boat trailers made launching our RHIBs a simple task. We practiced a couple of hasty recovery runs to make sure we could get the boats back into the trailers in seconds, and the loading proved to be just as easy as the launching. With the RHIBs in the river and our pair of EPA trailers nestled against the tree line, we pointed our bows to the north and made our first reconnaissance pass up the river.

The river was shallower than I expected, making speed our only option. With the boats running above thirty knots, the propellers and hulls rested less than a foot below the surface of the water, giving us the benefit of likely being the fastest boats on the shallow river, and speed would prove to be our greatest ally.

I motioned toward the west bank of the river. "There she is, boys. Welcome to Malcolm Wainwright's humble abode."

Hunter let out a whistle. "That's some kind of place. I'm really looking forward to disturbing a little peace over there tomorrow night."

Singer uncased the smallest of our four drones and brought it to life. He flew the tiny machine over the property, recording high-definition video of every inch of the compound. The surveillance took less than two minutes, and we owned a perfect bird's-eye view of target number two.

The high-speed run to the north dealt us an unexpected hand. Running just over thirty knots, the sound of the reinforced fiber-glass hull grinding against rocky shoals forced me into a decision I didn't like. Chopping the power would leave us aground in six-inch-deep water, and shoving the throttle forward might liberate us from the river bottom's grasp, but it also might chew the pro-peller off the engine. The decision was made in an instant, and I instantly regretted my choice.

The sudden stop threw Hunter forward and across the bow. He landed with a splash and a flurry of curses that left little doubt what he thought of my maneuver. With the boat resting in only a few inches of water, Hunter scrambled to his feet and challenged the RHIB to a wrestling match. The river bottom won the battle until Mongo joined the fight. We had the RHIB dislodged from the shoals and once again floating, but the problem of how to get both our boats across the dreadfully shallow stretch of river remained.

Clark said, "I'm glad you were the one to run aground, College Boy. Any ideas on how to keep from doing it again?"

"I've got one, but you're not going to like it. There are only two options. We can split the op into two separate missions—one upstream of the shoals, and the other downstream."

Clark grimaced. "You're right. I don't like that idea at all. We'd be cutting our team in half and eliminating any backup. Let's hear option number two."

I kicked at the rocky river bottom. "We could dredge the canal."

Mongo stood from the tube of our RHIB. "It's a long shot, but if that storm is big enough and produces enough rain tomorrow, it just might give us the depth we need to get across this spot."

"That's a big if," I said. "I like the way you're thinking, but we can't leave anything to chance. Let's start digging."

We tied the RHIBs to a pair of trees and settled in for the dreadful task of moving rocks by hand in cold water until we created a waterway deep enough to give us an avenue of ingress, but more importantly, a way out.

The team made short work of the task and had a trail blazed through the shoals in little more than an hour. By the time we remounted our RHIBs, we were wet, cold, exhausted, and only halfway through our recon run.

We motored upstream through our canal without so much as touching the bottom and came to a stop a hundred yards from the shoals.

I leaned against Mongo, "How are we going to find our little primrose path in the rain at midnight?"

He pointed into the trees. "Look at that spire on the church up there. Line that up with that cell phone tower in the distance, and that gives us a perfect range line right to our yellow brick road."

"I like it," I said. "I just hope it's not raining hard enough to hide those makeshift range marks from us."

We continued upstream until passing Richardson's property that looked remarkably similar to Wainwright's. Singer unleashed his drone again and collected all the airborne intel in record time.

Our high-speed run back downstream happened well after the sun shone on the other side of the world. Maneuvering the shallow river in the dark was challenging, but our night-vision nods made an otherwise impossible task manageable. We lost some paint and fiberglass from the bellies of the RHIBs, but the down-stream run was a success.

We recovered our boats into their trailers and settled in for the night. Pizza filled our guts, and exhaustion claimed our minds. Everyone was sound asleep before ten o'clock except Clark and me.

"Be honest," I said. "What did you think about the recon run?"

He studied the toe of his boots. "It wasn't what I expected. I know we studied the maps, but that river ain't no joke."

"I feel the same. I didn't expect it to be that much of an adversary."

"It's not too late to back up and come up with another plan," he said.

"No. I'm confident we can pull it off, but I was reminded of a valuable lesson tonight. Water always wins."

He said, "Yep. It's the most powerful force on Earth. You've got to work with it. Otherwise, it'll kick your butt every time."

"Speaking of kicking butt . . . We owe our bodies some sleep. This time tomorrow night, we'll be knee-deep in Richardson's and Wainwright's gray matter."

Chapter 12
Identically Different

For once, the weather-guessers got it right, and the predicted line of springtime storms arrived right on schedule. By the time the team rolled out of bed, the torrential rains had already begun, and the weather radar showed no end in sight.

As the team filtered down the stairs, one by one, I plated pancakes and sausage. "Good morning, guys. Have you looked outside?"

Mongo said, "Yep, and it looks like a perfect day for a little outdoor recreation."

We devoured stacks of pancakes, piles of sausage, and gallons of coffee. I parted the curtains in the dining room and studied the conditions. "Can you fly your little drone in this weather?"

Singer shook his head. "No, not the little one. The wind and rain would beat it to death, but I can put the heavy one up in thirty knots. It's stable and stout enough to power through it."

"Good. When you're finished eating, get it ready to fly, and we'll do a little harassing to warm up for tonight."

He shoved the last of his stack into his mouth. "I'll be ready in fifteen minutes."

We cleaned up the breakfast aftermath, and I said, "It's time for phase three. Planning is done, recon is behind us, and we have a nice little dredged course to get us upstream and back down. Now it's peek-a-boo time. Here's what I want to accomplish this morning. We need to know how sensitive the perimeter security is on the waterfront side of both Wainwright's and Richardson's property."

Singer said, "We can get part of that done with the drone, but we'll have to put a human on the ground to test for sensors."

I pulled out my sat-phone and dialed the ops center.

Skipper's voice filled my ear. "It's about time you bunch of lazy bums checked in. It must be nice to sleep as long as you want."

"We slept 'til we were finished," I said. "It's going to be a long night. I'm putting you on speaker so we can brief phase three."

I tapped the speaker button and laid the phone beside the laptop.

Skipper said, "Is everybody there?"

"All present," I said. "Let's mess with Wainwright's team, first. He's closer, and there are slightly fewer trees on his property. That'll give Singer some time to master the heavier drone."

Wainwright's property came into view on the laptop, and Skipper said, "Here's what we have from the cameras that can see the river. Fortunately for us, there's one camera array that seems to have taken a lightning strike overnight. Nobody's going out in this weather to rewire a leg of the camera network. I'm confident they'll live without it until the storm passes."

"That's good news," I said. "We need all the advantages we can beg, borrow, or steal. It's decision time, Singer. Are you going to fly that thing from here, or do you want to get wet?"

He peered through the blinds. "As much as I'd love to stay right here where it's warm and dry, this one requires a field trip."

Singer, Hunter, and I donned our wet-weather gear and hit the river. The rain came down in blowing sheets as if the heavens had melted and were pouring themselves out on the Potomac. We had the RHIB launched and headed upstream in ten minutes.

Hunter pointed up the river. "What do you think about hiding under the bridge?"

The Interstate 495 American Legion Memorial bridge loomed large in the rain-soaked mist. I turned to Singer, and he checked the map on the chart plotter.

He said, "I think Hunter finally has a good idea. That makes this a red-letter day. Let's set up camp in the driest spot we can find."

Paramilitary special operations work demanded that every possible advantage be exploited to its fullest extent, so my team would not shy away from operating in the deluge. But if our environment offered shelter, we certainly wouldn't turn it down as long as it didn't detract from our operational ability.

Hunter snugged us alongside a bridge column out of the wind and most of the rain. We secured our RHIB to the massive concrete column and felt the vibration of the vehicle traffic on the bridge overhead. As if the three of us shared one brain, we looked up simultaneously.

Singer said, "I sure am glad I don't have to live somewhere with traffic like that." He pulled the waterproof display from its Pelican case and set it up on the console.

The drone was next to make her appearance, and I lifted the coil of line from beneath the seat. "How much weight can that thing carry?"

Singer rolled the drone onto its back and opened its talons. "It claims to be able to carry ten kilos, but I'm sure that's in perfect conditions. Let's start light and see how she flies."

I uncoiled ten feet of rope and sliced it from the roll.

Singer held up the nylon cord and weighed it in his hands. "What do you think? Maybe five or six pounds?"

I nodded. "Sure, whatever you say. It's going to get heavier when it gets wet."

"Good thinking," he said, and leaned over the starboard tube.

He dunked the rope into the muddy Potomac several times and hoisted it back into the air. "Yep, you were right. It's a lot heavier now that it's wet."

He rigged the rope beneath the four-bladed drone and slid the controller toward me with his knee.

I pushed it back and reached for the drone. "Oh, no. I'm not going to be responsible for crashing that thing. You fly it, and I'll hold it."

He laughed. "Chicken."

With the controller in his capable hands, I held the flying machine at arm's length, and the propellers whirred to life.

He added enough power to fly the drone out of my grip, then hovered above the RHIB. "Give the rope a tug, and try to keep me from flying you out of the boat."

I squeezed the dripping wet rope as he added power. There was no danger of pulling me out of the boat, but the little drone put up an impressive fight.

He said, "Let her go, and we'll see what she can do."

I released the rope, and the flying machine rose and accelerated into the downpouring rain. Singer flew it up the river until it was out of sight, and he turned to the monitor. Several high-speed turns, climbs, and descents later, he said, "I'm happy with it. Are we ready to mess with our new friends?"

We donned our earpieces and patched into the comms with the ops center and the remaining team back at the rented house.

Once we'd established and tested our comms, I said, "Is everybody ready for round one?"

Skipper said, "We're watching and waiting. The cameras are high quality, but this rain is tough on the visibility. I hope we'll be able to see the drone when you bring it in."

Singer set his jaw as if he were stepping into a street fight. "Here we go."

We watched the monitor as the tiny camera in the drone's belly showed us where it was headed. Singer flew to the east and well above the tree line before turning west across the river and diving in. The drone picked up speed as gravity lent a helping hand. He flew across the rocky shoals at the water's edge until the end of the rope was only inches above the ground. When the drone was twenty feet onto the property and well inside the limits of the walled north and south boundaries, he pressed the button to release the rope, and it whipped through the air like an acrobat until landing with a splat onto the muddy earth.

He flew the drone away from the property and back downstream toward us as quickly as it would move.

I said, "What do you see, Skipper?"

"Nothing yet. Just be patient."

"Oh, yeah. Patience . . . that's one of my strong suits."

The drone arrived back beneath the bridge, and I caught it in my outstretched arms. "Anything yet, Skipper?"

She huffed. "I'll tell you when I see movement."

We loaded a second length of rope beneath the drone and drenched it in the river. As Singer flew the second route back up the river, Skipper said, "I've got movement. Stand by."

A few seconds later, Clark said, "I've got 'em. It's a team of two near the north wall and moving toward the river."

Skipper said, "Got 'em, but I can't tell if they're reacting to an alarm or just doing a roving patrol route. I've not been able to pin down any schedule for the patrols. They feel random to me, and this could be nothing more than a routine patrol."

Not being able to see what Skipper and the rest of the team back at the house could see was frustrating and almost painful. "What's happening?" I demanded.

Skipper groaned. "Give me the device ID from the drone's remote monitor. I may be able to feed the camera video to you so you'll quit being such a pest."

Seconds later, the screen split into halves, and the camera video played on one panel while the drone video filled the right half of the screen.

"Well done," I said.

Singer flew up the eastern side of the river and waited for the two guards to walk the length of the waterline and turn back toward the mansion. He said, "I think they're just patrolling, but let's find out for sure."

Once again, he climbed above the trees and made a beeline for the property at incredible speed.

"What if they see the drone?" I asked.

"They won't. If the drone's camera can't see them, they can't see it."

He flew across the shoreline and at least a hundred feet onto the property before bringing the drone to a descending hover.

"What are you doing?" Skipper asked.

Singer said, "I'm dragging the rope across the ground to test for sensors at the perimeter."

She let out a satisfied sound. "That's excellent thinking."

Singer said, "You keep an eye on the guards. If they turn, tell me immediately, and I'll run for the hills."

He dragged the rope across the muddy ground until reaching the shoreline, where he released it and let it fall. The guards never flinched.

Clark said, "I don't think they have any monitoring at all on the waterfront."

Singer landed the drone back in my arms and said, "I think you're right, but I'm not convinced yet. I want to try another pass or two and see what we can get away with."

We continued flying passes and dropping filthy sections of rope onto the ground, but nothing we did produced a reaction from the guards.

We recovered the drone and untied the RHIB. It took twelve minutes to cover the distance from the bridge to Richardson's home sweet home in the punishing rain. Our gear did a nice job of protecting us from most of nature's force, but the raindrops against my face felt like being pummeled by a thousand needles.

Hunter pointed across the windshield. "There's Richardson's place, but I don't see any bridges to keep us out of the rain up here."

We nestled into the tree line across the Potomac and from our target and repeated our exercise. Although the security companies may have been the same, the diligence was not. Within seconds of dropping the first length of filthy, soaking rope on the property, a three-man team of well-armed guards exploded from the rear of the property and scanned the waterline with rifles at the ready.

"Well, that was fun," Skipper said. "Something tells me Richardson takes his privacy a little more seriously than our boy, Wainwright."

I said, "Does this mean all the cameras are working here?"

Skipper said, "Yes, it looks like it."

"Play back the video of our first intrusion and see if you can pick out the drone in the video."

She did, and said, "I couldn't see the drone or the rope, but something set off the alarm. Let's try it again."

We rerigged the drone and sent her on her way back across the river.

Singer said, "I've got an idea. Instead of breaking the barrier at the river's edge, I'll fly over the fence and slowly bring the drone back toward the water. Let me know as soon as you get a reaction from the guards."

He did exactly as he described, and no one moved inside the compound until the drone and rope broke the imaginary line between the ends of the fence.

The guards alerted just as before and set up a three-man perimeter at the water's edge.

I watched intently on the small split screen. "Am I the only one who's curious about the dogs?"

Skipper said, "Oh, yeah. I probably should've told you. I let a little white lie sneak into the daily security briefing for Grand Star Security. It seems their kennels were somehow infested with a bacterium that leads to severe dehydration and often a terrible death for the dogs. Of course, it's completely false, but the company took it seriously enough to quarantine and test all of their animals, as well as the handlers, for the presence of the bacteria."

"Yeah, that's something you probably should've told us, but I'll admit it's a nice surprise. Nobody likes dealing with well-trained dogs in the dark."

Singer said, "That's good news, but we've still got these guards to deal with. Are we going to keep freaking them out, or do you have a better plan?"

"Let's give them one more pass just to keep them on their toes, and of course, to lead them to believe they're getting false alarms, then we'll let them brief the night shift on the situation before we come back out to play."

"So, that's your plan?" Singer asked.

I said, "Nope. That's just part one of my plan. You're going to love part two."

Chapter 13
Water World

We spent the remainder of the afternoon with our eyes focused on the intensifying storms, and for once, it appeared the environment would be on our side. Battling both our opponent, as well as Mother Nature, would've left us at a tremendous disadvantage, but fortunately, it would be our adversary who'd be left with the burden of dealing with the storms and the stalwart commandos hellbent on not only penetrating the perimeter, but also reaching the privileged men sleeping soundly in their beds and pouring terrified disbelief into their souls.

Just as the good news was piling up, my phone chirped, and Skipper wasted no time getting to her point. "I did it!"

I pulled the phone away from my head to protect my eardrum. "You did what?"

"I worked out the code in the alarm network at both houses. I can now feed the system all the false alarms I want."

"That's great, but we don't want to overdo it. With a system that sophisticated, they won't just assume the weather is causing false alarms. They'll troubleshoot it and find your fingerprints all over the code."

"That's just it," she said. "Getting into the system was simple. Any wannabe hacker could pull that off, but the real magic is not leaving any breadcrumbs behind. I wrote a shield into my code that detects when the system starts a self-diagnostic sequence. As soon as my software detects that someone is looking for the problem, my program deletes itself and rewrites the system code to appear perfectly normal."

She paused as I tried to understand what she was saying. Finally, she said, "This is the part where you tell me I'm a genius and promise me a raise I'll never get."

"Yeah, that," I said. "So, let me get this straight. You can mess with them all you want with system faults and false alarms, but when they go looking for the software glitch, there won't be any evidence you were there. Is that right?"

"Yes, exactly. It's a little more complicated than that, but you get the gist."

"If you're right, you're a genius and you deserve a raise, but if you're wrong . . ."

"I'm not wrong," she insisted. "You know I'd never do anything to risk your life in the field. I'm one hundred percent on this. Just give me the word, and I'll have those guards running themselves ragged in the pouring rain."

I leaned back on the sofa and threw my feet onto the coffee table. "Before I green-light your digital assault, explain it to Mongo. He's the smart one, and I'm the pretty one."

"I agree with half of that. Put him on."

I tossed the phone to the biggest brain in the world. "Listen to Skipper's story, and then explain it to me."

He caught the phone and stuck it to his ear.

Two minutes later, he put the phone back in my hand and nodded. "Let her do it."

I told her, "Mongo says do it."

She sighed. "That took too long. Next time, just let Mongo answer the phone."

"I do have one suggestion before you launch your electronic attack. It might be best if you didn't duplicate the alarms at both properties. I'd like for them to think they have separate issues and maybe even blame the rainfall."

"Just stick to being pretty," she said. "I've already got that worked out."

I stuffed the phone into my pocket, and Mongo said, "We couldn't do what we do without her."

"I know. It would take a thousand operators to replace her."

He picked a flake of something from his shirt. "You are paying her well, aren't you?"

I gave him a smile. "That may be the thing I like most about you, my friend. You always think of everyone else around you before you think of yourself. If I stopped Skipper's salary right now, she could live in luxury for the rest of her life without ever touching the principal."

His silent nod said it all.

The afternoon passed like molasses. The time leading up to the start of the mission felt like being a ten-year-old waiting for Christmas. Singer won *The Price is Right*, but Mongo dominated *Jeopardy*, as always. As night fell on the nation's capital, my team came alive.

One final check of the weather radar set our minds at ease. "It's going to pick up around midnight," I said.

Clark said, "You know what they say about the witching hour."

Oh, this ought to be good, I thought.

"The half hour before midnight is for working dark magic, and the other part is the better half of valor."

"I should really start writing these down," I said. "You're getting old, and you'll probably die pretty soon. The world can't afford to lose the wisdom of Clark Johnson."

He took a bow. "Thank you. It's good to know you recognize genius when you hear it."

The last supper, as we liked to call the meal before launching the action phase of a mission, was our traditional pizza and all the caffeine we could pour down our throats. Calories to keep us moving, as well as keeping us as warm as possible, were essential, and nobody was on a diet that night.

Hunter sidled up beside me and whispered, "We don't need one of your pep talks or another chance to back out of this one. Let's just go to work."

"All right, if you say so. But the boys are going to miss my pep talk."

"We've heard them all before, and they're stuck in our heads, so you can consider your talk given."

With that, I folded the lid of the pizza box closed and hopped to my feet. "I think I'll go put the fear of God in a stuffy old guy. Who wants to come with me?"

The team stood, donned their wet-weather gear, press-checked their weapons, and moved out.

I pulled four kits from my dry bag and tossed three of them to Hunter, Singer, and Mongo.

Hunter rattled his. "What's this?"

"Just a little something to help keep our bullets in our guns," I said. "They're tranquilizers. Bury the needle to the hilt and shove the plunger closed. They're not instant, but the fight will start to drain out of the bad guys within seconds. If we can get this done without firing a shot, that'll be the best possible outcome. What we're doing is that first half of Clark's witching hour. This is the black magic, and it'll put us in prison if we get caught."

Hunter planted hands on hips. "I thought we agreed on no pep talks."

"No, *you* agreed on no pep talks. I never signed onto your agreement."

He chuckled. "Okay, we've got it. Rock 'em to sleep if we can, and don't shoot 'em unless we have to."

With our waterproof comms in place, we conducted radio checks between the team and with the ops center.

Skipper said, "I've been running them to death all evening. I sent the last false alarm forty minutes ago. They sent one man to check it out at Richardson's place, and nobody took a look at Wainwright's."

I said, "It looks like you've sufficiently softened our target, at least as far as getting onto the property. The only problem I see is a concentration of guards inside or near the entrances to the house."

"You're welcome. Oh, and I have one more possible tidbit of good news. Since I'm roaming around inside the alarm software at will, I had the computer produce a likely floor plan. It looks like the same people who built Bonaventure built our target houses. The master is most likely on the second floor overlooking the back lawn and the river. There's some sort of solid structure in the center of each house that could either be chimneys or elevator shafts. That's the best I could do. Happy hunting, boys."

The collection of fun-loving goofballs who'd played *The Price is Right* all afternoon transformed themselves into rock-hard warriors, and the looks in their eyes said they were some of the deadliest and most capable operators on the planet.

"Time to run and gun, boys. Let's hit it."

We rigged a tactical kayak to the stern of our RHIB and headed upstream. The bilge pumps were barely able to keep up with the torrential rain, but the one element we hadn't considered was the near-zero visibility. I hugged the center console, taking full advantage of what little protection the plexiglass windshield offered. "It's darker than I expected."

Hunter glanced up. "Yeah, that happens when the sun goes down."

I gave him a little love tap on the back of his helmet as we bounced our way up the Potomac.

In what was a blatant display of frustration, my partner flipped his night-vision device up and away from his eyes. "The nods are useless."

To my surprise, Tony's voice filled our ears. "Bring up the GPS tracks you rode this morning. Even if you can't see, keeping the boats on the same tracks you ran before will at least keep you on the river."

"Why didn't I think of that?" Hunter said.

With our hulls following the magenta lines we left on our chart plotters, we were essentially flying our RHIBs exactly as we flew our airplanes in zero visibility, completely dependent on our instrumentation.

We raced beneath the I-495 bridge and enjoyed the two-second reprieve from the punishing rain, but as quickly as we sailed into the relief, we roared back from beneath the cover and once again into a relentless liquid world. Hugging the eastern shoreline, we continued northbound until the GPS showed us half a mile north of Richardson's property.

With the throttle pulled back just above idle, we cautiously motored across the river and into the receptive darkness of the western bank, and my mind drifted back two and a half centuries when George Washington, Jefferson, and a whole host of founding fathers likely pulled fish from that river before corruption, greed, and privilege dug its talons into the great experiment of democracy and made men like my team and me necessities in a jaded world.

Hunter stuck the bow onto a narrow rocky beach and surrendered the controls to Clark. He grabbed my collar and shook me from my stupor. "Are you ready?"

I put history back in its place and followed my partner across the tube and into the knee-deep water, determined to make a new piece of history no one would ever study in the years to come.

I slid into the rear seat of the tactical kayak and steadied the narrow boat while Hunter slithered into the front. My height gave me a line of sight Hunter wouldn't have had if he'd been behind me.

"Activate the strobe," Clark ordered, and Hunter thumbed the GPS device mounted on the hull in front of him that would allow us to recover the kayak after Hunter and I abandoned it on the edge of Richardson's property.

I said, "Hit 'em again, Skipper."

"I just did, and they're showing no signs of reacting. It looks like our harassment lulled them into that false sense of security we hoped for."

I tapped Hunter with my paddle. "Ready?"

He dipped the blade of his paddle into the river and tossed a splash of cold water into my face. "Ready!"

"Let's roll!"

We dug our paddles into the water and backstroked away from the shallows. The current of the Potomac carried us downstream without requiring us to stroke, so I let my paddle trail behind us act as a rudder, and the technique worked perfectly. At drifting speed, our nods were more effective against the darkness, and the northern wall of Richardson's property came into focus.

I said, "Let's put in about fifty yards short of the wall."

Hunter gently paddled toward the bank.

The kayak's bow brushed against the rocks, and I stuck my paddle straight down to test for depth. I hit the rocky bottom at two feet. "I've got the boat. Dismount."

He slipped from the coffin-like hold of the kayak and into the water, then he steadied the boat as I withdrew my legs from their imprisonment. He gave me a look, and I slid my hand through the kayak to ensure we'd left nothing behind. He shoved the kayak away from the bank and toward the faster current of the unrestricted river. In seconds, the Kevlar craft was out of sight downstream, and we were dismounted soldiers committed to the battlefield before us and at the mercy of our training, will, and determination.

Chapter 14
The Only Suspect

Just as we'd done in the kayak, Hunter took the lead, and I trailed one step behind and half a step to his left. We'd chosen to make our initial penetration with our M4s and switch to pistols once inside the house. Silence was impossible in the knee-deep water, but fortunately, it was also unnecessary since the rain made far more noise than either of us could, as long as we kept our fingers off our triggers.

I said, "It's time for a little tactical baptism."

Hunter gave me a nod, and we submerged ourselves in the sixty-degree water of the river while trying not to shiver. Keeping our bodies the same temperature as the environment was crucial to avoid detection by the thermal cameras. Drying wasn't a concern, but we would heat up a little with every stride once we were out of the river.

Back on our feet, we crept from the water perfectly in line with the northern perimeter wall of the compound, and Skipper said, "Turn your cameras on, boys."

Hunter and I pressed the activation buttons, sending what little we could see onto the displays back at the Bonaventure ops center.

"Cameras are alive," I said.

"Roger. It's nastier out there than I expected."

Hunter whispered, "You should be out here with us."

"No, thanks."

I gave him a nudge, and we slipped across the invisible electronic fence—our first spot of likely detection. Rather than waiting around for a pair of armed troopers to welcome us ashore, we continued our movement toward the house.

Hunter said, "I don't like being pinned to this wall. We've got no cover if they start shooting."

"I agree. Skipper, how far can we get away from this wall before the cameras pick us up?"

"It's impossible to say for sure, but staying within six feet of the wall is best, as far as the cameras are concerned."

My partner huffed. "Six feet doesn't give us any better escape routes, so let's continue."

The lights of the house came into view from fifty feet, and we paused to scan for bodies in front of us.

I whispered, "This is going far too well. I don't like it."

He nodded and reduced his posture to a crouch.

I followed his lead and lowered myself toward the muddy earth. "I know what you mean. I'd feel better if somebody ran out and picked a fight with us."

Skipper said, "I can ring their bell again if you really want some playmates."

"Thanks for the offer, but we'll stick with what we have for now."

As we drew closer to the house, the canopy of massive oaks deflected some of the cascading rain and gave us a clearer view of the back of the house.

I whispered, "I've got two at the door on the left."

Hunter said, "That's all I have. Are we going hard or soft?"

"Let's start easy and see how it goes."

We sloshed through the muck until Hunter reached back with a hand and stopped. I watched as the two guards by the door shuffled beneath an awning that offered pitiful relief from their drudgery. A small orange flame flickered in front of one of the men, and seconds later, a rising plume of cigarette smoke escaped his lips.

We moved, still doing our best to remain silent, but the closer we got, the weaker our defensive position would be.

Skipper's voice pierced the drone of the rain. "Freeze. You tripped an alarm, and there's action."

We eased ourselves to the ground and lay prone, hoping if the boys came out to play, we'd have the element of surprise long enough to disable the dispatched guards.

A guard in a dry uniform pushed open the door and issued an order, but the two posted guards made no move to obey. A heated discussion ensued, and the dry man seemed to win. The two guards drew lights from their sides and raised them beside their faces. Obviously against their will, the two men spread six feet apart and moved toward our position.

"This isn't good," Hunter said.

"Remember . . . don't kill them unless we have to."

"Should we retreat?" he asked.

"No, let's hold our ground."

As the two men approached, neither raised a weapon, but the beam of their powerful lights sliced through the rain and darkness like a sword. The two men posed a risk we didn't want to deal with. If discovered, any advantage we once had would vanish, and the fight would be on.

Hunter spoke into his mic. "Did we trip a proximity alarm?"

"Affirmative," came Skipper's reply. "They'll close on you."

"Roger." I crawled forward until my shoulder was in line with Hunter's. "When they break ten feet, we have to hit them."

He gave a nod, and neither of us took our eyes off the approaching pair. Their weapons stayed down, dangling at the extent of their slings.

One of the guards said, "I've had it with these alarms tonight. Everybody knows it's just the rain."

The other said, "Me too, man. This sucks."

Despite their displeasure at being dispatched into the weather, the two men kept coming, the beams of their lights crisscrossing the muddy ground in front of us.

They continued until discovery was imminent, and the instant their boots broke the imaginary ten-foot line in the sand, we sprang to our feet, closing the distance in an instant. Shock and disbelief filled their eyes, and they sacrificed their flashlights in exchange for their rifles. Before they could bring the weapons to bear on us, we hit them hard with our shoulders, landing just below each man's chin and sending them onto their backs.

My man groaned and squirmed backward through the mud, but I stayed on top of him, pinning his rifle to the ground with one hand while pressing my right forearm into his neck. He thrashed and jerked like an animal, but I outweighed him by at least fifty pounds, so his struggle only served to exhaust him and encourage me.

With my arm still restricting his breathing, and hopefully, some blood flow to his brain, I raised my left hand into a hammer fist and sent it down hard on his weapon hand. The sound of small bones giving way beneath the blow left me certain he wouldn't use that hand for the rest of the night.

The commotion beside me sounded nearly identical to the fight I was in, and I gave my partner a glance just to make sure he was winning. He was. Somehow, Hunter had made his way behind the armed guard and laced his arms around his neck and head in the perfect choke hold. Before I turned back to my opponent, Hunter's man fell limp in his arms.

I raised my fist to deliver a second blow, this time to the man's wrist, but before I could drop the hammer, Hunter rolled toward me and plunged a syringe into the guard's neck. Seconds later, the man drifted off to sleep.

Hunter rolled back over in the mud and slid a second needle into his foe. "We'll leave these two here to sleep it off."

"Agreed," I said. "But let's at least roll them on their sides so they don't drown."

We hurriedly repositioned the bodies, climbed to our feet, and sprinted for the door. The jig was up, and our mission was no longer covert. We were on the verge of making a lot of noise and a gigantic mess inside Richardson's quaint little cottage on the river.

Hunter hit the door and butt-stroked the first man he saw. The guard melted to the floor as my partner stepped over him and continued for the main staircase.

A uniformed guard came through the front door of the house just as we tracked mud, rain, and adrenaline across the main foyer. It was my turn to welcome another guest into Chase and Hunter's wonderland. I sent the heel of my hand beneath the man's chin, forcing his head up and back with enough force to rattle the hinges of the massive oak door he'd come through. To my surprise, he didn't wilt. Instead, he reached for his sidearm as he staggered a foot in front of me.

The man was only doing his job, but he chose to turn a fistfight into a gunfight, and I wasn't interested in that game. I trapped his hand before he could draw the weapon, and I swept his legs with my robot foot. The maneuver worked in spades, and the would-be gunman's head crashed to the marble floor like a bowling ball. I couldn't be sure he survived the collision with the floor, but there was no time to assess the damage.

Hunter took the stairs two at a time, and I followed at a sprint. The double French doors into the master suite were closed, and judging by the unyielding resistance of the knobs, they were locked.

Hunter looked over his shoulder with a wry smile. "Do you want to pick it, or shall I?"

"I'll take this one," I said. An instant later, I landed my left heel just above the doorknob, and the doors exploded inward.

Two forms rose from the bed, one broad and balding, the other slim and obviously confused. Hunter drew his Glock with one hand and his fighting knife with the other as he lunged toward the woman. He pressed the muzzle to her forehead and forced her back against the pillow.

Gibson Richardson shot a hand toward the nightstand, but his illusion of superiority melted when I crushed his hand between my robot and the front edge of his bedside table. He gasped in pain, and I shoved the barrel of my pistol into his gaping mouth. He recoiled, forcing himself backward until his head and shoulders met the ornate headboard.

Before his brain could form an accurate picture of what was happening in his own palace, I cinched a pair of flex-cuffs against his wrists and planted a knee on the inside of his right elbow. The self-important DC elitist found himself, perhaps for the first time in his life, completely at someone else's mercy.

With my balaclava hiding my identity from him, I moved to within inches of his mortified face. "We're not here to hurt you," I hissed. "We're here to hurt *her* and make you watch. How does that feel, Gibson?"

He grunted and continued squirming as I shoved my pistol farther into his mouth with every move he made.

I growled. "You made a terrible decision, and now the people you love will pay."

Still gagging on my muzzle, he struggled to utter a few words.

"You're not making any sense, Gibson. Use your words."

I withdrew my pistol from his mouth and pressed it against his right eye. "Now, try again."

Blood poured from his lips, and he spat into the air. "You're dead men, you son of a—"

My elbow collided with his nose before he could finish his empty threat, and blood sprayed in every direction. I yanked my muzzle from his eye and pressed it between his destroyed nose and upper lip. "Now, do you want to try that again with a little respect in your tone?"

Watching Hunter sink a syringe into the woman's shoulder, I formed a plan and softened the pressure against Richardson's upper lip. "This is the part where you offer us money."

"Is that what you want?"

"Yes, that's exactly what we want. Let's hear it."

He swallowed a mouthful of blood and spittle. "I have cash. At least a hundred grand. It's yours. Just let me open the safe."

Hunter and I roared with laughter.

I said, "A hundred grand? That's hilarious, Gibson. We spent ten times that amount just to get to this little impromptu meeting of ours. Do you really believe a hundred grand will buy your lives?"

"How much?" he begged.

I pressed a little harder with my pistol as the woman's breathing became regular and slow. It was almost showtime. "I don't think you understand, Gibson. We don't want your money. We just wanted to hear you beg. Now you get to watch your wife die because you think your life has more value than anyone else's. You think just because you're wealthy, you can do anything you want to anyone you want, but we're here to make you understand that isn't true."

He trembled, his mind obviously imploding in terror.

Taking advantage of his horrified stupor, I pulled his pistol from the nightstand and tossed it onto the bed. In a calm, measured tone, I said, "Kill her."

Richardson jerked and writhed, but I wouldn't let him turn to his wife.

Hunter lifted the pistol from the bed, pressed his forearm against the woman's head, and fired two shots into the pillow. The tranquilizer did its terrible work the instant Hunter pulled the trigger, and the woman slumped across the edge of the bed.

Gibson Richardson whimpered and begged. "Please don't kill me. Please. I'll give you anything you want."

I laughed. "You can't give us what we want. You don't have enough money or power or influence to give us what we want, but I'm going to give you a little gift that keeps on giving. Your wife is dead. Your men are dead. And you're the only suspect. We shut down your security cameras with your access code, so you're the only survivor. The only living victim. The only suspect. Sweet dreams, you worthless coward."

I grabbed what little hair he had left on his head and used his skull as a battering ram against the headboard until he fell unconscious in my grip.

Hunter said, "Stick him, and let's get out of here."

I pumped enough tranquilizer into his neck to leave him all alone in the spirit world for hours to come.

We descended the stairs even faster than we'd climbed them and headed through the back door.

I said, "We're coming out. We'll be at the water in thirty seconds."

Clark said, "Roger."

I'd almost forgotten the torrent of rain cascading from the heavens, but Mother Nature reminded me as soon as we hit the muddy lawn. Sprinting as hard as our legs would carry us, we crossed the yard and continued running into the waiting river. I heard the RHIB's engine before I saw it, but Clark kept his word. As if we'd planned the timing of our rendezvous perfectly, without breaking stride, I lunged over the bow of the RHIB, landing with a thud on the deck. Hunter was next over the tube, and the two of us panted, sucking in air as fast as our lungs would take it.

Between heaving breaths, Hunter said, "Maybe . . . we should . . . have . . . done . . . more running."

Clark's calm tone filled my earpiece as he provided the situation report. "Sitrep . . . team recovered. No friendly casualties. En route to target number two."

Chapter 15
One of These Is Not Like the Other

When we caught our breath, Hunter and I dragged ourselves into the bow of the RHIB.

I said, "I think that went well. How about you?"

"Better than expected."

Clark said, "Now would be a good time to brief Mongo and Singer on what they're going to see when they put boots in the mud."

Our open-channel comms allowed each of us to talk to everyone else as if we were standing side by side.

I said, "Sorry, we're a little amped up. Here's what you can expect."

Hunter and I spent the next several minutes covering every detail we saw on the ground and answering questions until Clark pulled the throttle back, and I leaned up to see where we were.

He said, "I think we've lost the kayak."

That got my attention. "What?"

"We're on the coordinates last reported by the beacon, but it's not here."

I scanned the area with my nods in place. "I got nothing. Do you think it sank?"

Clark said, "I think it sank and tumbled downstream, most likely shredding it."

"Shredding it? It's made of Kevlar."

"Yeah, but the seams aren't. They're just hot-glued together for the most part."

"That's a terrible flaw."

He said, "I agree, but we don't have time to redesign a tactical kayak in the middle of the night. We've got work to do. I want to trade one of you guys out for Disco. I'd rather have you or Hunter at the helm for the infiltration. Disco's great in an airplane, but RHIBs aren't his specialty."

Our chief pilot said, "I couldn't agree more. I'm coming alongside to starboard."

A second later, his RHIB bobbed against the left side of ours. "Uh, that's the port side, Flyboy."

He said, "See? Clark was right."

I leapt aboard, and Disco took my place with Clark and Hunter. "Are you guys ready to have some fun?"

Singer and Mongo had their game faces on, so I cut the shenanigans and headed for Wainwright's place.

Mongo shot a finger into the rain-soaked air. "There it is."

I maneuvered the RHIB upstream of the northern wall and let the current drift us toward a small beach I'd noticed on the original recon run, but the billions of gallons of water the heavens poured onto Virginia in the previous twelve hours had buried the beach beneath whitewater.

I said, "There's no beach. Do you want to hike in from the north or swim ashore?"

They discussed the options, and Singer said, "Put us as close to the rocks as you can, and we'll deal with the water."

"You got it," I said and headed for the bank.

The relatively straight banks left the Potomac running swiftly, unlike the terrain at Richardson's place. With the bow pointing upstream, I milked the throttle to control our downstream progress until we were abeam the spot where Singer said, "Hit the bank."

I cranked the wheel to the left and added power. The RHIB's bow rose against the current and fell off sharply when the steering finally responded. Once broadside in the current, we picked up speed I didn't like, so I turned slightly back upstream and added more power. The boat danced and surfed across the whitewater rapids created by the submerged boulders, and I was suddenly thankful for Clark's decision to put me instead of Disco at the controls. Nothing about the coming seconds would be easy for anyone at the helm, but I had a better chance of getting our men ashore than anyone else on the team, except for maybe Tony.

"Get ready!" I yelled, and Singer and Mongo poised in the bow.

Mongo gave a thumbs-up, and I hit the throttle. The sickening feeling hit my gut the instant Mongo and Singer left the boat. Their combined weight had kept the bow low until they jumped. The bow shot skyward, and the stern sank, sending the engine and propeller against the rocky bottom. The RPMs revved through the roof as the propeller and the foot of the engine collided with the boulders beneath the boat. I was now sideways in a whitewater river with no power, no steering, and no way to know if my teammates had survived the plunge into the Potomac.

I remained calm enough to tell Clark what was happening. "I'm dead in the water, package overboard. Stay with them!"

"Roger. Stay with the boat as long as you can."

I didn't have time to answer. With the paddle in hand, I beat against the roiling river with all my strength, in wasted hopes of pushing what was left of the RHIB against the rocks and getting her stopped.

With everything in my world accelerating, I braced against the console while still digging at the water with my undersized oar. Just as I sent the blade back into the water for another wasted effort, the left-side tube crashed into a jagged boulder, halting the RHIB and sending me careening across the boat. I grabbed anything I could find and stayed with the collapsing vessel, but my paddle continued its traverse of the raging river. The sound of fiberglass grinding against rock told me the portside tube had collapsed, and I was seconds away from capsizing and likely being pinned against a massive rock with the mighty force of God and the Potomac River tearing at my helpless body.

What will become of my robot?

I'm supposed to understand the ridiculous things the human mind does in times of trouble, but trying to understand what was happening inside my head at that moment could lead to nothing other than insanity. Oddly, I wasn't afraid. I'd been shot at, blown up, lost part of a leg, stabbed, had my tongue sliced in half, taken my own brother's life, and after all the living I'd done while knocking on death's door, I never imagined my end would come in the bulging tumult of the Potomac River on the edge of the capital of the greatest country to ever grace the planet.

No matter what I did, I was only seconds away from being in the water, and perhaps only seconds longer from having the water inside me. I had to make a choice, and doing nothing was, in that moment, a choice. I could cling to my dying boat and hope to survive as it was torn apart on the rocks. I could abandon my boat and make my stand on the rocks that were grinding the RHIB into minute bits of its former self. But it was a third option that called to me—an option that was only slightly less dangerous than my predicament at that moment. My choice was made, and I leapt from the dying boat, bounding off the boulder that was the temporary home and joining my brothers-in-arms on the assault of Malcolm Wainwright's home.

I made both the decision and leap simultaneously. My comms were gone. My rifle was gone. My sense of direction was nearly gone. And any hope I had of surviving the river was gone. Land was my only option, and perhaps it was only a temporary reprieve from death's desperate claw reaching from within the abyss for my body and soul.

I wasn't cold, afraid, or panicked. I was doing exactly what I was placed on Earth to do: fighting for my life so I could fight for something bigger, something greater, something that must be forever preserved. Freedom called to me that day, and I answered her cry. I'll never know how I survived the clawing, grasping, punishing journey from the river to the mud of Wainwright's estate, but survive I did, and I found myself facedown in the mud beside my brothers—beside the men who loved the same things I loved and who would give their last breath to defend.

Breathless and nearly exhausted, I reached for Singer. "Tell Clark I'm alive and with you."

He relayed the message and helped me to my feet.

Mongo stepped beside me and threw a mighty arm around my shoulders. "I've got you, Chase. But what are you doing here?"

"The boat," I said. "I ripped off the prop on the rocks, and I had to get out."

"Are you hurt?"

"I don't think so, but let's do an assessment."

He hefted me and half-carried, half-dragged me to the perimeter wall. "Your pupils look good. Breathing and heart rate elevated, but that's normal under the circumstances. We couldn't see any blood even if it were present, but I don't detect any broken bones. Are you hurting?"

"No. I feel okay. My vision is good, and I know what's going on."

Mongo said, "In that case, I guess I should say welcome to the party. Let's go rattle a rich guy's cage. What do you say?"

I climbed to my feet. "I say let's do it."

Since I was left with only my sidearm, Singer was on point, Mongo trailed him, and I was in the back, completely blind behind the mountain of a man in front of me. As we moved up the lawn, everything about the place looked different than Richardson's. The trees were bigger. The lot was narrower. And the rear of the house was well lit.

I tapped Mongo's shoulder. "If it's anything like the other place, we've got about twenty more feet until we set off the bells and whistles."

No sooner than the words left my lips, the perimeter around the house exploded in brilliant white light as if the sun itself had risen solely for the event.

Singer ordered, "Retreat for cover!"

We backtracked toward the river until each of us had found a tree for cover and concealment. My tree and I were twenty-five feet from my teammates' positions, and I had no comms. Peering around the tree, I saw the worst possible contingency evolving. Heavily armed men poured from the light with their muzzles trained downrange . . . exactly in our direction.

We were seconds away from the firefight of our lives with our backs against a raging river and walls on our flanks. We were not only sitting ducks but also flightless. I inventoried my assets and found only a knife and five full magazines—one in my Glock.

I'll never know who fired the first volley of automatic rifle fire, but I'll never forget the sound of the explosions in the chambers and the projectiles cracking as they left the muzzles and broke the sound barrier. The thud of the rounds striking the ground around me echoed through my head as I stuck my pistol around the tree and poured lead toward the aggressors.

Singer and Mongo opened fire as well, and I squinted against the glaring lights to see man after man collapse to the muddy ground, but for each man who fell, two took his place and kept coming.

Mongo yelled over his shoulder, "Fall back! We'll cover!"

Retreating wasn't in my blood, but living to fight another day is always better than martyring oneself in the name of a temporary cause. Against my instinct, I low-crawled through the mud and muck toward the river that had, only minutes before, tried in vain to kill me. Now that same water looked and sounded like my only salvation. I'd rather take my chances in the raging water than against supersonic lead in the air.

To my surprise, I made the riverbank without taking a round. Perhaps the gunmen hadn't seen me, or if they had, maybe the wind and rain robbed them of their marksmanship. I'll never know, but I was only one third of the team who was pinned down, and I lay helpless without any way to get the rest of my team to relative safety.

My training, instinct, and common sense told me to keep my head down, and all three were right. Just when I believed my team would be overrun and captured or killed, the air behind me exploded with the electric staccato of an M60 machine gun. The weapon belched fire, expelling 7.62 mm rounds at five hundred per minute, and that was the sweetest sound I'd ever heard. In seconds, the incoming fire from the guards was hushed, and Singer and Mongo retreated to my side.

Singer said, "We're on the beach and coming to you. Stay off the rocks!"

I grabbed his sleeve. "That water is roaring. There's no way to get to the RHIB in that current."

He pointed toward the house. "Would you rather deal with that or the river?"

The platoon of guards who were getting a dose of their own medicine still held the upper hand against the three of us on foot.

Clark could only have so much ammo for the M60, and when that was expelled, the surviving guards would resume the fight, and we'd be cut to ribbons at the water's edge.

"Let's hit the water," I said.

Although I couldn't see his face, somehow I knew Singer was smiling and probably singing "When the Roll Is Called Up Yonder" or maybe "The Old Rugged Cross."

One thing I knew above all else in that moment was how thankful I would be if we survived the next few minutes of our lives.

And survive, we did, but the swim was no fun. Calling it a "swim" wasn't appropriate, but I don't know how else to describe the escape in the frigid water. We floated on our backs with our feet extended downstream to absorb any contact with rocks. Our arms and hands were of little use other than frantically flailing to keep our heads upstream of our boots. Staying together was a pipe dream that didn't happen. Seconds into our floating egress, none of us could see the others, but I remembered the time I spent studying the details of the river. Just around the next bend would be a relatively deep, slower-moving section of the river, where we could hopefully find our way into Clark's RHIB, or at least make our way to the eastern side of the river and onto drier ground.

I felt the vibration of the RHIB more than I heard the engine, and Disco grabbed my arm. He hoisted me aboard the boat, and I looked up into Clark's face.

He stared down at me. "Any idea where the other two are?"

I rolled onto my knees, scanning the darkness over the bow until I saw three orange flashes in the middle of the river. "There they are! Ten o'clock and thirty meters."

Clark turned the RHIB and motored toward the flashes. It took all three of us to get Mongo in the boat, but soon he was leaning against the portside tube and catching his breath.

Clark gave him the same look he'd given me. "Where's Singer?"

Mongo motioned toward the western bank of the river. "Last time I saw him, he was headed that way and still slightly upstream."

We motored toward the bank, with every eye on the boat scanning for any sign of our sniper.

Clark suddenly slammed his palm against his ear. "Yeah, we're here. Where are you? . . . Okay, we'll be right there." He sighed and sank onto the seat behind the console. "He's at the site where we dug the trench, and he's okay."

When we picked him up, Singer was humming "Old Gospel Ship" and looking for his lost boot.

Back at the ramp where we'd launched the RHIBs, Clark said, "I think we should ditch the RHIB and the trailers and head south."

No one protested, and we set the RHIB adrift, lit both of our Environmental Protection Agency trailers on fire, and backed them toward the water. We gathered our gear from the rented house, dropped our soaking wet clothes in a dumpster, and settled in for the long ride home down Interstate 95.

Chapter 16
Keys to the Castle

With my lost commo gear bobbing somewhere in the Potomac, I pulled a new, dry set from our kit and fit it to my ear. "Clark, how do you hear?"

"Loud and clear. Are you ready for the debrief?"

"I don't know if I'm ready, but it has to be done. I'll be the first to say it out loud. The mission was a failure."

"That's a little harsh," Clark said. "I think it was only a partial failure."

I scoffed. "That's like being a little bit pregnant. You either are or you're not, and we most certainly failed. I'll take the blame, though."

"That's not how this works," Mongo said. "We either succeed together or fail together."

Clark jumped in. "Let's break it down. We accomplished our mission at Richardson's property with no casualties."

I said, "We don't know that. When I put the guard down inside the front door, he went down hard."

Clark said, "You lost your earpiece before Skipper reported that he was on his feet after you and Hunter exfilled, so we're certain phase one was accomplished without casualty. Now, let's talk about Wainwright's compound."

I started the conversation. "I misjudged the current and bottom composition of the river. I put us in a deadly position and forced Singer and Mongo into the water when it wasn't safe."

Our giant said, "Hold on a minute. You didn't force anybody to do anything anywhere. We stepped overboard knowing full well what we were getting into. Everybody on this team has made infiltrations that were more dangerous than ours. You didn't kick us out of that boat. We stepped out."

"Regardless of that," I said, "I still put us in the position that resulted in me losing the RHIB and ending up in the water with you."

Clark said, "Chase, what happened to the boat that made you lose power?"

"That's the misjudging the bottom composition I mentioned. I was right on top of some monster rocks when Singer and Mongo stepped overboard. When the bow came up, the foot of the engine struck a boulder, and that was all she wrote. Being sideways in the current pinned me to the rock that destroyed the boat, and I chose to put myself in the water instead of on the rocks."

Clark said, "That covers the deployment and loss of the RHIB. Now, let's talk about what happened leading up to the ambush."

I said, "I'll take the blame for that one, too. I made the call to hit Richardson first, and that was the linchpin. The guards at Richardson's place had plenty of time to warn Wainwright's security element before we got there. If we had hit them simultaneously, like I originally planned, this wouldn't have happened."

The comms went silent until Clark finally said, "Maybe that's what happened, or maybe Wainwright's guards are just better prepared than . . ."

Skipper's voice came on. "Unfortunately, Chase is right. The warning came from Richardson's contingent, and the company deployed backup guards. It was a bad call, but we made it together."

"How many casualties were there?" I asked.

Skipper said, "We don't know. As soon as the warning came, the guards at Wainwright's locked down the cameras through a secondary network I couldn't access."

Clark said, "The casualties are on me. I opened up with the machine gun to get our men out of there. It worked, but when all this washes out, I'll still be the guy who pulled the trigger."

"Let's change the subject for a minute," Skipper said. "Is anyone hurt?"

No one answered, so I said, "I'm beat up a little from my fight with the rocks, but nothing serious."

Clark said, "We may have some minor nicks, but we're operational."

"That's good. How about equipment losses?"

Clark ran down the list. "We lost the first RHIB when Chase sank it. We intentionally scuttled the second one, so those are our major losses. We burned and sank the two trailers, and Chase lost an M4 and a commo set. Can anyone think of anything else?"

Skipper asked, "You still have both trucks, right?"

Clark said, "Yes, the vehicles are fine, and we're moving south."

"Have you thought about putting some distance between the two trucks in case you're being pursued?"

Clark groaned. "I hadn't thought about it until now, but you make a good point. What do you think, Chase?"

"I think the chances of them chasing us are pretty slim, but not zero, so splitting up sounds like a good idea. It only costs us a little time and some diesel fuel."

Clark said, "I agree. You head west and work your way through Charlotte, and we'll stay on Ninety-Five."

I said, "There is one more thing to consider. If they are chasing us, and they catch either of us without the other, we're only half a team, and I don't like starting a fight at half strength."

To my surprise, Clark laughed. "If they hit us, let's hope they hit my truck instead of yours. We've got three Green Berets in this truck, and you've got a civilian and two Air Force pukes over there."

Instead of playing into his hand, I said, "Good thinking. In fact, maybe we should head for the West Coast instead of Charlotte."

Skipper reined us in. "Stop it, boys. This is serious. I'm tracking both of you. Just be careful, and report anything suspicious. In the meantime, I'll monitor everything I can in Virginia and keep you posted."

The detour through Charlotte only served to give my mind more time to torture me. The deeper into my self-imposed mission I took the team, the more I regretted making the decision. I'd cost us hundreds of thousands of dollars in equipment losses, but most painfully, I was likely responsible for the deaths of several Americans who were simply doing their job in the middle of a rainy night on the Potomac. Was I guilty of the same sin I believed Wainwright and Richardson had committed? Had I taken a personal vengeance too far? Was I the immoral beast who deserved not only my own wrath, but also that of God? How deeply into my core would my recent decisions cut, and could I survive the gaping wound that razor would inflict?

I watched the sun break through the trees to the east, casting her ever-increasing light on a new day, and I widened my eyes to ward off the sleep trying to consume me. Disco and Hunter had long succumbed to the siren call of the sandman, and they were both breathing the rhythmic cycles of sleep. I surveyed the faces of my partners and wondered how many people slept with such comforted abandon because men like us fought their fights for them. Had I allowed myself to devolve into less than those people who unknowingly relied on us deserved?

Stopping at the diesel pump drew my passengers from their slumber, and they yawned and stretched to life.

Hunter grumbled. "Are you okay, Chase? Do you need me to drive?"

I pushed open the door. "Go back to sleep. I'm fine."

His answer came in the form of a return to rhythmic breathing, and I slid the pump handle into the mouth of the tank.

The truck stop coffee tasted like kerosene, but it wasn't about flavor. It was about the caffeine, and the sludge in my cup suffered from no shortage of that particular drug.

As I crossed the parking lot back to the truck, Disco leapt from the back seat and yelled, "Chase! Where are your comms?"

"In the truck. Why?"

"Clark's looking for you."

I picked up my pace to a jog and slid back into the driver's seat. I didn't remember pulling out my earpiece, but I snatched it from the center console and stuck it back in place. "I'm here, Clark. What's going on?"

He said, "I just got a call from the Board."

I swallowed hard. "That doesn't sound good."

"No, it's not good, but it could be worse. Of course they know about what we did last night, but they don't know it was us . . . yet."

"That's a huge relief. Did you get the impression they had any suspicion it might have been us?"

"No, and here's why. They asked if your team might be interested in a dignitary protection detail."

I said, "For Wainwright and Richardson?"

"You got it."

Perhaps it was my lack of sleep or maybe my expenditure of adrenaline in the previous few hours that made the situation suddenly funny, but the laughter came and wouldn't stop.

Clark finally said, "I know. It hit me the same way. They want to pay us to protect them from us. Sometimes truth is stranger than facts."

Instead of calling him out on whatever that sentence was supposed to mean, I asked, "So, what did you tell them?"

"I told them I'd pitch it to you and see if I could get you back in the game."

"Are you sure it's not a fishing expedition?"

"That was my first thought, too, but I asked the right questions, and they gave good answers. I believe they've been caught on their heels, and the whole Board is nervous."

"That throws a whole new twist into this operation," I said.

"It sure does. And my initial thoughts are that it offers an opportunity we didn't have before. It sounds like they're unwittingly willing to hand the bandits the keys to the castle. So, bandit . . . do you want the keys?"

I let the idea rattle around in my head for a moment. "I'm tired, mad at myself, and uncertain of a lot of things right now. This isn't the time for me to make that decision. Let's get home, get some rest, and talk about it later."

"That's reasonable," he said. "I bought us at least a couple of days by telling them I'd have to sell you on the idea. Oh, and we'll talk about this later, but from my perspective, it's a good sign that they still trust you enough to want your team shielding them from the unknown threat."

I pulled back onto the interstate. "There are a couple of ways to look at that. It could be that they trust us, but we can't rule out the possibility that they're laying a trap for us."

"I thought of that, too, but I didn't get the feeling it was sinister."

"As if my brain needs something else to think about, I want your opinion on whether the whole Board is corrupt or if it's just Wainwright and Richardson."

He sighed. "The whole world is corrupt, College Boy. It's just a question of *how* corrupt. Power is the most addictive drug the world has ever known, and those guys have power in spades. That's part of the reason they're so nervous. We burst their little bubble and let some of that power leak out on the ground. Now they're sniffing and fetching to get it back and keep it."

"I'm not sure what sniffing and fetching means, but I get your point. Where are you right now?"

"We're just outside Florence, South Carolina. How about you?"

"We just bought fuel about half an hour north of Columbia, so we're not far behind you."

"Any sign of a tail?" he asked.

"Not yet. You?"

"Nothing, and the call from the Board made me believe there's no pursuit. It sounds like they're circling the wagons instead of sending out raiding parties."

I said, "I'm not ready to believe we're in the clear yet, but that sounds like a good sign. I hate to bring this up, but did they mention casualties?"

"They didn't. In fact, they said Wainwright's place got shot up pretty badly, but they didn't say anything about anybody getting dead."

"Maybe they're keeping that fact under wraps for now. I guess we'll find out in due time. We'll see you back at Bonaventure."

He said, "We'll see you there. You didn't buy fuel on a card, did you?"

"I'm not the wet-behind-the-ears rookie you took under your wing a dozen years ago. Even I am smart enough to know this trip is all cash, all the time."

Chapter 17
Mom?

The so-called coffee didn't do the trick, and Hunter ended up behind the wheel while I dozed in and out of consciousness. The waking moments were filled with doubts about my ability to make critical decisions, and the sleep was consumed by nightmares of the results of my decisions. Despite the war being fought inside my head, Hunter parked the truck at Bonaventure sometime after noon, but without consulting my watch, I had no ability to determine the day of the week.

The shower felt nice, and the telephone conversation with Penny almost made me feel human again. I told her enough about the operation for her to understand it hadn't gone as we planned, but worrying her while she was working in Hollywood would serve no practical purpose.

Migration at Bonaventure resulted in the team landing in one of three places: the ops center, the kitchen, or, as it happened that afternoon, the gazebo.

"So, what now?" I asked when Clark finally settled into his chosen Adirondack chair.

"I'm still thinking on that one," he said. "Part of me wants to do nothing and see what unfolds, but inaction isn't what we do."

"It's been what we've done for the past two years," Hunter said. "That's why we were all fat, slow, and sloppy."

"I've got a better question," Singer said. "What were we going to do next if our little scare tactic had worked?"

Singer always had a way of bringing the world into perspective, no matter how screwed up things were in my noggin.

I silently ran the logical answers through my head until I said the stupidest thing imaginable. "I believed we could rattle those guys hard enough to make them do the right thing and take an honest look at what they'd become."

Most people remember what it was like when our parents were deeply and truly disappointed with our behavior at some point in our youth. That was the look I earned from Clark Johnson that afternoon.

After he spent several minutes staring at me in disgust, he said, "Let's pull our heads out of Chase's little wonderland of fairies and butterflies and look at the reality of this thing. We pissed in a hornet's nest, and now, no matter how fast we run, we're going to get stung . . . a lot."

The mood was already dismal, but putting the reality of our situation into words only served to bring the gloom a little closer.

Clark pushed himself from his chair, and I asked, "Where are you going?"

He checked his watch. "I'm going back to Miami, where I belong. Good luck, guys."

With speed I never imagined possible, Mongo leapt from his chair, folded Clark in half, and deposited him back onto his seat.

Clark shook off the surprise. "I wasn't really leaving. I was just going to the head, but thanks to you, you big ape, I don't need to go anymore."

Mongo waggled a finger toward the rest of us. "Anyone else have visions of jumping ship?"

No one flinched, so the big man squeezed back into his over-sized perch.

"Let's deal with things one at a time," I said. "First, does any-body believe they know it was us who hit Richardson's place and attempted to hit Wainwright's?"

Hunter shrugged. "I think it's a possibility, and as such, it's something we have to consider."

Singer nodded. "I feel the same. The Board isn't a bunch of id-iots. They've been around the block enough to know how the world works. Especially our world."

I turned to Clark. "You know them better than any of us. Do any of them have a tactical background?"

He studied the framing in the top of the gazebo for a while. "I'm ashamed to admit that I don't really know, but I know some-one who would know."

"Get your dad on the phone," I said.

Disco suddenly looked concerned and surveyed the yard and river. "Do you think we should take this conversation into the ops center?"

I spun my head in hopes of seeing whatever had spooked our chief pilot. "What did you see?"

"Maybe I'm just being paranoid, but sound carries a long way over water, and if I were doing the listening, that's where I'd be."

I stood. "You're going to make a fine spy someday."

"How do you know I'm not already?"

Mongo pounced and had the pilot upside down by his ankles before he could spread his arms and declare, "It was a joke!"

Our circus freak let Disco live, and we reconvened in the ops center. Needless to say, Skipper was hard at work in her lair when we slipped through the door.

I asked, "Where have you been?"

She said, "I was asleep. You bunch of night owls kept me up all night making sure nobody was chasing you, and a girl's got to have some sleep."

"Thank you for babysitting us. We're having our what's-next discussion and thought we should bring it up here."

"Good plan. I'm just cleaning up some files, so it can wait."

We found our places at the table, and I said, "Okay. *Now* get your dad on the phone."

Skipper said, "Whose dad?"

"I was talking to Clark."

She spun back to her keyboard. "Here. I'll get him for you."

A few seconds later, the speaker in the center of the table came to life with the sounds of a phone ringing.

A woman's voice came on the line. "Hello?"

Clark recoiled, then flashed a look at Skipper and back at the speaker. "Mom?"

"Is that you, Mudpie?"

Clark shook his head. "Yes, ma'am, it's me. But we must've dialed your number accidentally. We meant to call Dad."

"No, honey, you dialed the right number. He's just getting out of the pool now. Hold on just a minute."

Clark stretched forward, pressed the mute button, and whispered, "That's my momma answering the phone at Dad's house."

"Hey, Clark. What's up?"

He thumbed the mute button. "Uh . . . hey, Dad. What's Mom doing answering your phone?"

Dominic chuckled. "What's it matter to you who answers my phone?"

"It doesn't matter until it's my mom doing the answering."

Dominic said, "We spent some time together while your brother was in the hospital, and we sort of remembered what we liked about each other forty years ago. Things happen, and people change. And for the record, she was my wife long before she was your momma. You know how it is. Anyway, she came down to the islands for a few days. All of that is beside the point, though. You were obviously calling for some reason."

Clark settled back into his chair, but his face was still twisted out of shape. "Okay, Dad. I'll tell you why I'm calling, but this conversation isn't over."

Clark spent the next several minutes detailing our operation in Virginia with special emphasis on the train wreck it turned into.

When he finished, Dominic said, "That is interesting, son. So, what are you going to do next?"

"That's part of the reason we called. I . . . we . . . need to know a little background on the members of the Board. Are any of them former operators?"

Dominic cleared his throat. "Son, I've been out of the game a long time. I'm not sure—"

Clark interrupted. "They offered us the job of providing private security for Wainwright and Richardson. We need to know if it's a trap."

The line went silent for a moment until he said, "It's definitely a trap, son. You'll have to . . ."

Before Dominic could finish whatever he was going to say, the house shook violently as if an earthquake were born in the basement, and a thunderous roar echoed, even through the soundproofing in the walls of the ops center.

The entire team sprang to their feet, and Clark said, "I'll call you back."

We descended the stairs as if the house were falling down around us, and we sprinted through the kitchen and onto the back gallery.

To my horror, flaming debris fell like rain onto the yard and the black surface of the North River. What was left of the boathouse Kenny had spent so many hours building was engulfed in orange flames, and my beloved gazebo lay flat and burning like a massive campfire.

My world stood still as I tried to digest what was happening right in front of me. As it slowly sank in, I turned to Disco and grabbed his shirt with both fists. "What did you see on the river when you suggested we should go upstairs?"

He trembled in front of me. "I don't know, but something caught my eye. I swear I didn't see anything specific. It was just a flash, maybe, but more of a feeling than anything else."

The longer I stared at him, the more my brain pored through the possibility of Disco being a spy.

Did he move us from the gazebo because he knew the explosion was coming? Was he feeding information to the Board? Did he warn Wainwright? And did he manipulate Clark into getting him out of the RHIB that took me into the rocks on the Potomac?

I stared into his soul, but there was no treason in his eyes. He probably saved our lives by getting us out of the gazebo before the explosion. I trusted every member of the team more than I trusted myself in that moment, so I shook him by his shirt that was clenched in my fists. "Get Irina and Tatiana on the Citation right now, and put that thing on the ground in L.A. as fast as it will fly. Penny will meet you at the airport, and you are to take them some-place safe. You got that?"

"Yeah, Chase, I've got it. But what about Maebelle?"

I spun on a heel, and Clark yanked his phone from his pocket. "She's good. I'll take care of her. But go!"

I let go of Disco's shirt and stared at Skipper.

She threw up a hand. "I'm not going anywhere. You need me here, and right here is where I'm staying."

Disco landed a hand on the gallery railing and leapt across it, landing in a sprint on the lawn below. The rest of us headed for the armory to retrieve the tools with which we would make someone pay.

Chapter 18
I Guess They Know

Armed to the teeth, we sprinted up and down the riverbank in search of anything that might give us an idea of who we were dealing with. If they blew up the boathouse, they could've just as easily blown up the main house with all of us inside. Obviously, they wanted to make a point without piling up bodies. A rational man would've found comfort in that fact, but I did not. I wanted an enemy who'd come out and fight like a man—not one who was as calculated and devious as we were. I've never shied away from a fight, but chasing down a smart, plotting, well-trained opponent like us often meant walking into a trap, and I'd walked into far more traps than I wanted in the previous forty-eight hours of my life.

Thinking logically in the minutes following the explosive destruction of a beautiful boathouse and a couple million dollars' worth of vessels wasn't something my brain was prepared to do. As if the whole event had occurred in a vacuum, I didn't think about anyone else hearing or seeing the explosion. That was, of course, ludicrous, and a whole flock of emergency vehicles poured onto Bonaventure from every direction. Firetrucks plowed across the lawn as if it were a superhighway, and blue lights flashed atop every St. Marys police car on duty that afternoon. I wasn't prepared to answer questions, but from the looks of things, I wouldn't be given the option to say "no comment."

The first question surprised me, and it came from a fireman wearing captain's rank on his jacket and helmet. "Sir, do you want us to fight the fire or let it burn?"

I turned away from the scalding heat of the fire. "Keep that pile in the middle of the yard wet. There's a three-hundred-year-old cannon under that rubble, and I'd like to protect it."

The captain nodded. "How about what I assume was a boathouse?"

"Let it burn."

"Was there anyone inside the structure when the fire started?"

My initial reaction was a confident no, but honesty required that I say, "I don't know for sure, but no one was in there with my permission when it went up."

The captain pulled a handheld radio to his lips. "Possible victims inside the structure. Cool it off and get in there."

I laid a hand on his forearm. "I said I don't *think* anyone was in there."

He pulled off his helmet. "If you don't know, we have to assume the worst, sir."

"But no one could've survived the explosion."

"Explosion?"

I held up a hand to shield against the heat. "Yeah. We were in the house when the explosion shook the whole world."

He placed his helmet back on his head and frowned. "How much gas was in the boathouse?"

"There was no gas, but there may have been as much as a couple hundred gallons of diesel fuel."

As if his helmet were more burden than protection, he fidgeted with it until it was resting on the back of his head with the shield pointing skyward. "And the explosion was massive?"

"Yes. It was loud enough to rattle the house, and you can see the debris scattered everywhere."

The radio came back to his lips. "Belay my last order. Remain clear of the boathouse. Possible explosives in the remaining structure." He looked down at the M4 strapped across my chest. "Let's move to the front of your house where it's a little quieter. I'll get the arson investigator headed this way. And sir, what's with the rifle?"

I glanced down. "Oh, it was just . . . I mean, we heard the explosion and . . ."

"I get it, but you might want to put it away before you talk to the cops. It makes them a little antsy when they have to interview folks with rifles hanging around their necks."

"Thanks. I'll do that. Do you need anything else from me?"

"No, but the arson investigator will need to speak with you as soon as he gets here."

"That's fine. I'm not going anywhere."

I locked my rifle back into its cage in the basement armory and climbed up the stairs to see a welcome sight. The St. Marys police chief ambled across the front lawn with his cowboy hat in hand.

"Hello, Chief."

Chief Bobby Roberts shook his head. "Don't 'hello, chief' me. What under God's Heaven have you done now, and why are there armed killers roaming around on the bank of my river?"

I said, "I didn't do it. I'm the victim."

"Victim's ass. If you didn't do it, you did something to cause it. Now, spit it out."

I motioned toward the front door of the house. "Let's go inside and have a chat."

He followed. "A chat? Is that what you're calling a government coverup these days?"

We closed the door of the library and settled into the wingbacks.

"All right, Chase. Let's have it."

"Are we off the record, Bobby?"

He threw his hat onto my desk. "Do you see a pad and pencil in my hand? Just tell me what's going on, and I'll help you clean it up."

I crossed an ankle over my knee, and Bobby looked surprised. He said, "What happened there?"

"Oh, my robot?"

"How did I not know you were missing a foot?"

"It's a relatively new development. I lost it a couple of years ago overseas, and the folks at UAB built me this high-speed thing."

"How did you lose your foot?"

I cocked my head. "Come on, Bobby. You know I can't tell you about that."

He chuckled. "Ah, to live the life of a double naught spy."

"Shaken, not stirred."

"Exactly," he said. "Now, tell me about the boathouse."

"The truth is, I'm not sure who did it yet."

"I'm not so much interested in the *who* as the why."

"The why is easy. I pitched a hissy fit and slapped an important guy around a little bit in DC. I'm sure he sent some low-level nobody with a pound of C-four to retaliate. They weren't trying to hurt anybody. If they were, they would've hit the house and not the boats."

He chewed on his bottom lip. "Are you planning to file an insurance claim?"

"I'm self-insured, but why do you ask?"

He stared at the floor. "I'm sorry to have to ask this, Chase, but when did you move your boats out of the boathouse?"

"What are you talking about?"

"Your boats . . . They weren't in the boathouse. Your Cat is downtown by the Cumberland Island Ferry, and your Mark V is up at the Navy base. You see what I'm saying, right?"

"I didn't move my boats."

He screwed up his face. "Somebody did, and it's going to look like you moved your boats out and blew up your own boathouse to collect the insurance."

I leaned back in my chair. "That boathouse is worth a hundred fifty grand, maybe two, tops. And I don't carry insurance on it. I told you, I'm self-insured. There's not going to be a claim."

He took a long breath and held it. "It still looks bad, Chase. Do you think whoever blew it up was the same person who moved the boats?"

"Boats are easy to steal, but I don't know why anybody would do that. My boats are easy to identify, especially the Mark V, and moving them would risk being spotted. That's not logical."

He lowered his chin. "Someone blew up your boathouse. What's logical about that?"

"Good point. But logic in your world isn't the same thing as logic in mine."

As if there were no door at all, Skipper came bounding into the room without so much as a knock. "Oh, hey, Chief." Without giving the city's top cop a chance to reply, she said, "Nobody got hurt, right?"

I said, "Not that I know of. All of us are good, but somebody moved the boats before they blew up the boathouse."

"Oh, yeah. Tony did that."

I raised an eyebrow. "Tony moved the boats, or blew up the house, or both?"

She scowled. "No, he didn't blow anything up, but he did move the boats. The Mark V was in the way when Earl was working on the RHIBs, so he stuck it under the cover up at the base."

"What about *Aegis*?" I asked.

"He and I were the last ones to use *Aegis*, so we called to have the fuel truck come top off the tanks, but the truck was down for maintenance, so we had to take it to the fuel dock downtown, and something was going on down there, so we left it until the gas guy could get to it."

I turned to face the chief, and he shrugged. "So, do you want to file a report?"

"A report of what? You think I blew up my own boathouse? That's not a crime, is it?"

He picked a piece of ash from his pants. "That depends on how rigidly I interpret the law. Intentionally setting off an explosion inside the city limits without a license and a permit is a violation of more than a few ordinances."

I held out my hands toward the chief with my wrists together. He withdrew a pair of cuffs from his belt and called my bluff. When he walked out, I was left sitting in my wingback with my wrists firmly cuffed and confident that no police report would ever exist for the Bonaventure boathouse explosion.

Skipper pulled a handcuff key from my desk drawer and freed me from captivity. "Don't you think that's enough messing around?"

I threw up my free hands. "The chief of police was interviewing me. What do you want from me?"

She pointed through the kitchen. "I want you to get out there with Clark and come up with a plan to deal with the fallout from the train wreck that followed you home from DC."

I headed for the armory to reclaim my rifle, but it was a wasted venture.

The team met me before I made it back up the stairs, and Clark said, "There's nobody out there, and if there was somebody, he's long gone by now. Did you talk to the cops?"

I pointed toward the cruiser pulling away. "I had a nice chat with Chief Roberts, and he arrested me . . . sort of."

"What?"

"Okay, he didn't really arrest me, but he did handcuff me. It's a long story, but there won't be a police report. And we've got a nice new pair of handcuffs."

The fire captain—minus his heavy turnout coat—rounded the house. "Mr. Fulton, I talked to the police chief, and he said you gave him all the information. He instructed me to have the arson investigator come straight to him. Is that how you understood it when he left?"

I gave Clark a wink and turned to the captain. "Yep, that's exactly what I expected."

He said, "We had to back off the fire until we knew there was nothing left that could explode. It's burned to the waterline, and there are no signs of people or explosives, so we're going to send a diver into the water for a quick look around before we go."

We secured the weapons back in the armory and parked ourselves in the ops center.

I reopened our meeting. "I guess this means they know it was us, huh?"

Almost before I finished my statement, Clark's phone buzzed. He pulled it from his pocket and thumbed the speaker button. "Hey, Maebelle. What's up?"

Instead of the Southern drawl of Maebelle's voice, a man said, "Mr. Johnson, this is Lieutenant Ortega. I'm a detective with Miami Beach PD. Can you verify for me that you are, in fact, Maebelle Huntsinger's husband?"

"Yes, I am. What happened?"

"There's been an accident, sir, and Mrs. Huntsinger is being transported by ambulance to the ER at Mount Sinai Medical Center."

"What accident? What happened? Is she—"

"There was a fire at the restaurant, el Juez, and Mrs.

Huntsinger suffered smoke inhalation. She was stable when the paramedics placed her in the ambulance, but that's all the information I have at the moment. Can I have an officer pick you up and take you to the hospital?"

Chapter 19
To Be a Spy

Clark Johnson was one of the coolest-tempered men I'd ever known, but when the Miami Beach PD detective delivered the terrifying news, the fury in his eyes could've been the rage of the devil himself.

He exploded from his chair and froze for a moment as if trying to decide what to say.

I pointed toward the door. "Go! We've got this. Are you okay to fly?"

"Yeah. I'm okay. I'll call you when—"

"Just go!" I ordered.

He bolted through the door, leaving Singer, Mongo, Hunter, Skipper, and me still huddled around the table.

I leaned forward onto my forearms. "I want to hear ideas. Mongo, you go first."

The big man stared down at the table before saying, "There are three possibilities. One, the fire at Maebelle's restaurant could be completely unrelated to this, but that's unlikely. Two, the boathouse explosion could be someone other than the Board, but that's also unlikely. Off the cuff, I believe Wainwright and/or Richardson sent a couple of guys to rub our noses in the spot where we peed on the carpet. If that's the case, our careers are over, and they'll leave us alone as long as we leave them alone. I doubt they intentionally hurt Maebelle. They probably didn't know she was in the building. It feels like a warning shot over the bow that accidentally landed amidships."

I played his scenarios through my head. "Singer? Let's hear it."

He didn't hesitate. "The fire and the boathouse are the same incident, so I think we have to rule out the possibility of it being an accidental coincidence. I agree with Mongo that we're done when it comes to working for the Board. That chapter is closed, and I figure we're all okay with that. The question is, what happens next? I'm not sure I agree that they're finished firing shots. We hurt their privileged little elitist feelings. I wouldn't be surprised if they keep dropping mortar rounds at our perimeter just to remind us what they're capable of doing." I turned to my partner. "Hunter, what have you got?"

"I'm with Singer, but I think there's another question we're not asking. Who cares what *they're* going to do? What are *we* going to do?"

I spun in my chair. "Skipper? Thoughts?"

She twisted her hair into a pile on top of her head and stuck a pencil through it. "I don't deal in guesses, and anything other than facts is a guess. We'll probably never be able to prove Wainwright and Richardson are behind the attacks, but that doesn't matter. It's not like we're going to court. We need a plan that's not based on emotion. We need an if-then plan. If they hit us again, then we'll do X. And if they directly attack one or all of us with intent to hurt or kill, then we'll do Y. We just have to determine what X and Y are."

Singer said, "It's your turn, Chase. You're the captain. The rest of us are just pulling oars."

I said, "No, we're way beyond that. We're in this together, and we're going to wade through it together. At this point, we have to assume we're down at least two men and maybe three. Tony is sidelined as far as action goes, but he's usable in the ops center. Clark is welded to Maebelle's side while she's in the hospital. And Disco is playing high-security chauffeur. That leaves the five of us, so we have to base our plan on the manpower we have."

Skipper said, "If we were going to strike back, what would that look like? I mean, we can't exactly roll into DC and start piling up bodies. I guess if Anya was still around, she could pull it off, but not us. We're not playing in some third-world cesspool. We've started a war on our home turf, and the first world has real prisons for real people who break real laws."

I asked, "Did we have any security cameras in the boathouse?"

Skipper spun around and pulled out her keyboard. "We have— or rather, we had—two. One was on the water side, and the other was an interior cam. Here's the split-screen video of the last forty-eight hours before they got blown to the moon." The video appeared on the monitor above her head. "I've already been through it, and there's nothing, and I mean zip, zero, nothing on the tapes. It looks like a normal day until this . . ."

The screen flickered ever so slightly the instant before going black, and I said, "Hold it. Back up to the ten seconds right before the explosion."

She did and played the video in ultra-slow motion.

"There," I said. "Look at the ripples on the water the second before the explosion. What caused those ripples?"

Hunter stood. "I don't know, but it's worth having a look."

Fifteen minutes later, he and I slid into the black water of the North River with our rebreathers, comms, and torches. We finned beneath what had been our boathouse and inched across the muddy bottom, our torches illuminating a few inches ahead of us as we moved.

"What are we looking for?" I asked.

"When I went through the combat diver course in Key West a hundred years ago, the SEALs and a bunch of SF guys were testing a device that would hold a buoyant explosive charge on the bottom until the timer ran out. Then it would release the charge attached to a rubber ball. The ball was just buoyant enough to float the charge to the surface or into contact with whatever was above it that needed to go boom."

"So, you're thinking the charge was planted by a diver beneath the boathouse and released either on a timer or a remote trigger?"

"Exactly. Something made those ripples you saw, and I'm betting it was a floating rubber ball attached to a charge."

We crawled around on the filthy bottom of the North River for an hour before giving up.

Hunter said, "That bottom is blown to bits. Whatever *was* down there is either blown to St. Louis or driven so deep in the mud we'd never have a chance to find it."

We climbed from the river where our floating dock used to be and shucked off our dive gear.

I kicked a piece of timber that had once belonged to the now-demolished gazebo. "I'm mad about the boathouse, but I didn't have any emotional attachment to it. The gazebo is another issue."

"It's just material stuff," he said. "We can rebuild it."

"You're starting to sound like Singer."

"That's not such a bad thing, right?"

"No, it's not bad at all. We could all use a dose of Singer in our heads."

We dodged the debris and made our way onto the back gallery. I grounded my dive gear on the steps and grabbed the water hose to rinse the mud and muck off our gear and bodies.

"Any luck?" Skipper asked as she came through the door.

"No, but Hunter has a theory."

He told the story of the time-delayed, buoyant charges, and

Skipper said, "I've never heard of anything like that, but it sounds like just the contraption for what happened here." She stepped back through the door and retrieved a pair of towels. "Your phone's ringing, Chase. Want me to get it?"

"Yes."

She stuck it to her ear, then tossed it to me. "It's Clark."

"How's Maebelle?" I asked almost before catching the phone.

"She's shaken up, and her lungs are full of smoke, but she's going to be all right. The doctor says she can go home tomorrow, but I'm not digging that."

"You're opposed to her being released from the hospital?"

"No, I'm opposed to her going home. I want her as far away from this as possible. Do you get what I mean?"

"I do. I'll make it happen. And how about the restaurant? Did it survive?"

"No, it was a total loss, but Maebelle was the only one in the building when it went up. She wasn't supposed to be there. They were closed because she's having some new stove or something put in."

"That's fortunate for the rest of her employees."

"Yeah. Have you done a roundtable yet?"

"We have, and the consensus is that this was a well-planned, coordinated attack with no intention of hurting anyone. We think it was orchestrated by W and R, but not the whole Board."

"What makes you believe that?"

"Just a gut feeling," I said.

"I see. What did you decide about a response?"

"We've not gotten that far, and I've got to be honest. I don't know what to do. If we do nothing, that might end the whole thing, and it would be over, but by doing nothing, we're making ourselves sitting ducks. We could use your input."

"I'll be there after I know Maebelle is headed someplace safe with somebody I trust, but you have to know that doing nothing is *not* an option."

After I shared the good news with the team, Skipper said, "The sat-phones are clean. I checked them myself, so you don't have to watch what you say."

My watch said it was time for Disco to be on deck in California, so I dialed.

"Perfect timing," he said when he answered. "They just topped us off with fuel, and we'll be airborne in fifteen minutes. Has anything changed?"

"Everything has changed."

It took five minutes to bring him up to speed, and when I was finished, he said, "That changes my schedule a little, but it's not a problem. I'm glad Clark changed his mind about Maebelle. It'll make us all feel better knowing she's safe with the others. I'll be in Miami early tomorrow afternoon, and I'll coordinate with Clark."

I said, "Skipper cleared the sat-phones, so they're secure."

He grunted. "That's good, but I'd like somebody to go over the Citation."

"Excellent idea. I'll have Clark arrange that while you're in Miami. Anything else?"

"Yeah, there's one more thing, and it's pretty important. Stand by."

The next voice on the line was Penny's, and she was far calmer than I expected. "You're not letting them get away with this, are you, Chase?"

"We're still working on a plan, but no, we're not going to lie down. Something has to be done, but we're not sure what that something is yet."

She said, "Thank you for sending Disco to get us. He won't tell us where we're going, but I guess that's some of the operational security you're always harping about."

"Yes, it's OPSEC, and it's important. I don't even know where you're going, but I trust Disco to make sure you're safe."

"I've got to tell you, I'm a little scared about what's going on. We've never had to run and hide before. Is it going to be this way for, I don't know . . . like a long time?"

"I don't like putting you in this situation, but for now, it's necessary. We will resolve this, and life will return to normal soon. I promise."

She laughed. "Normal? What has ever been normal about our life? I wouldn't know what to do with normal. We'd both be bored out of our minds. The truth is, I haven't really enjoyed the past couple of years with you playing psychologist instead of super-spy."

I chuckled. "I've not been *playing* psychologist. I *am* one. The state of Georgia gave me a license, you know."

"I know. That was the wrong choice of words. I didn't mean to imply you're not . . . well, you know. I just meant I kind of liked it better when you let your beard grow out and you killed people for a living."

At that point, I couldn't control my laughter. "There's a couple of points in there that I'd like to clear up. First, I've never killed people for a living, and second—"

"Hold up, Big Boy. Unless you lied to me, your very first mission was to kill a buck-toothed Russian in Havana, and you got paid very well for doing it."

"Okay," I said. "I'll give you that one, but in general, I've not been a hired killer. The second thing is this. I need to help you understand what a spy is. When an intelligence operative—like a CIA case officer—recruits another person to gather and report intelligence covertly, the person recruited is the spy, not the case officer. That's why we always deny being spies."

"Are you telling me all this nonsense so I won't worry? Because if that's what you're doing, it's not working."

"That wasn't my intention, but I would like for you to avoid worrying as much as possible. I truly don't believe this is going to turn into a life-threatening situation."

"They blew up our boathouse and Maebelle's restaurant, Chase. They already made it a life-threatening situation."

Chapter 20
The Lights Went Out in Georgia

According to Clark, Disco landed in Miami the next afternoon and surrendered the Citation into the capable hands of a pair of textbook geeks who'd worked for his father on more occasions than they could remember. As always, the pair arrived in black concert T-shirts. The first boasted Iron Maiden, while the second bore a disturbing graphic of Black Sabbath. The inspection lasted just over an hour, and the pair emerged from the plane with three devices resembling microphones and had said they weren't active, and probably weren't sinister, but that there was no reason to leave them in the plane.

"What were they doing in the airplane in the first place?" I asked.

Clark said, "It's pretty common for business jets to have some speakers and mics for airborne meetings. The geeks didn't find anything that would transmit or record anything except the stuff we need to fly."

"That's a relief. When will you be here?"

I could almost see him checking his watch. "I'll be there inside of two hours."

"I'll pick you up at the airport."

* * *

St. Marys, Georgia, is the quintessential quiet Southern town. The only thing missing is a town square with a courthouse and statues of sword-wielding men on horseback. There's no significant crime, no major industry, and locked doors are the exception rather than the rule. There were probably more weapons and ammunition in my basement armory than the rest of the town possessed combined. When my mother's family settled in the Low Country of coastal Georgia, they simply never left. I was merely the latest generation to call Bonaventure home. Perhaps I would be the last.

I suppose my inattention during the seven-minute drive from the Bonaventure driveway to the airport could've been directly related to the relative absence of criminal activity in my small town —the recent demolition of my boathouse notwithstanding. I didn't notice the three other cars until I turned on the half-mile-long access road to the airport.

They each made the turn with me, and the lead car accelerated hard. At the very least, I was in for some damage to Dr. Richter's beloved VW Microbus. The hundred-year-old oaks four feet off the right shoulder of the road made that spot perfect for the three-car pinning maneuver that lay only seconds in my future. There wasn't enough horsepower in the VW's buzzing engine to outrun itself, let alone the V-8 engines beneath the hoods of my pursuers' rides. We were going fisticuffs at best and gunplay at worst.

I watched the scene play out as it had in training a hundred times. The lead car pulled ahead with its rear bumper in line with my front tires. The two occupants of the lead vehicle were both on the left side—one in front and one in the rear seat. The back-seater gripped an H&K MP5 as if he'd been trained by the SEALs.

The second car in the stack pulled alongside me with only inches between the right side of his car and the left side of my microbus. Just like the lead vehicle, the two men occupied the left side of the car. That meant they were willing to sacrifice the right sides of their vehicles to bring me to an undesired stop, and there was nothing I could do about it.

My only hope lay in the hands of the trail vehicle. If executed correctly, car number three would nose behind me within inches, but the view in my mirror said he'd not done so yet. That might be a small window to build time and create an escape back toward a part of town where a witness or two might come in handy. Just like in the movie *Top Gun*, I hit the brakes hoping he'd fly right by, but I apparently don't have much in common with Maverick. Instead of flying by and giving me an exit route, he spun the wheel hard left and locked up his brakes. The lead and second vehicles reacted in concert with their trail man. The lead turned sharply right and slid the car to a stop. The driver of the car immediately to my left grinned like the Cheshire Cat and squeezed against me, giving me no way out of the microbus except the passenger side exits.

These guys are good.

I have to assume my reaction was subconscious. I shot a scanning gaze through the windshield, praying I'd see Clark's King Air on final approach. With any luck, he'd see the commotion and come to my aid, but there wasn't a cloud in the brilliant blue sky, let alone a King Air.

I thumbed the seatbelt the instant before drawing my Glock and rolling from the driver's seat. I had a better chance of surviving a gunfight inside the VW than in the open field of oak trees.

Did I see a suppressor on the MP5? Will these guys start a gunfight without suppressors a thousand feet off the main street of St. Marys?

My pistol would make a lot of noise, and a few full-auto bursts from an unsuppressed MP5 would wake the dead. These guys were clearly pros, but they wouldn't draw attention unless it was absolutely unavoidable. That left only one option for me. They started the fight, and I was in fear for my life. The shooting would be justified when I pressed the trigger, but I'd counted at least five men and probably six. My odds weren't great, but they were going to pay for picking a fight with me.

Cornering myself was a terrible tactical maneuver, but my choices were being made by whomever the assailants were. I pinned my back to the left side of the van with my feet poised beneath me in that old familiar catcher's crouch. From that position, I could see, shoot, lunge, dive left or right, or explode forward into the face of the first man through the door.

The decision was made. The instant the side door of the bus came open, I'd pump two rounds into the first face I saw. I'd then thrust my body to the right and clip the second man in the column. If I were hitting a van occupied by only one shooter, I'd send two men to the side door and one to each of the front doors. If I had a fifth and sixth man, I'd position them at the rear of the bus, ready to fill the interior with lead if the occupant put up much of a fight.

Wait a minute. This isn't a hit. It's a grab. They're not going to shoot me. They're going to take me. Come on, Clark. Where are you?

I slid my sat-phone from my pocket and thumbed the ops center number. Pulling the phone to my ear would likely get me shot, so I eased the phone onto the seat at my right shoulder and waited. Skipper would answer, maybe on the first ring or possibly the fifth. When I believed she was on the line, I said, "I'm going to be taken from the airport access road. Six men. Three cars. Full-size sedans, all dark in color. Florida plates on one. Others unknown. MP-Fives. Pros."

Without ending the call, I shoved the phone back into my pocket and moved my index finger from the frame of my Glock to the trigger.

All right, catcher. He's running on you. Gun him down at second!

The door flew open, and I pressed the trigger twice. The roar of the weapon inside the van had to be deafening, but I never heard it. My first shot went a little high and a little right, striking the man in the left shoulder. The force of the impact turned his torso to the left, I put one more just beneath his arm, and he went down. Dude number two appeared, and we pressed our triggers simultaneously. He felt my bullet, but I didn't feel his until I realized it wasn't a bullet at all. It was a pair of barbs at the end of a pair of copper wire leads connected to a high-voltage Taser. I held on to consciousness as long as possible, still praying for Clark—or even better, Singer—but consciousness wasn't enough to make my index finger reset the trigger and press it again. Every muscle in my body tensed and turned to iron. I had no control over my trigger finger or any other part of my body. The more I resisted and clung to life, the stronger the pulses of relentless electricity became until my body could take no more and the lights went out.

With no idea how long I'd been unconscious, I blinked in a wasted effort to clear my head. The brightest light I'd ever seen thrust itself into my brain, and I squinted to stop the beams from burning through my skull.

They must be flex-cuffs. They're too pliable to be steel. Listen, Chase . . . listen. Is that duct tape or packing tape? Whatever it is, they started at my ankles, and they must be near my thighs. Calm down. Calm down. Just breathe.

Trying to suppress the panic rising in my throat, I took a long breath and felt the cloth bag draw itself against my nose and mouth.

Okay, I'm bagged, cuffed, and taped. Is my sat-phone still in my pocket? I can't feel it, but that doesn't mean it's not there. How many hands are touching me? Two on each arm, and one man with the tape. That's three. Did I kill two of them? Were there only five? What's that sound? That's the microbus. Where are they taking it?

Survive, evade, resist, escape . . . survive. Above all else, survive. Fight, Chase, fight!

With my faculties back in place, I opened my eyes to see nothing but a wall of darkness. The bag over my head meant the piercing light had been electrical inside my mind instead of an outside source. The muscles in my legs ached, but they worked, so I gave them free rein to do the work they willed. I kicked, thrusted, and twisted like a furious mermaid on the deck of a shrimp boat. With my legs taped from ankle to thigh, there was little harm I could do, but giving them the pleasure of my submission wouldn't happen. My torso worked, too, so I twisted like a black tornado in the North Texas sky until the calm voice of one of my abductors cut through the air like a knife. "Go ahead and fight, hotshot. I've got plenty of battery left in my Taser. Want another hit?"

I drew a lungful of air and tried to curse my tormentor, but that only brought the realization that not only was I bagged, I was also thoroughly and completely gagged. My yelled aggression came out as a muffled cry from a wounded animal, and he must've taken it as a formal request for another jolt of electricity. I held on longer that time by controlling my breathing and focusing on the light that didn't exist. I offered no more yelling—just feigned submission—and it worked. The pulses stopped, and my eyes stayed open, but there was no fight left inside of me. I listened and felt for the world around me in hopes of staying alive and gathering as much intelligence as possible.

The telltale sound of the props reversing on Clark's King Air a thousand feet away reverberated through my ears, but that glorious sound was hushed by the trunk lid slamming only inches above my head.

Chapter 21
My Would-Be Coffin

This was not my first time to be bound, gagged, hooded, and tossed into the trunk of a car. The technique was the preferred method for snatch-and-grab teams when the environment supported the operation. On the street, the classic style of forcing a hostage into the sliding side door of a van was extremely effective, but if used to grab a well-trained victim, the technique resulted in a violent battle inside a moving vehicle. That scenario was effective but often resulted in significant injuries to both the captors and the kidnap victim.

Stay calm. Regulate your breathing. Listen to the tires on the road, and remember the surface quality. Count the turns. Time the legs between turns. Remember elevation and speed changes. Stay alive!

We made a 180-degree turn followed by a 90-degree turn to the right. Interstate 95 lay less than ten minutes away. Once on the interstate, the possibilities were endless, and the probability of my team finding me before I became a corpse was minuscule.

Left turn, three seconds. Right turn, two seconds. Left turn. Acceleration followed by two sharp right turns. A stop, reverse, one-eighty, acceleration. Two rapid left turns.

The series of maneuvers reiterated the fact that I had been taken hostage by an elite, highly skilled snatch-and-grab team.

Even if I were comfortable, calm, and unbound, the route they were running would've made it impossible for me to keep track of where we were. After only a dozen turns and rapid maneuvers, I lost any spatial orientation I had when my captors closed the trunk.

I had no choice but to assume I was alone and no one was coming to rescue me. Every move I made in the coming minutes had to be predicated on that assumption. With orientation gone, the next essential task was to free myself from my confinement, and that process had to start with the flex-cuffs behind my back.

Everything, without exception, can be abraded to the point of failure. The only requirements are a stronger surface, mechanical movement, and time. To abrade a pair of handcuffs of any kind requires one additional element: tolerance of pain. My process began with a search for an accessible, stronger, hopefully sharp surface on the inside of the trunk. I pawed at the carpeting until I was sure blood was dripping from beneath my fingernails, but the blood and pain had to be ignored. Finally, the carpet gave way, and I pulled it from the steel framework of the trunk.

Was that the sound of the interstate?

We were cruising at a moderate speed on a smooth, quiet road with rapidly passing traffic that sounded like it was overhead. If we'd just passed beneath the interstate . . .

That's definitely a left turn . . . acceleration . . . a new road sound. Smooth, moderately quiet, bumps every four seconds. That's the concrete of Interstate Ninety-Five south. We're headed for Florida. Stop it, Chase! It no longer matters where we're going. Survival is the only concern. Get yourself out of the cuffs.

With my focus back on my flex-cuffs, I continued my search for a suitable surface to penetrate my bindings. What I found was a relatively sharp bend in a piece of thin steel near the trunk's lock, and I began the long, tiring process of sliding my cuffs and the flesh of my wrists against the metal. I ground the plastic flex-cuffs against the steel until my shoulder and upper arms spasmed in exhaustion, but stopping was not an option. I had the rest of my life to get out of my bindings, and the cuffs had to go first.

Ignoring the pain, I continued grinding, and sweat poured from my skin. The liquid on my wrists and hands may have been sweat, but more likely, it was crimson blood flowing from the wounds the sharp metal edge inflicted. It didn't matter how badly I was bleeding. Death was in my near future if I didn't free myself, and I couldn't allow pain, exhaustion, or blood loss to distract me from escaping.

Wait . . . Deceleration. Left turn, followed by a one-eighty. We're definitely off the interstate, but where? How far south have we traveled? Has it been ten minutes or two hours?

More high-speed turns, more speed changes, more confusion.

Focus, Chase! Stay in the fight. Survive, evade, resist, escape. Keep grinding.

Survival was an unending process—until it wasn't. The time for evasion had long passed. I had resisted, and I would continue to do so if and when the trunk came open. Escape was the key— the ultimate goal of every breath. The sawing continued, against the protests of my arms and shoulders. Having no way to know if my efforts were producing results other than pain and exhaustion, I had no choice but to continue.

Believing I'd reached the limit of my body's ability to continue the push and pull, it happened. The snap was barely audible, but inside my head it sounded like the crack of thunder. The plastic cuffs lost the battle with the edge of steel, and my hands were free.

I allowed myself a few seconds of mental celebration. Victories in captivity are rare and should be acknowledged.

With my temporary excitement complete, I twisted and turned to bring my left arm between my body and the floor of the trunk.

At 6'4" tall and 220 pounds, I consumed most of the volume of the trunk, so getting both hands in front of my body cost energy and time. When I finally worked my hands to the front of my body, my shoulders and arms throbbed and burned with pain shooting from my neck to each wrist. Ignoring the pain was my only option, so I quickened my pace of work and attempted to untie the drawstring of the hood covering my head. The knot served as further proof that I was dealing with professionals. It wasn't a bow. Instead, it was a knot tied half a dozen times with the remaining string cut, providing no way to remove it except with a knife . . . or another abrasion.

I felt the cuffs still locked solidly around my right wrist with a long strip extending from the previous left cuff. I threaded the plastic strip through the knot and began sawing. The smell of blood on my hands filled my senses, and my arms raged in agony with every sawing stroke.

The grooved plastic of the cuff made relatively short work of the cotton string, and the bag came off my head. My brain expected light when I pulled the hood from my face, but the trunk provided none. That didn't matter. I'd accomplished another victory. There was no time to celebrate that minor accomplishment, so I yanked the gag from my mouth and worked my jaw until the cramps were gone.

I really need some water. I've never been so thirsty. Get it together, Chase. Focus!

I licked my lips and the inside of my mouth in a wasted effort to get some relief from the dehydration, but it was in vain. The next step was freeing my legs. I prayed the tape would be gray duct tape. Tearing through duct tape only requires the smallest of tears in any edge, and it splits with ease, but when my fingertips came in contact with the binding, it was smooth with a raised thread every quarter inch.

Reinforced packing tape presents a collection of problems. Just like anything else, it will abrade, but the plastic tie wasn't long enough to pass between my legs to saw through it. I couldn't over-power the tape, so my desperation turned to hope as I slid my hand into my pocket where my knife should've been, but of course the pros had taken it. Abrasion was my only option, but finding a tool in the trunk would be a nightmare.

I searched every corner of the trunk, but it was empty except for my body. My belt was missing, and only two assets remained. The problem was the distance to the assets. They were attached to the other end of my body, and I had no choice but to get at least one hand to the laces of a boot. I twisted and extended my hand as far as it would reach, but the tape acted almost like a cast on my legs, limiting my ability to bend my knees to draw my boots closer. The tape, coupled with the confines of my would-be coffin, made it next to impossible to reach my goal, so I devised a new plan.

Did I just feel a turn? Are we slowing down? No! Stop it! Focus!

With the toes of my boots pressed against the side of the trunk, I reached above my head and planted both fists against the oppo-site sidewall, pushing with every ounce of strength in my body while pulling my ankles toward my butt. The force worked, and my knees bent almost 90 degrees, giving me precisely the access I needed. The lace slowly came out of the boot as I worked with my fingertips stretched as far as possible. I prayed I wouldn't drop the lace, if it ever came free. Thankfully, it came free but didn't fall. I passed one end between my thighs and pulled it from behind, leav-ing one end in front of my legs and one end behind. With an end in each hand, I sawed, and my arms redoubled their protests.

Slowly, the lace sliced through the tape until I had enough to un-wrap. Pulling the tape around my legs in the space I had was no easy task, but it was working. Once below my knees, the job became ex-ponentially easier because I had the freedom to bend my legs farther, and my prosthetic leg was much smaller than my natural leg, so the tape came off easily and quickly. Finally, I was free of my bindings, but I was still locked inside a steel box doing seventy miles per hour somewhere in South Georgia or North Florida.

In a maneuver that would've made Houdini proud, I rolled over until I was facing the back of the car. To my delight, the roll had torn away another piece of carpet, revealing access to the left taillight from behind. Reaching through the small opening, I discovered the housing of the light to be heavy plastic. I pressed on it, hoping it would pop free of its mount and fall to the road beneath us, but no such luck. After several minutes of pondering how I could convince the light to part ways with the car, it finally came to me.

I twisted my torso and curled my legs until I could reach my stump and the top of my prosthetic ankle and foot. With several minutes of time spent twisting the connecting coupling, my robot was free of my stump. I slid the metal end through the small opening in the trunk until it contacted the plastic body of the taillight. I raised an elbow above my head and drove it into the sole of my boot still attached to the fake foot. The light didn't break, but it cracked. Another half dozen thunderous blows from my elbow shattered the plastic and opened a six-inch hole through the fixture, and my first taste of light poured through my new window on the world.

It took several seconds for my eyes to adjust, but when they did, I felt like I'd broken out of Alcatraz. I was still stranded on an island in San Francisco Bay, but I wasn't behind the concrete walls anymore. Now all that lay between me and freedom was a frigid bay with a six-knot current . . . and a few sharks. My Frisco Bay turned out to be what I believed was Interstate 95. Based on the shadows of other cars being cast to the east in the afternoon sun, we were headed north and remaining in the jurisdiction of the

Georgia Highway Patrol—a law enforcement agency that loved writing tickets for damaged taillights. I was still deep in the woods and far from freedom, but my odds were improving.

While I had my robot foot in my hand, I re-laced and tied the boot before putting the whole contraption back on my stump. With my foot back in place, it was time for an assessment of my situation. A team of professionals was still kidnapping me, but I was no longer bound, blinded, or gagged. I knew roughly where we were and the direction we were heading. I'd opened a small window into the world outside my captivity, and I was relatively unhurt. A couple of bloody hands and sore muscles from the pair of tasing events were my only real medical conditions, and I could deal with both of those without any problems.

With the assessment done, I needed to focus on a plan. I could signal through the broken taillight with a torn strip of carpet or even a piece of my shirt, but that would likely only put a civilian in danger when they tried to get involved. If I were fortunate enough to spot a highway patrolman, I'd stick everything I could find through the hole to flag him down, but I couldn't depend on that possibility. I needed to spot an exit sign with the name of a town to further narrow my position, and I had to find a way to open the lock on the trunk lid. I now had a plan and a list of tasks. Those would be my focus for the coming minutes and hours.

I slid my hand through the small opening into the cavity that held the broken taillight and felt for small strips or shards that might work to manipulate the trunk lock. I found several small pieces and retrieved them one by one. The small column of light through the broken taillight gave little usable illumination to the locking mechanism, so I was limited to working by feel. Before inserting a makeshift plastic shim into the works, I explored the lock with my fingertips, trying to draw a mental picture of how it worked. To my delight, I discovered a curved hook with a cable attached, and I sent up a silent prayer of thanks for the beautiful gift. Somewhere inside the car, near the steering wheel, was a small plastic handle attached to the other end of the cable I'd discovered, and above that beautiful small plastic handle was a placard that read "Trunk Release."

I pulled the cable, and the lock clicked, releasing its hold on the latch of the trunk lid. Holding the lid tightly, I allowed it to open a few inches. A broad beam of light rushed in, along with the roar of wind and road. Daring to peek through the crack, I saw a smattering of cars, but none with blue flashing lights on top. The second thing I noticed was the speed at which the road was passing beneath the car. There would be no chance of surviving a plunge from the trunk onto the interstate. If the initial collision didn't split my head, I would break at least both arms and legs in the resulting tumble. Adding insult to injury, the driver would quickly notice the trunk flying open and cars dodging my body bouncing across the road. Escaping at that speed was not survivable, so I'd let time and distance pass with as much patience as I could muster before attempting to run.

The pros who successfully got the jump on me would, undoubtedly, have filled their fuel tanks before shoving me in the trunk, but they probably hadn't counted on me freeing myself. My moment would come . . . if I had the patience to wait it out.

Chapter 22
Knock Knock

I spent the next half hour trying to get a glimpse of an exit sign or anything I recognized. Knowing where I was felt critically important, even though I couldn't understand why. Perhaps it was my psychological need to gain control of something—anything— in my life.

It became an exercise in frustration, so I pulled the trunk lid until it latched, and I tried to relax, which is nearly impossible inside a trunk. My patience was finally rewarded when I heard the right taillight click in rhythmic staccato. A turn was coming up. The car decelerated, but only slightly. The off-ramp felt steep, but there was likely at least a yield sign at the bottom of the ramp, if not a stoplight. My window was opening, and I would take full advantage of it.

I slipped a pair of fingers back into the locking mechanism and pulled the cable. The click came, and once again, the broad beam of light filtered through the long, horizontal opening. We were still moving too fast for me to endure a leap and roll without serious bodily harm, so I held on, waiting for the bottom of the ramp and slower speed.

The right turn signal stopped clicking, and I anticipated a left turn that would require even slower speed than a right, so I slid one knee through the crack and prepared to make my roll. If I could pull it off, I'd close the trunk on my way out and hopefully leave the driver none the wiser. The turn came, but the speed reduction didn't. If anything, the driver accelerated through the long, sweeping left turn.

Does he know I have the trunk unlocked? Was there a warning on the dash, or did he catch a glimpse in the change of the angle through the rear-view mirror? That's the only explanation for a maneuver like that.

He was obviously determined to keep me inside the vehicle as long as possible, and it was working.

We were doing at least the same speed as we'd done on the interstate, but the road was much rougher. After several minutes, we made a hard, high-speed right turn, and the road became a washboard, but the driver never relaxed his right foot. The speed was still high, and the rough road made it impossible to avoid being thrown around the trunk. Unable to hold the lid barely open in those conditions, I pulled it until it latched, and I braced myself with my feet and arms. Dust boiled through the broken taillight, indicating we were no longer on a paved road. Things were not looking up.

My new plan was to be ready when one of my kidnappers opened the trunk. I'd overpower him with the element of surprise, take his weapon, use him as a human shield, and take down his team as violently as necessary. It was a dangerous plan, but desperation often demands force over fear. I'm not ashamed to admit I was prepared to impose my will with all the force I could deliver, but there was no shortage of fear inside my chest, either.

Of all things to pop into my head, I could almost hear Clark saying, "Everybody's got a plan except horseshoes and hand grenades." I never knew what he was talking about, so that one was as good as anything in the moment. I would've given a million dollars to hear his voice right then, but I was alone in a deadly scenario with only my own wit, will, and fortitude to rely on. If I was to survive, it would be accomplished at the barrel of a gun that wasn't mine.

The car began to slow, but not much. The road remained full of ruts and ridges, but I had the insatiable need to look outside. I squirmed until my eye was aligned with the broken taillight, and when I peered through a wall of red clay dust, my stomach turned. There was another car trailing us only a few feet behind. Rolling out of the trunk was definitely off the table.

Finally accepting my fate, I abandoned any thought of escape and hardened my mindset for a gunfight. All I needed was a gun and a few targets. The targets wouldn't be hard to acquire, but the gun would be a different story.

To both my delight and horror, the car slid to a stop, and the sound of a slamming door reverberated through my capsule.

"Get him out, Parker."

I'd just gained a piece of intel I didn't have. Parker was the chosen bandit to get me out of the trunk. That meant he wasn't in charge. I hoped it also meant he was a junior member of the team with limited experience because I didn't want to face off with a hardened warrior when the trunk came open. I wanted a rookie who wasn't expecting to be attacked. Maybe, just maybe, Parker was exactly what I wanted.

A pair of knocks came on the trunk. "Come out, come out, wherever you are, hotshot. I'm gonna open this trunk, and you're going to behave. Otherwise, you're going to die."

He inserted the key into the lock and counted in a loud voice. "One . . . two . . . three—"

I lunged through what should've been an open trunk on three, but the rookie outside wasn't nearly as green as I'd hoped. Instead of springing through open space and attacking Parker when he threw open the trunk on three, I collided with the steel of the trunk lid and knocked myself goofy. Stars encircled my head, and I worked to shake them off, but Parker didn't waste my moment of dazed confusion. He threw open the trunk on the count of five or six and thrust himself backward and away from the car. I raised an arm to shield myself from the blinding sun, but I didn't spring from the coffin. If I had, there would've been no one to attack. Parker was ten feet away with a submachine gun trained on my head.

A pair of men grabbed my ankles, rolled me facedown in the trunk, and forcefully yanked me from the vehicle. When my chin hit the lip of the trunk on the way out, it felt like Mike Tyson had landed a perfect uppercut. My vision narrowed, but I didn't go out as I held on to my tenuous grip on consciousness. I hit the dusty earth facefirst and felt the air leave my lungs. Before I caught another clean breath, a boot landed on the back of my neck, and dust and dirt filled my mouth.

Soon, the boot was replaced by a knee, and a real pair of handcuffs secured my hands behind my back. "So, you're the infamous Chase Fulton. I've heard a lot about you, but none of it really impressed me, civilian."

I coughed, spat a mouthful of dirt, and growled, "What do you want? Maybe I can give it to you before I yank off your arm and beat you to death with it."

"Oh, good," the man said. "I was hoping you wouldn't be a pushover. Games like this are always more fun when the mouse still thinks the cat just wants to play."

He bounced and shoved his knee even harder into my neck. "Is that what you want, little mousey? Do you want the big bad cats to play with you and let you believe you can escape?"

I struggled to fill my lungs. "What I want is for you to surrender before I have to kill you and your buddies."

Laughter roared, and I kicked at the ground, hoping to find enough purchase to get the man's knee off my neck. My efforts were rewarded, but only for an instant. I threw the man off-balance, and he collapsed to the ground beside me, but he didn't stay down. He bounced like a rubber ball and was on his feet in an instant. The fall hadn't injured him, but it granted me the greatest gift I could've asked for in that moment. His cell phone fell from his pocket and landed on the dirt beside my hip. Believing no one else noticed what could be my only link to survival, I rolled, grabbed the phone, and prayed it was upright in my palm. My thumbs went to work dialing what I hoped was the Bonaventure ops center number, but I didn't know for sure. Before the next pair of hands grabbed me, I pressed the phone into the dirt and rolled away.

Hands weren't the next contact. It was a booted foot landed squarely between my legs, and for a moment, my will to fight left my soul.

While I was reeling from the kick, someone looped a length of rope across my feet and cinched my ankles together. He pulled the rope over my handcuffs, lacing my feet to the cuffs behind my back. An instant later, two men grabbed my arms and dragged me across the filthy ground. I bounced across a threshold and onto a concrete floor. The dragging continued for twenty more feet before a man I couldn't see laced a chain behind my knees, and an electric motor whirred. The motor foretold a bad evening to come. As the chain came taut, my body left the floor until I was suspended upside down beneath an electric hoist.

I had to retain my composure and continue resisting. In seconds, my vision would clear enough to identify the men, but I'd begun to doubt I would live long enough to describe them to anyone. My belief that my eyes would work was shattered in an instant when someone emptied a canister of pepper spray in my face.

Blind, drowning in snot, gasping for breath, and gagging on the pepper, I regretted a great many decisions I'd made in my life.

I didn't see it coming, but I recognized the old familiar feel of a baseball bat when it collided with my gut. What breath I had in my lungs exploded from my mouth in a forceful spray of spit, pepper, and blood.

An angry voice spoke just above a whisper within inches of my ear. "How's that pepper taste, hotshot? Want some more?"

Even though I was blind, I knew exactly where his mouth was, so I bucked wildly and sent my forehead into the man's face. I'm certain the damage was minimal at best, but the psychological victory of scoring a single blow boosted my spirit, regardless of the nightmare to come.

The man roared. "Hit him with the cattle prod!"

I took several short breaths to prepare for the punishment, but it didn't matter. The shock sent my body convulsing like a wild animal, and every muscle in my body ached.

"Wait!" I yelled. "You're doing it wrong." I gasped and labored to regain my breath. When I could speak again, I said, "You've obviously got the prod for calves, not full-grown cows. You've got to get your team under control, man. They're playing whiffle ball, and you and I are in the major league over here."

To my surprise, the man whose nose had to be pouring blood laughed. "You're a funny guy, Fulton. You know that?"

"Yeah, that's me," I gasped. "A regular barrel of laughs."

"How do you feel about soccer since you're such a big sports fan?"

It was my turn to laugh. "Soccer? That's not a sport. That's communist kickball. It's not a sport unless you hit a ball with a stick."

My sarcasm was rewarded with a demonstration of soccer kicks using my head as the ball. I'm sure I went out, but I have no idea how many times. When I regained enough of my senses to open both eyes at once, I coughed and gagged until blood from my mouth ran up my nose.

"Clean him up!" someone ordered, and before I could turn to see who it was, I was pounded with a stream of water from a massive hose. The force spun me and stung almost as badly as the pepper spray. The barrage of water was agonizing, but I kept my wits about me enough to capture several mouthfuls and force them down—or rather, up—my throat as I hung there inverted, bloody, soaking wet, and desperate.

"Spin him!" came the next order.

A pair of men shoved me in circles until the chain wound itself into a twisted knot, and then they let me fly. The spinning was disorienting and uncomfortable, but it was a lot better than the soccer demonstration. At least I thought it was until it continued for ten minutes or more without interruption. It only ended after I vomited, wasting every precious drop of water I'd swallowed. In that moment, I would've loved to replay the soccer match.

A man in a low rolling chair wheeled himself toward me with his hand extended. "Strap!"

Someone laid a long, thin strip of leather in his palm, and my brain exploded trying to guess what he would do with the strap. But I didn't have to wait long to find out. He rolled behind me, stuck his knees in my back, and laced the strap around my neck. Then he wrapped the leather around each of his hands and leaned back, cutting off air from my lungs, blood from my head, and the belief that I'd ever escape.

"It's time for a little man to man, Chase Daniel Fulton, born January first, nineteen seventy-four . . ." He eased the pressure on the strap and continued quoting facts about me—everything from the name of my first girlfriend to the middle name of my innocent wife.

I growled. "If you touch my wife . . ."

The man pulled the leather again. "What? Just what are you going to do if we do whatever we want to your wife? You don't look like you're in any position to make threats."

I coughed and struggled against the strap. I'd been tortured before, but never by anyone as good at it as those guys. They beat up my mind and spirit at least as much as my body. Their blows were perfect, with just enough force to inflict terrible agony without killing me.

I twisted my neck and ducked my chin in a desperate effort to breathe. I croaked, "What do you want from me?"

With that, he released the leather strap with one hand and let it fall to the floor with my blood, sweat, and vomit. "That took longer than I expected. Let me tell you . . . I'm impressed. The last few guys we trussed up like this didn't last as long as you. You should be proud, Chase. Maybe I'm wrong about you. Maybe you're not quite as civilian as your CV suggests."

I heaved, filling my lungs and relishing the blood flow back to my head. "What . . . do . . . you . . . want?"

"Oh, that's an easy one, Chase. I want to punish you for your sins."

I let my breathing calm. "You're going to need more time and a lot more men. My list of sins is long and sickening."

He smiled. "It's a shame. I think I would've liked having you on my team. You're quite the fighter. I like that in a man. Tell me, Chase, are we north or south of your pitiful little town?"

"North."

"Very good. How far north?"

"I don't know."

"Tell me about the taillight. I'm curious. How did you manage to break it out from inside the trunk?"

"Let me down, and I'll show you."

He let his head fall back and let out a long laugh. "Oh, did you hear that, boys? He wants us to let him down."

Nervous laughter filled the room, and I tried to steal their moment. "Just tell me what you want, or kill me."

The laughter died, and the man said, "Be careful what you wish for. We just might make your wish come true."

I took the moment to think about holding Penny in my arms, on a beach somewhere no one has ever heard of, with waves lapping at the sand. I could almost smell her hair blowing on the breeze and feel her perfect skin beneath my fingertips. Hanging upside down would eventually kill me, but I would leave this world with thoughts of Penny Fulton instead of the fear those men wanted to force inside my head.

Chapter 23
Who's Side Are You On?

The longer I hung upside down, the more my mind grew to accept my situation. Blood was pooling in my skull and struggling to return to my heart and lungs. The chain wrapped around my knees made circulation to my one remaining foot almost nonexistent. My wrist locked inside the steel shanks of the handcuffs grew numb from the pressure, and the rope binding my ankles to my handcuffs pulled so violently against the muscles, ligaments, and tendons of my shoulders that my neck spasmed as if my body were enwrapped in an unstoppable convulsion.

My interrogator and chief torturer pressed the cattle prod against the center of my chest and glared into my eyes. "Sometimes interrogations end immediately after applying this particular method of encouragement. Sometimes the electrical current this close to the heart stops the pump, and there's nothing we can do to bring you back."

Drawn back from my waterfront daydream with my beautiful wife, I whispered. "Push the button, asshole."

And he did.

My heart didn't stop pumping, but every other muscle attached to my skeleton contracted with a force of unbelievable magnitude. My diaphragm leapt and convulsed, forcing my lungs to gasp, jerk, and beg for air. I roared like a lion until the pulsing torture ceased and my body relaxed.

In that moment of hyperventilation, relief, and terror, a realization flooded my already overloaded brain. They let me shoot two of their men without shooting back. Using a baseball bat, they pounded my abdomen, where there were no bones to break. They jolted my body with electricity, but not enough to stop my heart. They'd sprayed me with non-lethal pepper spray and high-pressure water. All of that added up to only one conclusion: they weren't trying to do serious bodily harm, and more importantly, they weren't going to kill me.

But what I was enduring almost made death a preferable alternative.

I hissed, "How are your two men I shot during the grab?"

The question brought immediate laughter from my tormentor and his clan, and two sets of body armor landed on the filthy concrete floor just in front of me.

The man said, "You didn't shoot two of my men. You shot two of my vests. Thanks for not aiming for the T-box."

The emotions whirring inside me battled as I tried to decide if I was angry for having failed to kill my abductors or if I was thankful my rounds hadn't been lethal. My predicament wasn't conducive to moral turmoil, so I fought to push the thought from my head.

Survive. Evade. Resist. Escape. I'm still alive . . . check. I hadn't evaded . . . fail. I resisted at every turn . . . check. Escape . . . do it no matter what the cost.

Escaping conventional handcuffs is an essential skill, and with almost anything small enough to insert into the keyhole, I could pick the lock in seconds, but the chances of finding a hairpin were nil. The second option required twisting the chain connecting the two cuffs until it bound against itself, and then applying enough pressure to either break the chain or pull it from its connection to one of the cuffs. That was the option for me.

I whimpered with feigned sounds of exhaustion and fear while I worked the links of the connecting chain, hoping someone would hit me again to cover the sound and motion of breaking it, but they were ignoring me. If my effort produced results, I would likely fall to the floor in the second after the break. My hands would be free, but my head would contact the floor harder than I wanted to endure. The requirement to escape demanded doing so whenever possible, not whenever convenient, so I focused on the necessity to escape instead of the pain of the cuffs digging into my wrists as I applied the force that should've snapped the chain. Instead of the restraint surrendering to my will, the tension from the rope around my ankles and pulling on my handcuffs was enough to prevent me from twisting the chain far enough to break. After more attempts than I could count, it became time for option three.

The only remaining possibility of slipping my cuffs was to dislocate my thumb and force my compacted hand through the steel ring. The agony associated with the effort would be indescribable, but the benefit of reobtaining the use of my hands far outweighed the coming pain. The event wouldn't be quiet or covert, so I made the decision to wait for another distraction . . . and I didn't have to wait long.

Only minutes later, the man rolled his squatty chair back into position beside my head, and my theory about his unwillingness to kill me crumbled into dust. He drew a Colt 1911 .45-caliber pistol, pressed the muzzle to my temple, and thumb-cocked the hammer.

Is he going to shoot me, or is he just trying to scare me?

I wanted to believe he was going to pull the trigger. That belief made what was to come not only justifiable, b ut a lso t ruly required.

"What do you want from me?" I yelled as I jerked and twisted in my suspension. "Do it! Either tell me what you want or pull the trigger."

My thrashing sent him backing up a foot to avoid my flailing shoulders, head, and torso, and my screaming had become routine, so the men paid little attention. I set my jaw, prepared for the nearly unbearable pain, and yelled at the top of my lungs. "Do it! Pull the trigger! Do it!"

As I screamed, I forced my left thumb into my palm and pulled with the strength of a thousand men. The thumb joint collapsed, and everything in my world happened in ultra-high speed. My hand slipped through the cuff, raking flesh from bone, and my body twisted like a spinning top as my freed arm flailed through space. Almost in the same instant, the rope to my ankles slid off the now-empty left cuff, and my legs straightened. I threw my chin against my chest as violently as possible, hoping to take the impact with the concrete floor on my shoulders instead of the top of my head. With both arms free, my final spin sent my right hand toward the man, and I clamped down on the frame of his pistol like a vise, ripping the gun from his hand.

My chin-tuck worked, and I found myself on my side, both arms free, pistol in hand, and only inches from the man on the stumpy rolling chair. I threw out my left arm with the bloody dislocated thumb and hooked the man's waist, pulling him from his chair. The adrenaline-driven dire effort to survive and escape gave me the strength to draw the man against my chest as a human shield. My situation had improved, but only slightly. I'd escaped my confinement, but getting out of the building alive would require that I kill every man in front of me or convince them to surrender and allow me to leave. It was time to create my balance sheet.

I had a weapon and a hostage. There were likely seven, and maybe eight rounds in the .45. I was facing five armed men inside an open building, not counting my hostage.

Eight bullets against six men. Maybe I should've stayed in my previous position, hanging from the rafters.

Perhaps my incessant need to escape drove me to make the most poorly timed move in history.

All five men drew and spread out. I was suddenly facing a fight I couldn't win. If they were willing to kill me, I'd be dead inside sixty seconds, but if they were under some strange set of orders to keep me alive, the coming seconds would prove to be some of the most bizarre moments in my life.

They spread out in an arc, making it impossible for me to see all of them at the same time, so the decision of who to kill first loomed large in my mind. As my adrenaline subsided, the pain in my left hand grew to almost debilitating levels, and the man in my arm must've sensed the change.

He spoke in a soft, confident tone. "Listen to me, Chase. Nobody is going to kill you unless you start the fight. Lay the gun down, and nobody gets hurt. It's that simple."

I drew him tighter against me and tried to make myself as small as possible behind my shield of flesh and bone. "When was the last time you laid down *your* gun in a situation like this?"

He took a long breath. "I've never been in a situation like this. We're plowing new ground here. You don't know what's happening, do you?"

I didn't like his technique of directing the conversation to make me question everything I thought I knew. "What are you talking about?"

He seemed to relax. "I'm talking about why we've not broken any bones or put any bullets in you. Don't you think that's a little strange in a situation like this?"

I grunted. "I thought you said you've never been in a situation like this."

"Not this situation. The one when you were still my prisoner.

I've been in that position more times than I can remember, but this is my first time being held hostage by an ally who doesn't realize I'm on his team."

Two things happened at precisely the same instant: My mind turned itself inside out trying to make sense of the man's comment that we were allies. The other thing that happened was three simultaneous explosions from the exterior of the building. The breaching charges ripped holes through the walls and blew doors from their hinges.

Yelling filled the air. "Hands! Hands! Hands! Get 'em up! Drop your weapons! Do it now!"

My abductors raised their hands as ordered, but they didn't drop their weapons. Instead, they lowered their rifles to hang on their slings across their chests and kept their pistols firmly in their grips.

Mongo hit the first man at the far right with a blow so hard the man's booted feet left the ground, and he was unconscious before his body hit the floor. Moving faster than should've been possible, my giant ripped the pistol from the second man's hand and landed a perfect temple blow with the butt of the weapon, sending the man melting to the floor. Simultaneously, Hunter swept the feet of the man on the far left and landed with a knee in his crotch and the barrel of his rifle beneath the man's chin. Singer put two rounds into the concrete at the fourth man's feet, forcing him to leap backward until he collided with the wall behind him. Our Southern Baptist sniper closed the distance and bounced the man's head against the wall until he crumpled to the floor.

Clark charged across the room, but his target surrendered before contact. The fifth man fell to his knees and slid his weapon across the floor, but his submission didn't stop Clark's attack. He hit the kneeling man squarely in the forehead with the butt of his

M4, sending him onto his back with blood pouring from the open flesh covering his skull.

My team had the five men flex-cuffed and dragged into one pile of bodies before I realized what was happening, and Clark turned to me with his weapon trained on the human shield in my arms. "You're not looking so good, College Boy. Are you hurt?"

"Not bad," I said. "Just superficial stuff. Don't kill anybody. I think none of this is what it appears to be."

Chapter 24
Head Shot

Clark holstered his Glock, took a knee in front of me, and grabbed my hostage by his shirt. "Please lie to me just one time. Please refuse to answer me just one time. I've been chasing you all day while you've been torturing my brother, so please give me an excuse to turn you inside out."

The man held up his hands in apparent surrender. "What do you want to know?"

Clark relaxed his grip, and the man sprang forward, trapping both of Clark's wrists. As he lunged to drive his forehead into my handler's face, I swung the 1911 in a descending arc until the butt of the grip contacted the man's temple and his body went limp.

Clark pulled away. "Why would you do that? I wanted to take him down. Now who's going to answer my questions?"

"I think I know the answers you're looking for. I don't know any of these guys, but I'd put money on them being another tactical team directed by the Board—or at least by Richardson and Wainwright."

Mongo dragged the newest unconscious victim onto the pile with his buddies and turned back to me. "Let's take a look at that hand."

I held up my left hand, and he took it in his. "I can't do much about the cuts, but I can reset that thumb if you've got the stomach for it."

I turned my head away and took a deep breath. Mongo's massive hands gripped mine, and he started counting. "One . . . two . . ."

Before I could tense up on three, he yanked my thumb and shoved it back into the joint where it belonged. I howled in pain and jerked my hand from his grip.

He chuckled. "Nice. I expected you to pass out. I'm impressed."

I rolled my eyes. "After what I've been through in the last four hours, you could've cut off my hand and I would've stayed on my feet."

"Speaking of staying on your feet," Clark said. "Let's get that guy up."

"Which guy?" Mongo asked.

"The one you just put on the pile. Something tells me he's the boss."

I nodded. "I get that impression, too. He seemed to be in charge. There's a handy little firehose right over there if you want to wake him up."

Clark put on his grin. "Oh, yeah. I like that idea. Truss him up, Mongo. I'll get the hose."

Mongo rolled the man onto his side and cuffed one hand in front of his body and one behind with the chain running between his legs. The handy-dandy chain that had been my connection to the overhead winch made a perfect noose. Mongo thumbed the button, pulling the chain just far enough to bring the man to his toes. Clark hit him with a blast of cold water that would've awakened the dead.

The man came to, gagging and straining against his restraints.

Clark stuck his nose inches away from our victim. "Welcome back, old buddy. Ready to play nice?"

It took him several seconds to realize the position he was in. With his heels off the floor and only his toes still touching, the strain required to keep the tension off his neck was substantial. Being cuffed between his legs eliminated any possibility of him escaping.

The man glared down at Clark. "Who are you?"

Clark gave him an open-handed slap across the face. "That's the punishment for talking without being asked a question." He sent a violent shot to the man's gut. "And that's the punishment for asking questions." Clark motioned toward me. "Only he and I ask the questions. Got it?"

The man choked out the words. "Got it."

Clark started the interrogation. "Tell me your name, and if you lie . . . well, let's just say you really shouldn't lie."

"Warren McHenry."

"Excellent start," Clark said. "Why did you grab my boy?"

"It was my job."

"Why didn't you kill him when he became too much for your goons to handle?"

He hesitated, and Clark grabbed the winch control and hovered his thumb above the button. The threat worked.

"We're on orders not to kill him."

"Orders from whom?" Clark gave me a wink and whispered, "You liked that fancy talk, didn't you, College Boy?"

"I did."

Warren said, "The same people you work for."

"Names," Clark demanded.

"You know I don't have names to give you."

Clark pressed the button for an instant. The chain grew tighter, leaving Warren on the absolute tips of his boots.

"You wanna reconsider that answer?"

Choking even more than before, Warren said, "Okay, okay. Let me down, and I'll tell you what I know."

Clark drew his pistol and stuck the muzzle under the man's chin. "So help me God, if you so much as stutter, I'll splatter-paint this place with your brain. I'm in this thing neck-deep, and I don't care what happens to me. You got me, Warren McHenry?"

He groaned. "Roger."

Clark thumbed the button and drew McHenry's feet off the ground an inch. The man kicked and choked, and his face flushed bright red as terror filled his eyes. For the first time in my life, I was afraid of what Clark Johnson was about to do.

My handler grinned up at his victim. "Oops. I must've pushed the wrong button. Sorry about that, Warren. Come back down here with the rest of us, and we'll have a little chat."

His feet hit the floor, and he drew in what had to be the most delicious breath of his life. Clark unwrapped the chain from his neck and shoved him to the floor. He landed on a hip to avoid crushing the hand cinched between his legs and let out a sound as if the life had just abandoned his body.

Clark placed a boot beneath the man's chin and locked eyes with him. "Don't get me wrong, Warren. I respect your defiance. You're a fighter like us. Please tell me my boy didn't whimper like a scared little girl when you put the screws to him."

McHenry squirmed beneath the foot. "I've put a lot of men through nine miles of hell, and until Mr. Fulton, I've never had one who wouldn't break."

Clark lifted his foot. "I wouldn't have expected anything less. Now, let's get down to the part where I get to cut off your fingers if you lie to me."

Warren huffed. "You've got my men piled up like cordwood

and me cuffed up like a pedophile. I think it's safe to say we've been bested, and we can talk like grown-ups now."

Clark gave me a glance. "Any shots you'd like to get in before we dust him off?"

"No shots," I said. "But I do have a question. What were you going to do to me next? How long were you going to leave me hanging upside down?"

Warren looked down at his cuffed wrist. "Threats and physical violence weren't working, so believe it or not, I was going to take your prosthetic foot off and beat you with it."

Clark chuckled. "That's some cold, psychological stuff right there. Did you come up with that all by yourself?"

"Actually, I was resurrecting it. I cut a guy's arm off just above the elbow in Tierra del Fuego, tied the tourniquet myself, then beat him nearly to death with his arm."

"Did he talk?" Clark asked.

"He would have, but I couldn't keep him alive long enough."

"Been there," Clark said. "As the old saying goes, it's time to quit circling and sniffing butts and get down to the Nutter Butter."

Warren blinked a hundred times in rapid succession and turned to me.

I threw up my hands. "Don't look at me. I'm just a civilian, re-member? What makes you think I'd have a clue what he's talking about."

Clark gave the man a shove. "You know what I mean. I guess you want out of those handcuffs, huh?"

"That would be nice."

Clark tossed a handcuff key onto the floor in front of him. "You get sixty seconds from the time you pick up the key. If you're not free in that time, I'm taking my key back."

Warren scampered to the key, retrieved it from the floor, and began the arduous task of unlocking himself while cuffed between his legs.

As the unlocking fiasco was underway, Warren's men returned from the spirit world and back to the land of the living. Mongo and Singer sat each of them upright in a hodgepodge collection of chairs with their cuffs still in place.

Clark was a little lenient on his timekeeping task and gave Warren the extra time he needed to escape.

With his hands finally free, he asked, "Could I get one of those chairs?"

Mongo pulled another seat from a stack in the corner of the room and slid it beside the last man in the row.

Warren took the seat. "Thanks."

Clark met my gaze and raised an eyebrow. "Are you doing this, or am I?"

"I'll take it," I said, and he stepped away.

Doing the traditional crowding and looking-down method of psychological intimidation would've been wasted on our guest, so I dragged a chair slightly in front of him and offset toward his men.

"All right, Warren McHenry. We're going to keep this friendly. Soldier to soldier. At least we're keeping it friendly until you decide to make it otherwise. Capisce?"

He nodded, and I gave his shin a love tap. "We're going to use our words, as well."

"Got it."

"Don't be ashamed, Warren. This isn't an interrogation. It's a conversation between like-minded combatants who found themselves temporarily on opposing sides of an issue. I'm not going to embarrass you in front of your men. That's over and behind us. Are you tracking?"

He nodded, and I moved to offer another love tap, but he caught himself. "I'm tracking."

I crossed my legs to demonstrate a relaxed posture and leaned back to appear non-threatening. It worked. His shoulders relaxed, and he unclenched his fists.

"Let's start with something simple, Warren. What did Wainwright tell you to get you to hit an American the way you hit me?"

Back to the floor went his eyes, and back to his shin went the toe of my boot. One of McHenry's men jerked out of his chair while still cuffed and moved to defend his boss. Hunter calmed him down with a nicely delivered butt-stroke to the base of his skull, sending the man to the floor in a heap.

I studied the man lying motionless on the deck. "Admirable. Your men seem to be loyal. That says a lot about the leader you are. I can respect that, but let's agree to agree that we're through beating on each other's teams."

Warren glared down the line of his warriors. "Stay in your seats, men. This is almost over."

"This is *far* from over," I said. "We've got a lot to cover, and you get to decide how long it takes. Now, back to my question. What were you briefed, Warren?"

He closed his eyes, took a long breath, and started talking. "We were briefed that you went rogue and hit one of the Board member's houses. They said you drilled through the security team, leaving a dozen dead bodies on the ground, and then they said you shot his wife in the head."

I gave Clark a glance and a wink. "And you believed that?"

"Why would they lie about something like that?"

"To get you to hit another American."

Warren lowered his chin. "I noticed you didn't say another *innocent* American. Does that mean you did what they said?"

I motioned down the line of men. "You watched my team hit your team. My men were armed to the teeth with everything from MP5s to M4s, and not a single man got shot. They blew a couple of doors off their hinges, but they took the room with precisely the required degree of violence. Does that sound like a team who's gone rogue? If we're murderers, why is everybody on your team still breathing?"

He shook his head and immediately withdrew his shins from my striking range. "No, your team doesn't appear to be rogue. They're obviously well-disciplined, efficient, and serious."

"Let's move on," I said. "This briefing you got . . . Was it from the Board or just Wainwright?"

He cast his eyes to the right, and every student of neurolinguistic programming knows that indicates the subject is recalling a memory and not fabricating a lie. When he came back from his stroll down memory lane, he said, "It was just Wainwright, but now that I think about it, he clearly wanted me to believe it was a mission from the Board."

Clark let out a sound that could've been his lunch talking back, or more likely, his inability to suppress his disgust with Malcolm Wainwright.

I checked my partner. "Can I tell him?" My handler nodded, so I said, "Sit back and relax, Warren. I'm going to tell you a story."

He repositioned in his seat just as the man Hunter sent to the floor came back to join the living. Hunter helped him back into his chair.

I began my tale. "The same thing happened to us, but it was on a bit of a grander scale. Wainwright had a coconspirator for our adventure. They told us a big story about a guy who claims to be a descendant of the Astor family with some crazy connection to the Titanic."

Warren frowned. "Like, the ship?"

"Yes, exactly like that. Anyway, he was supposed to be some international arms dealer who'd committed some unthinkable atrocity. We accepted the briefing and took the mission. We committed millions of dollars in assets toward the operation, and we found the long-lost child of the Astor family on Saint Barts, where he was living the good life."

"So, you caught him?"

"That's where I'm headed. He wasn't the real target. We were set up to stumble onto a Russian arms dealer whose father had done some particularly nasty stuff to Wainwright's and the other guy's granddaughters."

"Granddaughters?"

"Yes. The two Board members have children who are married to each other. Apparently, this Russian's father killed two little girls, and I can understand the rage attached to that, but they didn't have to lie to get us to go after the bastard. The lie got a couple of my men hurt badly and put one on the disabled list for the rest of his life."

Warren sighed. "I see. Can I ask a question?"

"You just did."

He ignored my quip. "Did you hit Wainwright's house?"

"Not exactly," I said. "But we did hit the other guy's house pretty hard. We put a bunch of guards down, but we didn't kill any of them. We put two rounds into an expensive mattress beside the wife's head, but we didn't kill anybody. Well, we didn't kill anybody at that house."

Clark slid in beside me. "I'll take it from here. By the time we egressed from the first target site and landed at the next, they'd circled the wagons and brought in some extra shooters. We got pinned down pretty hard and had to shoot our way out. There may have been some casualties, but they weren't intentional. We just wanted to keep their heads down long enough to get outta Dodge."

Warren dropped his head. "That's not the story we were briefed."

Clark motioned toward our sniper. "You see that humble-looking guy over there with the oversized optic on his rifle?"

Warren eyed Singer. "If I were betting, I'd say he's your sniper."

Clark said, "He's a lot more than that. He's the moral heart of this team, and every move we make is scrutinized to the nth degree by that man's devotion to what's right. He likes to say that the beauty of the truth is that it's still the truth, no matter who tells it."

My handler paused to give Singer's wisdom time to soak in before continuing. "Who has more to gain by the story they told you? Wainwright is crooked, and so is his cohort. Our team is burnt, no matter how this washes out. We're done, so from our perspective, there's nothing you can do to change the outcome. Now, I'd like for you to think about what Wainwright and his co-conspirator stand to gain by the story they're telling you."

Warren sighed, and Clark asked, "Who's your handler?"

"You know I can't divulge that, but I can tell you that he bought the story Wainwright told."

Clark grunted. "Call him, tell him what's going on, and hand me the phone."

McHenry patted his pockets. "I don't know where my phone is. It's been an exciting afternoon, to say the least."

I pulled a phone from the stack we'd seized from his team and tossed it to him.

He dialed a number and stuck the phone to his ear. "Shannon, it's Warren. I need you to listen."

He spent several minutes laying out the story, then he handed the phone to Clark.

"Clark Johnson here."

The conversation became intricate and complex but turned on a dime as it seemed to draw to a close. Clark lowered his tone and almost growled. "You put my wife in danger, and there's only one penalty for that. I know who you are. I know where you are. And I know how to get to you. Every time you fall asleep for the rest of your life, no matter how short that time is, you can plan to wake up with everything in your world on fire, and the last thing you'll see before leaving this world will be me holding the match and the empty gas can."

Instead of handing the phone back, Clark opened his hand and let it fall to the floor. In the same motion, he drew his Glock and press-checked the chamber for a round. "Look at me, McHenry. We don't need you. We've got every skill set we need, and we're not interested in dragging anyone else into our swamp. But what we do need is for you to stay out of our way. Are we clear?"

Warren chewed on his bottom lip. "I'll do what my handler instructs me to do."

Clark leaned in. "I've got no beef with you. You were following orders. That's what we do, but now you know the truth of what really happened, so your mission is over."

The man seemed to consider what Clark was saying, then asked, "Was it Richardson?"

Clark gave me a glance as if my input had any value, and I gave him nothing in return. He asked, "What makes you say that?"

"Just a hunch," Warren said. "We won't get in your way, but if you change your mind about needing or wanting our help, give me a call."

"That won't happen," Clark said.

Warren nodded. "For the record, his name was Cain Fitzgerald."

"Whose name?"

"The guy who torched the restaurant. He's a contractor, not a teammate."

"Thank you," Clark said. "He owes Maebelle at least three million dollars, and you owe Chase a new boathouse."

He didn't say a word, but he glanced at the man in the last chair, and I followed his line of sight. I put my boot between the boots of the last man in line. "I'm sending you the bill, but I've got one question . . ."

He interrupted before I could ask and said, "It was a time-delayed floater. I set it in the middle of the night, twelve hours before it went off."

Without another word, I walked away. "What are we going to do with these guys, Clark?"

Hunter, Mongo, and Singer leapt into action, stripping Warren's team's weapons and tossing the parts into a bucket. When every weapon was in a dozen pieces and scattered in the tall grass beside the building, we mounted the truck and left the compound and the other team in a cloud of dust.

Hunter slapped a hand on my shoulder. "It's good to have you back, partner."

"It's good to be back. Those guys aren't big on hospitality, but they're top-notch when it comes to snatch-and-grab work."

"Speaking of grabbing," Clark said. "Dr. Richter's VW is back at Bonaventure, none the worse for wear. There were four nine-millimeter shell casings on the floor. I'm wondering why we didn't find four dead bodies."

I huffed. "Body armor."

In perfect unison, every man in the vehicle said, "Head shot."

Chapter 25
Good Old-Fashioned Espionage

My first question when we hit Interstate 95 was, "Does Penny know?"

Clark shook his head. "Not unless Skipper told her. They've been out of pocket since Disco left Miami. I don't want to know where they are as long as they're safe."

"Same," I said. "I'm sure they'll check in, and honestly, I'm confident that Irina has the skill set to keep them alive, even if they get hit."

"What are we going to do with her?" he asked.

"I don't know yet. Mongo, what are your thoughts?"

The monster of a man said, "She's no Anya, but it's clear she's got some skills. I'm with you, Chase. I think she'll put herself between any threat and the rest of them."

"Are you thinking about bringing her on board?" Clark asked.

I said, "Not yet. We've got a lot to do before we make any more personnel moves."

Clark nodded. "Agreed."

I drummed my fingertips against the center console. "Let's talk about what we're doing next."

"What do *you* want to do next?" Clark asked.

"I want to burn Wainwright and Richardson to the ground and play in their ashes."

"Don't hold back," Hunter said. "Tell us how you really feel."

"That is the filtered version. They launched a tactical team against us, and that's absolutely over the line."

Clark held up a hand. "Wait a minute. They launched us against the team in Montana, and we cleaned their clocks."

"That's different," I said. "That team was rotten to the core, and they had to be stopped."

Clark looked over the rim of his sunglasses. "We hit two houses in DC and sent about a thousand pounds of lead downrange. Admit it. If you heard another team did that, you'd be ready to cut 'em down, and you know it."

"You're probably right, but this is different. We didn't hit the Board. We hit two bad apples, and they started their own private war with us."

He said, "Look around. They didn't hit the team. They hit you and me."

Hunter jumped into the fray. "Hold on a minute! By hitting the two of you, they hit all of us. Our families are in hiding, and we're blowing holes in metal buildings in the middle of South Georgia to get our team leader back. This ain't just you and Chase. This is all of us."

Clark said, "You're absolutely right, Hunter. I didn't mean to imply it wasn't an assault on all of us. I was just making the point that it's a very different method of operation than the Montana thing. We went out there to mop up the whole team. So far, they've just hit me and Chase, and other than blowing up a boathouse and setting a restaurant on fire, they've not hit us hard enough to put holes in us yet."

Hunter lowered his gaze. "You said *yet* as if you think we're not done with these guys."

"I didn't mean it that way, but there's no way to be sure. I didn't get the impression McHenry and his guys were coming back after us. Did you?"

Mongo jumped in. "I didn't get that feeling until you threatened to burn his house down when he went to sleep."

Clark grinned. "Yeah, subtlety is one of my strong suits."

"Oh, I can tell," Mongo said. "So, if they hit us again, we put 'em down, right?"

Clark cleared his throat. "If they hit us again, it'll be a blindside and they'll hit hard. I'm not in charge. That's Chase's gig. But if he asks for my advice, I'll recommend hitting back as hard as possible. They've been warned, and they know we're not rogue. Another attack is a direct threat to our lives and the lives of our families. As far as I'm concerned, if they come after me or Maebelle, I'll put 'em in the ground."

I pointed at my handler. "Yeah, what he said."

Mongo spoke up. "Understood, but what's our next move? We're not just going to sit around and wait for these guys to come back, are we?"

I said, "No, we're definitely not. We're men of action. Waiting doesn't become us. I've got a much better plan . . . I think it's time for some good old-fashioned espionage."

The cab of the truck suddenly became silent as the team waited to hear my plan.

"I've had a lot of peaceful and quiet time to think over the past several hours while I was kidnapped and interrogated, so I came up with an idea. By the way, how did you guys find me?"

"It wasn't easy," Clark said. "I saw the microbus on the side of the access road while I was flying the approach into the airport. That's what rang my bell, so I called you a dozen times before calling Skipper."

"I thought Skipper was probably involved."

"Oh, she was," he said. "Those guys are pretty good. We tracked your cell phone at first, and I thought it was crazy that they'd keep it active. It turned out they were using it for a play. They headed south on Ninety-Five for ten miles or so before dumping your phone in a trash can at a truck stop."

"That's the southbound leg I thought I felt."

"Yep, must've been. Anyway, we recovered your phone and dusted it for prints. Nothing, of course. They turned north at that point, I suspect after running an SDR with a hundred turns."

"Oh, yeah. They rolled me around like a pinball back there. I had no idea where we were headed until I broke out a taillight."

Clark said, "This is the part you're going to love. Skipper called UAB and talked to the prosthetic lab about your foot."

"My foot?"

"Keep your pants on, College Boy. I'm telling this story. It turns out they have a telemetry device built into your robot foot to keep track of its performance and malfunctions. It reports to a satellite every thirty minutes and delivers a report to Birmingham. Of course, Skipper jumped all over that, and in seconds, she was tracking your foot every half hour."

I shook my head. "Ain't technology grand?"

"Yes, it sure is grand, but a thirty-minute report isn't very good when you're moving at sixty-five miles per hour. It was ultimately the phone you dialed when you got to that compound. I can't wait to hear that story, but even better, I can't wait to show you the video of you hanging upside down like a pinata."

"You took the time to take video instead of breaching and cutting me down? I'll remember that. Next time one of you guys gets kidnapped, I'll be sure to take some quality footage before saving your life."

Everyone laughed, and Hunter asked, "Is it still called *footage* when you've only got one foot?"

I gave him the look. "I may hang *you* upside down just for that."

He leaned back and crossed his arms. "You better bring some help when you try it."

Clark gave the steering wheel a solid smack. "Let's save the inverted hanging for another day. I want to hear Chase's espionage idea."

I spun in my seat. "Okay, here's what I'm thinking. We tried punching them in the face and learned they punch back. I say we find a weakness and exploit it."

Clark let out a chuckle. "That's a little vague, don't you think?"

"Just wait. I'm not finished. We all know Skipper can dig deep enough to find wives, girlfriends, boyfriends, aides, or whatever. If we can worm our way in and get one of those people in harness, I know without a doubt there's evidence to prove Wainwright and Richardson are rotten."

Hunter rolled his eyes. "Come on, Chase. Surely you're not naïve enough to believe we'll ever get either of those guys in front of a jury."

"I'm not talking about a trial. I'm talking about confronting them with the evidence we have, and I believe they'll crawl inside a hole and disappear rather than face the public and professional humiliation of having their sins scroll across the evening news."

Mongo narrowed his gaze. "That's not what we do. We're a team of hitters, not spooks."

"But we've all got the training. We know how to do it. Our style may be a little more aggressive than the CIA case officers', but I think we can pull it off."

Clark said, "Chase is right. Recruiting a spy isn't rocket surgery. I say we get Skipper to shake the sugar tree and see if any monkeys fall out."

Singer laid the back of his hand against Clark's forehead, and Clark recoiled.

"What are you doing?"

"I'm checking for a fever. I think you must be delirious or something. Everybody knows monkeys don't climb sugar trees."

"You know what I meant."

Hunter said, "I don't even think *you* know what you meant."

* * *

Back at the Bonaventure ops center, Skipper and Tony were huddled around a console when we walked in. Both leapt to their feet, and Skipper threw her arms around me. "It's so good to have you back. I knew it would work out, but you had us scared. Are you okay?"

I returned the hug. "Yeah, I'm fine. Just a little black and blue around the edges."

Tony was next to hand out a hug, and I asked, "How are you doing, sailor?"

"I'm all right, but my brain hurts."

"Your brain hurts? That's not good. Have you called the doctor?"

"Relax. Medically, I'm fine. It's the mountain of information Skipper's trying to pour down my throat that has me overwhelmed. There's a lot more to this ops center stuff than I ever knew. Forget a firehose. It's like drinking from Niagara Falls."

"I get it," I said. "And I'm about to hand the two of you a real-world mission that'll add a few thousand gallons to those falls."

Skipper's eyes lit up. "I think I know what you're about to say, and I'm way ahead of you. I'm already running backgrounds on everybody I can find surrounding the Board. It's going to take some time, but I'll find somebody misbehaving."

"It's like you can read my mind."

She pulled off her glasses. "It's not all that hard to read a kindergarten book." She paused long enough for her jab to sting a little. "The in-your-face technique turned into a train wreck, so the logical next step is corporate espionage. Give me twenty-four hours, and I'll have some possible targets."

I said, "You were seconds away from getting a raise, but the kindergarten comment blew that right out of the water."

She laughed and hooked a hand through Tony's arm. "Keep your money. I'm married to the next Picasso. He's already sold over a million dollars' worth of masterpieces, and he's only been painting for a few days."

"Over a million dollars?" I asked.

Tony stuck his hands on his hips like Superman. "The yacht club in Charleston commissioned a pair of paintings for at least a hundred thousand. The final price isn't set yet, but it turns out Skipper is just as good at selling art as she is at running the ops center."

She said, "It's easy when the artist has a history of selling a single piece for a million bucks. I think I'll get the yacht club up to a quarter million, but we'll see."

"That's amazing," I said. "Who knew?"

Tony pointed toward the ceiling. "It's gotta be a God thing, right? Until Mr. Hunter tried to kill me, I couldn't even paint Skipper's fingernails, and now I'm selling like hotcakes."

Hunter growled, "I told you to stop calling me mister."

Tony maintained his Superman stance. "And I told you I'd stop when you quit being older than me."

Skipper clapped her hands. "That's enough, boys. Seriously, is that what you were going to ask me to do, Chase?"

"You nailed it, like always. I don't have the scheme all worked out in my head yet, but it'll come when we get some target packages."

"Like I said, I'll have some names and their deep, dark secrets by this time tomorrow. I've got one other idea you're not going to like, but it's espionage gold if you'll approve it."

Chapter 26
Terrible Idea . . . Let's Do It

Twenty-four hours later, Skipper summoned us to her lair, and we dutifully obeyed.

She asked, "How tightly are you tying my hands on this thing?"

"No hands are tied. Dig as deep as you want."

She twitched her nose. "I'm not exactly talking about deep. It's really more about how wide I can go."

"Wide?" I asked.

"Yeah. Am I supposed to be looking exclusively at Wainwright and Richardson's staff and families, or are the other members of the Board in play, as well?"

I turned to Clark, and he said, "If you're asking this question, that probably means you've already done some wide digging. Tell us what you found, and we'll go from there."

Skipper hit some keys, and pictures filled the large display over her head.

I studied the pictures. "Who are those guys?"

"I know we're not supposed to know the members of the Board, but I'm really good at what I do, so, of course I know them. And I know some of them a little more intimately than they'd like."

"That's no surprise," I said. "But we still don't know who those people on the screen are."

Clark twisted in his seat. "I'm not sure this is such a good idea."

Every eye in the room instantly focused on my handler, and I asked, "Why not?"

He winced. "It's just that this is one of the core elements of what we do. We're not supposed to know who's dispatching us. It's a critical and intentional break in the chain. If we know them, that breeds familiarity, and that leads to breakdowns in operational security."

"You mean breakdowns like blowing up our boathouse and trying to kill your wife?"

Clark glared at Skipper. "Brief the pictures."

Our analyst cleared her throat and brought the first picture to the foreground. "This is Travis Kingsley. He's what you might call a factotum. For those of you who don't understand big words, a factotum is a person who's hired to do the things a rich guy doesn't want to do."

"What kinds of things?" Hunter asked.

Skipper glared at him. "If you insist on interrupting me, this is going to be a very long briefing. Good ol' Travis works for Bradford Rawlings III, and he literally does anything and everything his boss wants, from picking up dry cleaning to threatening congressmen who are leaning away from Rawlings's political position. He's not officially the driver, but he does some of the private driving when Rawlings doesn't want his real driver to see where he's going and who he's meeting. Needless to say, Travis is an absolute insider, and he's got a secret."

She paused, I assume for dramatic effect, because none of us was brave enough to ask a question. The pause was brief, and she continued. "He's married with three children, votes straight party lines, wears the right suits and power ties, but he seems to spend a little of his recreational time at a place called The Back Door."

She paused again and sent a collage of pictures to yet another overhead display. "This is The Back Door."

The pictures showed a darkened stone staircase leading beneath an aged building somewhere in the suburbs. The rest of the pictures were taken from a low-quality camera that appeared to be situated above the door to whatever was at the bottom of those stairs. Travis Kingsley appeared in nine of those pictures taken from the door cam.

Hunter said, "Okay, I give up. What's behind door number one?"

"That's the part you're going to love. As I said, it's called The Back Door for obvious reasons, but what I didn't tell you is that it's the premier bondage, domination, and sadomasochism club in the DC area, and it's no girls allowed."

"Oh," came Hunter's only comment.

She said, "Yeah, *oh*, indeed. If this isn't a way in, I can't think of a better one. All we have to do is pick Travis up, show him the pictures, and he's in harness for us."

Hunter couldn't resist. "I'm afraid he might enjoy being in harness a little too much."

We tried not to laugh but failed.

Skipper bit a lip and continued. "I've got his address, four phone numbers, and access to his electronic calendar. All that remains is picking him up. I'd recommend nabbing him on his way out of The Back Door."

I shook my head. "No. I don't like it."

Clark said, "What do you mean, you don't like it? There's never been a better espionage target. I can't believe he's made it this long without the Russians or Chinese waving the pictures in front of his face."

"That's exactly why I don't like it," I said. "He's probably already in somebody else's harness, and we don't need to butt heads with the Chinese, North Koreans, or the Russians. Let's move on to somebody else."

Clark threw up a hand. "Wait a minute. If you're right, and the communists are already working this guy, the Board needs to know. We have a responsibility to bring the pictures to Rawlings. There's no evidence that points to him as being in bed with Wainwright or Richardson. I think he's a good guy, and he needs to know."

"I'm with Clark," I said. "Travis is a weakness who's a cakewalk to exploit. Somebody's already put him in harness, and they're gleaning volumes of intel from him. Who knows? Our names and pictures may be in one of the files he passed to his handlers."

Skipper slumped. "Man, I blew this one. You're exactly right, but I didn't make the connection. How do you want to handle it?"

Clark spoke first. "I don't want to handle it yet. I want to table it for now, and I'll deal with it when this is over."

"Let's move on," I said.

Skipper rattled the keyboard, and a new collection of photos appeared. "Here's a little soap opera for you. Check out the guy wearing gloves. His name is Myron Valeska, and he's the full-time driver for Randal Cunningham, another member of the illustrious Board."

"Why's he wearing gloves?" Singer asked.

Skipper smiled. "I love that you always know exactly the right questions to ask."

She zoomed in on Valeska. "The gloves are part of his persona —his mystique, if you will—but it turns out their purpose is a lot more basic. You see, our boy Valeska has a history of mischief, in-cluding a decent career stealing cars. Those days are well in his past, but it seems that he never knows when his boss, Randal Cun-ningham, will ask him to do a little dirty work without leaving any evidence behind . . . evidence like fingerprints."

I was intrigued. "What kind of dirty work?"

Skipper scrolled through a few more pictures. "Intimidation stuff, mostly, but there's one little episode that looks a lot like an opening to me." She zoomed in on a close-up headshot. "Valeska's a good-looking, single-acting guy, but he's married to an heiress-to-be. While he's waiting for the windfall for when his father-in-law kicks the bucket, he likes to dabble in the ladies. The problem is, he doesn't agree with the laws of Virginia, Maryland, or DC when it comes to the age of consent."

"How young?" I asked.

More pictures appeared, and Skipper said, "The young lady on the left just turned fifteen, and the one on the right is seventeen now. Valeska paid for abortions for both of these girls, but only one of them used the money for its intended purpose. Amanda Pennington—she's the one on the right—is a member of Our Lady of Mercy and the daughter of the most conservative parents on the planet. She took the money, but her family intervened and sent young Amanda to live with some distant cousins in South Dakota for eight months. When she came back to DC, her stomach was flat again, like most sixteen-year-olds, and the cousins had a new addition to their family. Best of all, the baby was two thousand miles from Georgetown and Our Lady of Mercy Catholic Church. I'm not Catholic, so I don't know how it works, but I assume Amanda spent a little time in the confessional getting things right with the family's priest."

"How did you dig that up?" Clark asked.

Skipper threw up her hands. "Hey, it's what I do, but in the interest of full disclosure, it was the priest who likes to gossip and made most of the information accessible."

"Gotcha," Singer said. "Does Valeska know about the baby?"

Skipper said, "There you go again with the right questions, and the answer is . . . probably not. There's no way to know for sure, but I couldn't find any indication that he knows. Although this one isn't as strong as our boy playing in the dungeon, it's definitely exploitable. What do you guys think?"

Everyone slowly turned my way, and I asked, "Why's everybody looking at me?"

Hunter said, "Because you're in charge, and it's your idea."

I steepled my fingers. "Being in charge is overrated, but here's what I think. Valeska is a solid target, and I think we should keep him in our sights, but I don't love the idea of using someone not directly connected to Wainwright or Richardson."

Skipper smiled. "That's what I thought you'd say, but don't toss Valeska aside completely. We may still be able to get something useful out of him. As always, though, you know I saved the best for last."

She spun with a flourish and lit up the monitors with shots of a handsome couple walking hand in hand through what could be Central Park. The lady was fit, and some excellent plastic surgery work made her look like she was in her late thirties or early forties without the flawless makeup. The man obviously had a thing for cougars. He couldn't be a day over thirty, and I guessed mid-twenties.

"What do we have here?" I asked.

Skipper grinned. "Gentlemen, meet Mrs. Malcolm Wainwright."

I gave her a slow golf clap. "Well done. The bullseye has been hit. Tell us about Mrs. Wainwright's boy toy."

"His name is Bryan Tomlinson, and believe it or not, he's Mrs. Wainwright's personal security. He's twenty-nine, educated at USC, commissioned as an ensign in the Navy, made it through Naval Special Warfare Orientation, BUD/S, SQT, and then assigned to SEAL Team Two in Little Creek."

Hunter rubbed his hands together. "Oh, goody! We get to recruit a former SEAL. This is going to be like a trip to the county fair, with guns and grenades."

"Not so fast," I said. "There has to be more. Why isn't this guy still with the Teams?"

Skipper said, "Now you're starting to ask questions like Singer. He took some shrapnel under his left arm while on a mission in the Middle East, but he stayed in the fight. His team lost two men and came home with five more SEALs with holes in them. They lived, but it wasn't exactly a success. When the surgeons finally pulled all the shrapnel out of Tomlinson, his left lung wouldn't inflate, so his Navy days came to an end."

"It looks like he found a nice, soft spot to land," Clark said.

Skipper nodded. "You could say that. He went into private security right after leaving the Navy, and Wainwright picked him up full time after some contract security work, and he's been with them ever since."

Clark said, "I say we pay him a visit and let him know just how much Malcolm Wainwright appreciates him taking such good care of his wife. Even though he's a former SEAL, I think he'll be a pretty soft target. He has to love the pay and 'benefits' of his job, so he'll likely jump into our harness without too much resistance."

Hunter said, "I agree, and I'll volunteer to make the contact and the pitch."

I leaned way back in my seat. "No, I don't like it."

Clark scowled. "You don't like it? What don't you like about it? The SEAL is an easy target with a decent-sized secret. It's not enough to excite the Russians or the Chi-coms, but it's perfect for us."

"I like the secret," I said, "but not the target." Again, every eye was on me. "Bryan Tomlinson isn't our spy. Gloria Wainwright is the target. If we can get her harnessed up, she's a gold mine."

I could almost see the wheels turning inside the heads of my team as silence consumed the ops center.

Finally, Singer said, "I agree with Chase, but if we're going to grab a cougar by her tail, we'd better have a plan for dealing with her teeth. That SEAL will come at us hard and fast as soon as she reports our contact."

Clark groaned. "I like it, but it means recruiting both of them. There's no way we can run Gloria Wainwright without Tomlinson knowing. If he's her private security detail, they're joined at the hip."

Hunter chuckled. "I don't think that's exactly where they've been joining up, but it's close."

"That's enough out of you," I said. "Clark's right. We'll have to nab them both, but not at the same time. Did you say Tomlinson was married?"

Skipper said, "No, he's single, and Gloria Wainwright isn't the only recipient of his affection. This leads us directly into my idea that you're not going to like."

"Let's hear it."

She hesitated for a moment before saying, "Can you think of a more effective method of getting a guy like Tomlinson to cooperate than springing a Russian honey trap?"

"Who would be our bait?" I asked.

Skipper held up her phone and wiggled it ever so slightly. "I still have Anya's number."

Chapter 27
Fight Like a Girl

The thought of Anya coming on board for another mission bounced around inside my head just as I'd bounced around in the truck of McHenry's car—except my trunk ride was a lot more comfortable.

Still uncertain if putting Anya in our ball game was a good idea, I said, "Let's start at the DOJ. See if you can get that Supervisory Special Agent who's running Anya on the phone."

Thirty seconds later, Skipper had the speakerphone running, and the line was ringing.

"SSA White."

I'd spoken with Agent White less than half a dozen times, but he never sounded anything other than grouchy.

"Agent White, it's Chase Fulton."

He huffed. "This can't be good. Nothing good happens when you're on my phone, Fulton. What do you want?"

"I'm glad I made an impression. Listen, I'm running an op in your neck of the woods, and I thought it would be courteous to let you know." He didn't say a word, so I waited several seconds before continuing, "Are you still there, Agent White?"

"I'm here, but you've still not told me what you want. And for the future, don't pretend to be doing me a favor when you call and ask for something. You may be running an op in my backyard, but you had no intention of notifying me or anyone else."

"I want Anya."

"Tell me something I don't already know."

"It's not that kind of want," I said. "I actually need her for the op in your neighborhood."

He clicked his tongue against his teeth. "Wet work?"

"No, we're not killing anyone. We're recruiting a volunteer, so to speak."

"You're laying a honey trap to get a spy in harness. Let's call a duck a duck."

"Let's start over. Supervisory Special Agent White, this is Chase Fulton. With your unofficial permission, I'd like to use one of your operatives for a covert action in the DC area to recruit an informant. And, of course, this conversation never happened."

"That's better," he said. "It's not like I've got her chained to the wall up here at Justice. To be honest, I don't even know where she is. Her protégé, an agent named Gwynn Davis, might know how to find her. Do you want to talk with her?"

"No, thanks. We're not limited by the same restrictions you guys in Washington are. I suspect my analyst has already found her."

White said, "So, you were taking Anya, regardless of what I said. This little call was just a sideline formality."

"I'd like for you to think of it more as a show of respect."

"I think you mean honor among thieves rather than respect. Take her, Chase. Just don't get her killed. I've got a few more projects for her before I can cut her loose."

"I'll bring her back to you in the same—or better—condition than I find her. As always, it's good to talk with you, Agent White."

"Just one more thing, Chase. Take care that you don't fall into the honey trap you set."

"Goodbye, Ray."

Clark tapped the table. "That's sage advice, Chase. It's hard to get the taste of honey out of your mouth."

"That better not mean what I think it means," I said. "Get Anya on the phone."

It rang three times on the speakerphone before Anastasia Burinkova's voice filled the room. "*Privet, kto zvonit?*"

I dusted the cobwebs from the part of my brain that stores my Russian vocabulary. "*Eto Cheyz, i my mozhem govorit' po-angliyski.*"

"Chasechka! You are calling me, and I am saying hello. You are okay, yes?"

I wondered how much of her Eastern European accent was authentic. "Yes, I'm fine."

"This is very good. I think you are not calling for only hello and to know if I am well, yes?"

"Yes. It's good to know you are well, though. I called because I need you—"

She cut in before I could finish. "Yes, this is something I know. I think sometimes I need also you, Chasechka."

"That's not what I meant, and let's stick with Chase instead of Chasechka, okay?"

"This is for me difficult. Is easy for Chasechka to come from my tongue, but I will try. What is thing you need from me?"

I swallowed hard. "I need to set a snare, and nobody's better at that than you."

"Is dangerous?"

"I don't think so. We've got a guy who's sleeping with his boss's wife, and we'd like to get him to do a little snooping for us. He's a former SEAL, and he's working as private security for the woman he's sleeping with."

"This, to me, does not sound like he is primary target for you. I

think you want to trap woman and not SEAL. He is only necessary for control. This is true, yes?"

I chuckled. "See? I told you there was nobody better at this
than you."

"This is flattering, but for this thing, you do not need me."

"What are you talking about? I wouldn't have called if we
didn't need you."

"It makes, to you, sense for needing me, but this is false belief
for you. You have Irina. She is beautiful, dangerous, and knows
many of same things I know."

My eyes shot to Mongo, and he screwed up his face.

I said, "I don't know about that, Anya. She's not exactly
trained to do the things you can do."

Anya's tone turned bitter. "You are calling for me to be your
whore, yes?"

"No, Anya. That's not what I meant. I just wanted . . ."

"You do not have to say more, Chase. Is not good for me inside
mind when you think only of me when you need sparrow. This is
not how I need to be for you."

"Anya, I . . . It's not . . . I mean, I don't think of you like that.
I'm sorry I made you feel that way. I only need someone young
and beautiful to get this guy's attention. I wasn't suggesting that
you sleep with him."

"You think I am young and beautiful? This is how you think of
me inside mind?"

Skipper said, "Hey, hold on. This is getting out of hand."

Anya cut her off. "Who is also on call with us, Chase?"

"It's the whole team," I said. "You're on speaker in the ops center. We're planning the mission."

"Make call not on speaker for only you and me. You can do
this."

"Yes, I can do that, but—"

"Do not say *but*. I wish to talk only with you. Make this happen, Chase."

I looked up at Skipper, and she pressed a pair of keys, silencing the speaker and mics. She said, "You're on thin ice here. Don't mess this up. Get the headset from the slot beneath the table."

I pulled the headset onto my ears and adjusted the mic. "Are you still there, Anya?"

"Yes, I am here, but I am angry you did not tell to me others are also listening. Please do not do this to me."

"I'm sorry. I won't do it again."

"Is okay, Chasechka. I am no longer angry with you. Inside voice you sound not good. Is lie you said to me when you told me you are okay?"

"No, I wasn't lying. I'm okay. It's just that a lot has happened in the past few days, and we're all a little on edge. That's all."

"This is not mission that is so new, yes?"

"I'm not following. What are you talking about?"

She spoke just above a whisper. "This is something left unfinished from your mission in Morocco to capture Ilya Semenov, yes?"

"How could you possibly know about that?"

"Tell to me what you want, and if is necessary, I will do for you."

I cleared my throat. "We're not finished talking about how you know what we did in Morocco."

"Yes, we are. Now, tell to me what you need."

I sighed. "We need you to catch the attention of a personal security pro who used to be a SEAL. He's sleeping with his protectee, who just happens to be married to his boss. We're going to flip the wife to get to her husband, who hung us out to dry on our last operation."

"This is complicated mission. I will ask again. Is dangerous, no?"

"I don't think so. It would only be dangerous if we harnessed the wife and not the bodyguard. He'd be hard to manage without a fight. We want to approach the wife, sell our pitch, and nail her down to get the inside intel on her husband. Before she has time to tell her bodyguard about it, we want *you* to get his attention and get him alone just long enough for us to step in and recruit him, along with the wife. Nobody's asking you to take your clothes off."

"If this is not dangerous operation, why do you not have Penny or Irina do this thing?"

"They're not here," I said before stopping myself.

"They are gone for always or only for short time?"

"It's a long story," I said. "We decided to get them out of town while this thing was going on. Disco took Penny, Irina, Tatiana, and Maebelle somewhere safe while we work this out."

"So, this means you were afraid they would be in danger, but you said operation was not dangerous. You are talking two things at one time, and this cannot be. Is either dangerous or is not. I think you believe it is too dangerous for women you love, but not too dangerous for me."

"It's not like that. It's . . ."

She said, "You once loved me. If this was still true, if I was wife instead of Penny, would you send me away or ask for me to do this thing for you?"

"It's not the same. The two of you are very different."

"And still you say you love her now and loved me one time in past, so you love two people who are very different. Is this what you are saying?"

"We've gotten way off track. This is about a mission to distract a bodyguard long enough for me to flip him. That's all this is about. It has nothing to do with who I love or any of that. It's just a mission."

She said, "Okay, I will do this for you, but I have something I must do first. I am inside Disney World with . . . friend. You have been to this place, yes?"

"No, I've never been to Disney World, but what do you have to do before this mission?"

"I must finish seeing Disney World. Is promise to friend. I will then do this thing for you so danger will end, and you can go back to your Penny, and I will go away again."

"Thank you, Anya."

"You are welcome, Chasechka. But I have one demand before I do this."

"A demand?"

"Is not demand, but I cannot remember English word. Is something you must do for me before I will do for you this thing."

"Condition," I said.

"Yes, this is word, condition. I have one condition. You must tell me whole story of why this is dangerous. This does not sound like normal mission for you."

"I'll tell you the whole story when you get here."

"In this case, condition is finished, and I will do for you. I will come to your house in two days. And this is okay? Penny says is okay, yes?"

"I'll see you in two days."

Skipper ended the call, and I slid my headset back into its slot. "That got weird."

Skipper huffed. "Yeah, you could say that. I was listening in. She's never going to let go of you, Chase. I know she's really good at this kind of thing, but the more I think about it, especially after that conversation, I don't think it's such a good idea to bring her in on this."

"What else can we do? We don't have anybody else who can pull it off *and* handle a SEAL if it gets out of hand."

Skipper pulled off her glasses. "I can."

I froze in my seat. "What?"

"I can do it. I know I'm not some Russian sparrow, but I've never had any trouble turning men's heads, and I'm smart. I can have Bryan Tomlinson following me around like a puppy—SEAL or no SEAL."

Suddenly, my brain felt like it would explode. "No, you can't. I mean, you don't have the . . ."

To my surprise, Hunter said, "Hear her out, Chase. You might be surprised."

I glared at him as if he'd told me the Earth had stopped spinning, and Skipper stood from her chair.

She said, "Come here, Chase. I want to show you something." I stood, but I wasn't sure why, and Skipper hooked a finger. "Come on. Don't be scared."

I crossed the room and stood a stride in front of our analyst, who I'd only ever seen as the bratty teenager I knew fifteen years before. But before me stood an undeniably beautiful woman with eyes that could lead a man into the pits of Hell.

"Hit me!" she said.

I took a step back. "What? No! I'm not going to hit you. What are you talking about?"

Skipper took a step forward and landed both palms on my chest, sending me staggering backward. "Hit me!"

"Stop it. No, I'm not hitting you."

She stopped, leaned in close, and whispered, "I'll bet you a million dollars you can't hit me."

I turned to my team, who was still sitting silently around the conference table, none of them offering any support until Hunter said, "Go ahead, Chase. Try to hit her. I'll throw in another million on Skipper."

"What's going on here?" I demanded.

Skipper shoved me again, this time hard enough to send me crashing into the wall. With no intention of actually landing the punch, I threw a strong, fast right hook designed to pass an inch in front of her nose. To my disbelief, she stepped into the punch, spun on the ball of her left foot, and threw up both forearms. She trapped my fist, rolled my hand backward, and twisted my wrist far enough to send me off-balance. When our combined energy and motion ended, I was on my back, and Skipper had one knee planted immovably in the center of my chest and the point of her switchblade pressed against the skin of my neck, just above my jugular.

I pressed myself into the carpet and raised both hands in surrender. "Where did you learn to do that?"

"I've been training with Hunter while you've been listening to your psych patients tell you their woes."

She closed and pocketed her knife and then offered a hand to help me up. "Even a SEAL wouldn't think little-ol'-me was any threat, but he'd be wrong . . . just like you."

I glared at Hunter. "Why didn't you tell me you were teaching her to fight?"

"You didn't ask. Besides, you'd made the decision to be a plain old civilian while the rest of us needed a hobby. Mine just happened to be teaching our analyst to fight like a girl."

Chapter 28
Bring It

I motioned toward the door. "Let's have a chat, Hunter."

He grabbed the arms of his chair. "Nope! I'm not going out-side with you. Whatever you want to talk about, we can talk about it here, where there are witnesses and people who can pull you off me if you start some garbage. You don't scare me, but that bionic foot of yours freaks me out."

"Fine," I said. "But before the conversation is over, you'll wish we'd done it outside. It's up to you."

"Yeah . . . I'll take my chances in here. It's the robot foot, man. It gives you an unfair advantage."

I wanted to be mad at Hunter and the whole situation, but I couldn't stop laughing at the absurdity of it all. "Okay, here we go. Do you believe Skipper can manage the situation if the SEAL gets out of hand?"

He didn't hesitate. "No, because she won't kill him. Anya would, but there's an element you're leaving out."

"What's that?" I asked.

"The whole purpose of having a beautiful woman grab Bryan's attention is so she can lead him to us—or at least to you, right?"

"That's right."

"Then Skipper doesn't have to manage the situation if the

SEAL gets out of control. You'll be there, and you can handle him."

I said, "I have just one more question. Can you look Tony in the eye and tell him Skipper can do this without getting hurt?"

Again, Hunter didn't hesitate. "She put you on the ground, so you bet I can make that promise to Tony and anybody else."

I reclaimed my chair and spun to face Skipper with her hair back in a pile on top of her head and her glasses in place. "It's kind of like Wonder Woman turning back into Diana Prince. Nobody would suspect you could do anything like you just did to me. Look at me and tell me you want to do this."

She bit her lip. "I'll be honest. It scares me, but yeah, I want to do it."

"Does Tony know you've been training?"

"Yes, he knows, and he's incredibly supportive. To be honest, I think it turns him on a little."

I threw up my hands. "I don't want to think about that, but listen to me. There's a lot more to fieldwork than just being able to win a make-believe fight. A billion things can go wrong that you never anticipated, and at least one of those will happen on every op. I called Anya because I've seen her slice hearts out of men's chests and never lose her focus. I'm not convinced you can do that yet."

"I'm not either," she said. "But the only way to know is to put me in the field and find out. You'll be there, Chase. And I know you'd never let anybody hurt me. I can do this. I really can. And I really want to."

I lowered my head and took several long breaths. "I'm not giving this thing the green light yet, but I'm willing to put you through the paces to see if you can dodge real punches instead of those designed to miss."

She smiled. "Bring it."

I held up one finger. "There's one more caveat. I have to talk to Tony. I won't put you in harm's way if he's not comfortable with it."

She held up two fingers. "First, the feminist in me says I don't need a man's permission to do anything I want, but second, I really love that man, and I'd never do this if he wasn't okay with it."

* * *

The conversation with Tony went exactly as I expected. He was nervous but supportive. "I don't want her kicking my butt. She's scary good, Chase. You'll see."

Hunter had converted the second half of our workshop into a respectable gym with machines, pull-up bars, barbells, weights, and best of all, a collection of mats for hand-to-hand training. I started slow and easy. I wanted to see Skipper's footwork, balance, and intuition. With every passing minute, I turned up the intensity a little more until she and I were fighting at full speed and full force.

Even for fighters in perfect physical condition, fighting is an exhausting endeavor, and Skipper and I weren't immune. We collapsed to the mats, gasping for breath and pouring sweat.

Hunter tossed a pair of water bottles our way and took a seat beside us. "She's not bad, huh?"

I swallowed the water and wiped sweat from my face. "She's better than you."

He laughed. "I'll take that as a compliment."

I planted my prosthetic foot in the center of his chest and pushed him over. "Good. That's how I meant it."

Clark stepped in to fine-tune a few techniques and reemphasized the unpredictability of a real fight. He shoved her around a little and worked some Krav Maga into the afternoon. When the fire went out of Skipper's eyes and gave way to physical and mental exhaustion, Clark threw an arm around her. "Not bad, kid. I'm impressed, and that doesn't happen very often. Get some calories and rest. You're going to need both for tomorrow."

"What's tomorrow?" she asked.

"You'll see."

* * *

We reconvened at ten the next morning with mock fighting knives in hand, and Skipper grinned. "This is my favorite part."

I tossed a blunt training knife to her. "It won't be by the time we finish today."

She furrowed her brow. "Why not?"

As if on cue, Anya Burinkova stepped through the door to the gym with a knife in each hand and charged Skipper. Our analyst sidestepped the charge and sent a nice hammer fist to the Russian's shoulder as she passed.

Anya stopped, slid a hand across her shoulder where Skipper's punch had landed, and said, "Is very good punch, but look at arms and stomach."

Skipper frowned and looked down, inspecting herself. Across both forearms and her stomach were lines of pink paint glistening against the sweat. "What's that?"

Anya held out her knives. "It is paint from edges of training knives. I cut you seven times while you believed you were safely avoiding my attack. Punch was good, but you are now slowly bleeding to death."

Skipper pawed at her painted wounds as disbelief filled her eyes. "But how?"

The Russian said, "I will show this to you. Before I ran toward you from across room, I had already plan inside head. Your right hand was most dangerous part, so I attacked right arm first. If these were real knives, you would withdraw bleeding arm and turn body to right. From there, I drew both knives across stomach and followed those slices with continued cutting to left arm."

"But there are seven wounds, and you only described six," Skipper said.

"Seventh was cut of opportunity. Your left arm was still in position to be easily attacked, so I made one final cut while you were concentrating on hitting my shoulder. This proves that your instincts are to first hit and not cut. If you are to fight with knives, this must change. Strike with knife is also punch but does more damage. You understand this, yes?"

"Yeah, I get the concept. But actually doing it is another thing altogether."

"Is okay. I will teach to you how to think about having blades in hands instead of only empty fists."

The two women fought, sliced, punched, and kicked for several hours until Skipper's head was overflowing with edged-weapon fighting techniques.

When they took a break to allow Skipper's brain to digest what she'd learned, Anya took a seat beside me. "You look worried, Chasechka."

"I'm okay. How was Disney World?"

"It was . . . interesting. But too many people."

"Did your friend enjoy it?"

"Yes, is nice of you to ask."

"Was your friend the other agent from Justice?"

"No."

"A man?" I asked.

She grinned and raised an eyebrow. "You are jealous, Chasechka, no?"

"No, I'm not jealous. I'm happy for you."

"My friend was not another man. She is only friend. I believe you will love her."

That's a strange thing to say, I thought. "What do you think of Skipper's fighting technique?"

"She was trained by American man, mostly, I think. This was you?"

"No, it was Hunter. I didn't even know they were training together. It all came as a big surprise to me."

"She had also Krav Maga instructor, maybe a little."

"That would be Clark," I said.

"She is strong, fast, and aggressive, like me. This is good. There is only one thing I am nervous about. She has never killed anyone. It will be very hard for her after this happens. She will have worry and bad thoughts when she does this, but it must happen."

I grimaced. "I hope it never does."

"I hope same, but you are bringing her inside dangerous world with terrible people."

"I know. It's in my nature to protect her. She's always been like a little sister to me. I don't know how well I'll handle it when she's forced to stand toe to toe with something evil."

"This is wrong way to say this, Chasechka. It should be toe to toe with *someone* evil."

"You're right, but I don't think that's what this mission requires. I believe she'll be fine, but it makes me feel a lot better knowing you're working with her. How long can you stay?"

She leaned toward me until our shoulders touched. "How long do you want me to stay, Chasechka?"

"Don't do that. You're here to train Skipper. If you and I don't think she's ready, you're here to work the mission with us."

She pulled away. "I am sorry. Is difficult to see you and not . . ."

"Let's just focus on Skipper's training, okay?"

"Yes, of course. I will work with her one more day, and we will make decision on next day after that. This is okay with you?"

"Are you sure you can get her ready in two days?"

"She has fighting spirit. Is only for me to connect her body with this spirit inside her. This will happen quickly, or it will not happen at all."

I hadn't noticed Skipper back on her feet, but in true style, she nudged me over and claimed my chair. "So, how do you think I'm doing? Be honest."

Anya said, "You are doing well. I was just telling Chasechka—"

"Chase. His name is Chase."

Anya smiled. "Yes, Chase. I was just telling him how well you are doing. I believe you will become very good knife fighter. Is only important for you to know that everyone who gets inside knife fight will get cut. It does not matter who wins or loses. Everyone bleeds."

"I get that," Skipper said, "but I did a lot more bleeding than you."

Anya nodded. "Yes, this is true, but only because I have many years of experience, and you do not."

"Not yet," Skipper said. "So, what's next?"

"For today, we are finished. We will train again tomorrow, and I will bleed more for you, I promise."

Skipper said, "Sounds good. Come with me. You can sleep at my house tonight. Maybe Tony will paint something for you."

Anya furrowed her brow. "What does this mean, paint something for me?"

Skipper stood and reached for the Russian's hand. "Come on. We'll get cleaned up, and I'll show you. Chase, you should go home, read the Bible, and take a cold shower or something."

I passed on the cold shower, but I did a little light reading before falling asleep . . . alone.

* * *

The next day came and went with Anya and Skipper slicing and dicing each other while Tony, the rest of the team, and I spent the day in the ops center poring over the research Skipper had done on Bryan Tomlinson and Gloria Wainwright.

"It all looks pretty cut and dried to me," Tony said. "I'm not sure what could go wrong."

Clark yelled, "Come on, Coast Guard, you know better than that. Don't ever say things like that before a mission. What's wrong with you?"

Tony threw up his hands. "Sorry. It just slipped out."

I came to his rescue. "Tony's not entirely wrong. This one is a lot safer than most of the dumpster fires we jump into. Here's how I want to work it."

Everyone pulled their notepads close and clicked their pens.

I said, "When Skipper recovers from whatever Anya's doing to her in the gym, she'll go to work digging around for Gloria Wainwright's calendar. When she finds it, we'll pick an event where Tomlinson won't be pinned to her skirt, and we'll make our move. I'll work point, and I want Hunter with me."

Clark held up his pen. "I thought you wanted to cover Skipper."

"Originally, I did, but I've changed my mind. I want Singer on Gloria's heels when she leaves the meeting with Hunter and me. I want to know where she goes and who she talks to. If Tomlinson's not with her, I want to know where he is and what he's doing while we're recruiting his protectee. Chances are, she's going to run straight to him when we cut her loose."

"Agreed," Clark said. "But that doesn't account for Mongo and me."

"I'm getting to that part. I want you shadowing Singer in case Gloria makes him or he blows the chase. She's married to Wainwright, so she probably understands what it means to run a sur-veillance detection route."

Clark said, "So, that leaves Mongo to cover Skipper, and I assume Tony's going to run the ops center."

"You're partially right. I want Mongo close but invisible. If Tomlinson catches a glimpse of a man as big as him, his antennae will go up, and he'll start sniffing for a setup."

Clark lowered his chin. "So, you plan to leave Skipper in there without any direct cover? What do you think about that idea, Tony?"

Tony held up a finger. "Just wait. He's not finished."

I continued. "Like I said, I want Mongo looming in the shadows, but I'm not leaving Skipper dangling in the wind on her first field op. Anya's going in with her. Twice the honey only sweetens the trap."

Chapter 29
Honey Cake

Clark pushed himself and his chair back and threw his feet onto the conference table. "And you're going to tell us you've discussed this plan with Anya and Skipper, and they both agreed enthusiastically, right?"

"Actually," I said. "I was hoping you'd tell them."

He huffed. "Not a chance, College Boy. That's all you. I guess that means the hand's on the other foot now, huh?"

I squeezed my temples. "Not sure what that means, but since you chickened out, I'll do the heavy lifting again."

I wanted the walk to the workshop gym to magically deliver an infallible plan that would leave both knife-wielding women incapable of shooting down my plan, but no matter how slowly I walked, nothing came to me. I was left with no choice other than playing it by ear, but nothing could've prepared me for what I'd see when I walked through the door to the gym.

Neither woman looked up when I stepped into the room and froze in place. They were sitting six inches apart with their legs crossed and playing patty-cake. I couldn't look away, and as it turned out, I couldn't hold back my laughter, either. They had to hear me, but neither seemed to care. Finally, I stepped onto the mat and asked, "What are you two doing?"

They continued their unbreakable concentration on the game, but Anya said, "I am teaching to Skipper rapid hand drills, and she is teaching to me game of patty-cake. We did not have this game inside Soviet Union when I was child. I think is very good game."

"We need to talk," I said.

Skipper said, "So, talk. But we're not stopping."

Patty-cake morphed into a rolling hands drill of strikes, blocks, and counterstrikes. I suddenly had the unexplainable desire to see Hunter and Mongo play that game.

I said, "I've been thinking. There's a lot on the line, and we can't leave anything to chance on this one. I know you're doing well. You've learned a lot from Hunter, and I'm sure Anya has filled your head to overflowing with edged-weapons tactics and techniques, but I'm not ready to put you in the field by yourself. There are too many variables and . . ." Neither of them interrupted, but both smiled, and I wasn't expecting that. "Why are you smiling?"

Instead of answering, both women lunged toward me in unison, and I was taken completely off guard. Skipper hit me just above the knees, and Anya's shoulder landed beneath my chin. When I came to rest, the Russian was lying on top of me with her face only inches from mine.

I stared into her smoky blue eyes that hadn't aged a day in a dozen years. She slowly moved her lips closer to mine, and I was powerless to move. An inch before our lips met, she whispered, "You wish," and hopped to her feet.

"What was that about?" I asked.

Skipper said, "Believe it or not, we were planning to talk with you about that tonight. I thought I was ready, but after the past two days, I'm not even close to being ready if Tomlinson turns this into a knife fight."

Before I could respond, Anya said. "I think she is very good, but it would be better if I am with her for first mission in field. This is suggestion you were going to make, yes?"

"It sounds to me like the two of you aren't giving me any choice. How much is this going to cost me?"

Anya said, "We will negotiate price for this when mission is finished. If is easy, price will be expensive for you, but if is bloody and fun for me, I might do for free price."

I sniffed at the air. "The two of you need showers, then you've got a date in the ops center."

* * *

Showers, dinner, and two hours in the ops center resulted in a solidified plan.

I settled into my chair. "Brief it, Skipper."

She plucked the pencil from between her teeth. "It looks like the stars have aligned for us. This is almost too good to be true. Gloria Wainwright serves on the board of directors for the PWPS, and their annual fundraising gala just happens to be Saturday night."

"I've got two questions," I said. "First, what is the PWPS?"

Skipper said, "It's the Potomac Wildlife Preservation Society. What's question two?"

"What makes you think her husband won't be at the gala?"

"Oh, Chase. You'd think you would've learned by now, but I'll tell you just one more time . . . I do my homework."

A collage of pictures of immaculately dressed societal elitists filled both monitors above Skipper's head. "Take a look at those and tell me when you find Malcolm Wainwright in any of those pictures from the last six years of the gala."

Hunter said, "I'll tell you who I do see, though, and that's Bryan Tomlinson. Check him out in the picture on the top right.

He's putting the moves on that woman in the red jacket. Is she some kind of waitress or what?"

Skipper said, "I noticed that, too, but I'm not sure what she is. The waitresses are in white tops and black skirts. Maybe she's an usher."

"Could be," Hunter said. "Regardless of what she is, she's got Tomlinson's attention, and she's not remotely in the same league as Skipper or Anya. This is going to be a piece of cake."

Anya laughed. "I think maybe you mean piece of honey cake."

I said, "It looks like we'll need to dust off our tuxedoes for this one."

"And I will need new dress," Anya said. "Perhaps Penny has one I can wear."

I shuddered. "In the interest of keeping me alive, you're not trying on *anything* that belongs to Penny."

Anya smirked. "Maybe some things that are now Penny's were once mine to try on anytime I wanted."

I pointed at the Russian. "Maybe you should never say anything like that again."

Skipper said, "If you two are going to keep this up, I'm putting a mic on both of you, and I'm sending Penny a receiver so she can listen in. So, are we finished with this petty stuff or not?"

"We're finished," I said.

"Good. That means we can get back to business, and Anya, I have plenty of dresses that'll fit you, so you don't have to go shopping or raiding Penny's closet."

I said, "I'm sure we've got plenty of questions, but I have a pretty important one. Is there any chance you can score us some passes to get into this fancy gala?"

Skipper rolled her eyes. "Really? That's your question?"

"I'm sorry. I should've known you had that taken care of long before I asked the silly question."

She ignored me and scanned the room. "Any more questions?" No one spoke up, so she said, "I've got one. Are we driving or flying?"

"Why would we drive?" I asked.

"Because the Citation is in parts unknown with Disco."

"Oh, yeah. I forgot about that. But we can still take the Caravan. It won't be as comfortable, but it beats driving. If you'll make arrangements for three black SUVs, we'll gear up and be ready to go in an hour."

"Consider it done," she said. "Where do you want to stay?"

"Some place nice, and book an extra room connecting to at least one of our rooms. We may need a place to do a little negotiation if Gloria or Bryan decides not to play nice."

"You got it," Skipper said. "Now, get out of my ops center, and pack a bag."

It didn't take the full hour. We were packed, geared up, and taxiing to the runway in just over forty-five minutes. The two-and-a-half-hour flight in the Caravan wasn't bad, but it made me miss the speed and comfort of the Citation.

We stepped from Suburbans, and Singer looked up at the elegant entrance to the Waldorf Astoria on Pennsylvania Avenue, just three blocks away from the White House. "Skipper sure knows how to book a hotel."

I threw an arm around our sniper. "I can't think of anything she's not good at. Can you?"

"Nope."

Singer's confidence in Skipper's hotel-booking ability was further cemented when we stepped into our suite of rooms on the seventh floor. He let out a long, low whistle. "Not bad."

Anya apparently couldn't resist. "Which room is yours, Chasechka?"

Skipper sprang into action. "One more word out of you, and you're staying at the Days Inn by yourself."

Anya said, "I think I will like this hotel better, so I will be good . . . for now."

Skipper assigned rooms with mine as far away as possible from the room she would share with Anya.

I said, "Get settled in, and we'll have dinner downstairs at seven-thirty."

As seems to be our custom, dinner lasted two hours, and surprisingly, my team managed to behave like sophisticated ladies and gentlemen. Mongo only broke one glass, and Anya didn't kill anybody, so I chalked that up as a win.

"Let's plan to do a little scouting in the morning," I said. "We'll start at ten to avoid the morning rush hour. Until then, sleep well, folks."

We dispersed and hit the sack, but sleep wouldn't come. I lay awake staring at the empty pillow beside me and longing to see the long, flowing hair and flawless features of the woman who was too far away to touch, but who never left my thoughts. I longed to reach for her and trace my fingertips across her skin as she lay sleeping beside me, but it was not to be. Too many forces kept us apart. Too much had happened, and too much had gone wrong to rest her head on that empty pillow. As badly as I wanted her, I couldn't take that step. I couldn't do that to her or to myself. I had no choice but to leave her in Disco's care somewhere on Earth and pray Penny Fulton wanted to be on that pillow as badly as I wanted her there.

Chapter 30
Party Dress

Meridian House was an astonishing, over-a-century-old structure at 1630 Crescent Place, just off 16th Ave, near the cascading waterfall of Meridian Hill Park. Fortunately, traffic around the property wasn't the same degree of terrible as the bumper-to-bumper mayhem less than two dozen blocks south around the most famous—and infamous—house in the country.

"What do you think?" I asked as Clark leaned forward and peered through the windshield.

"I think it's doable but not ideal."

"When was the last time we worked under ideal conditions?"

"Excellent point," he said. "I think we should operate out of two Suburbans with the third one staged on the other side of the park."

"I couldn't agree more."

We made six passes around the Meridian House and made notes of every choke point, alley, exterior door, blind spot, shadow, and perhaps most importantly, every camera.

Clark said, "I hope we don't have to run. With that many lights and four cameras on every angle, if we run, we'd better keep our heads down."

"Better yet," I said, "let's just play it cool like James Bond and stroll out with a beautiful woman on our arm."

"There's only one problem with that plan. We've got ten arms, and we only brought two beautiful women with us."

"Ah, they'll have some of those inside. And look at us . . . I mean, who could resist us?"

He shook his head. "I think we should come up with a better plan."

"How's this for a plan? I say we go recruit a few spies and get this party started."

"Now you're talking, College Boy. Let's make it happen."

I made the radio call. "Let's rendezvous back at the hotel. It's time to put on our party dresses."

Back in our suite, we took turns tying each other's bowties and trying to find places to hide pistols in our evening attire. Seeing Mongo in a chauffeur's cap and black suit was a treat worth celebrating.

"I'm sorry you don't get to go to the party, big man, but you'd look like Paul Bunyan in there, and nobody would struggle to describe the eight-hundred-pound gorilla in the room when questions start popping up."

"I get it," he said. "I'm just as happy outside with the vehicle. If you need me, I'm just a radio call away, and I'll burst through that place like the Kool-Aid Man."

I said, "With both Gloria and Tomlinson there, there's no reason to involve all three vehicles. We'll stick one on the east side of the park and operate out of the other." Nods approved my plan, and I asked, "Has anybody heard Skipper or Anya mention being ready?"

Clark asked, "How often do you remember a woman being ready on time?"

I checked my watch. "Penny's always ready on time."

"She doesn't count," Hunter said. "She's some kind of freak from outer space or something. Maybe she can teach a ready-on-time class when we get all this behind us."

"Great idea," I said. "Why don't all of you go home to your wives and girlfriends and recommend they attend that class? We'll see how well that works out."

Anya was first through the door in a black dress that looked as if it had been tailored precisely for her every curve. Regardless of what was on the inside— the deception, the refusal to play by the rules, the likelihood of killing somebody at will—the exterior of Anastasia Burinkova was flawless, and she had everyone's speechless attention . . . until Elizabeth "Skipper" Woodley floated in wearing a red version of Anya's dress, and no one remembered the Russian was in the room.

Our analyst spun on a heel and encouraged Anya to do the same. "Okay, boys, that's enough gawking. We're the same women who've been in jeans and T-shirts all day. Has anyone called Tony yet?" No one spoke, and Skipper rolled her eyes. "Do I have to do everything around here?"

Seconds later, Tony was on the speakerphone, and Skipper had on her game face. She said, "We're ready to roll. Do you have anything new to report?"

"I do," he said. "In fact, I was just about to call you. It looks like they've thrown a monkey wrench into our plan. Tomlinson just picked up Gloria Wainwright."

"How do you know?" I asked.

Skipper said, "Remember those security cameras I crawled into at Wainwright's house? We've still got them online in the ops center."

"Of course you do," I said. "What's their ETA?"

Tony said, "With traffic, it'll be at least thirty-five minutes. Can you beat them there and get in place before they arrive?"

"It'll be tight," I said, "but we can try. Anything else that can't wait?"

"Nope. That's all. We're on open-channel comms, right?"

"Yes, we'll do our radio checks on our way to the dance. Wish us luck."

Tony chuckled. "You don't need luck. You've got Anya and Skipper. By the way, is she wearing the red dress or the black one?"

Five male voices answered in perfect unison. "Yes!"

"God help the men in the room tonight. They're going to need it. Go get 'em, guys."

We cut the connection and headed for the Suburbans.

Once on the road, I briefed the new plan. "With Tomlinson in the picture tonight, that actually makes everything a little cleaner for us. We can run the whole operation at one site without scattering the team all over the city. Here's how I want to run it. Clark, I want you and Singer to work overwatch. Skipper and Anya, I need you to catch Tomlinson's attention and get him cornered. As soon as you've got him, Hunter and I will nab Gloria and have a little chat with her. Any questions?"

"I have question," Anya said. "If Tomlinson person becomes dangerous, how long do we have to wait before we kill him?"

"Nobody gets dead tonight, no matter how dangerous they become."

"This is also true if SEAL is trying to kill one of us?"

I said, "Okay, there are no absolutes, but please don't kill anyone unless it is absolutely necessary."

"This is much better rule than previous one."

I sighed. "Skipper, please don't let her kill anybody."

Our analyst said, "We'll see."

We pulled into the circular drive, and Mongo stopped at the reception stand. One by one, we stepped from the Suburban with Anya and Skipper leading the way. No one would notice the five commandos dressed like penguins behind the ravishing beauties. No one asked for our invitations. Instead, they handed us numbered paddles and a glass of champagne at the door. The paddles, I assumed, were for a charity auction to be held at some point during the evening, but something told me we wouldn't make any purchases.

Inside the opulent house, the attendees were a study in elite status. Although I couldn't pull any of their names from my skull, at least half a dozen congressmen roamed from group to group shaking hands and telling lies about their accomplishments on the Hill. Two secretaries of obscure departments trailed in the congressmen's wakes, obviously engaged in a little OJT for the jobs they wanted next. None of that interested me. My only goal was to cut Gloria Wainwright out of the herd and ruin her night.

Skipper and Anya could hear every member of the team through their earpieces, but their dresses made it challenging to situate a microphone out of sight. That left us with no choice other than to place the mics slightly below the plunging neckline of each dress, but that brought up another problem of its own. The design of the dresses, as well as the design of the women wearing them, led most men's eyes directly to the microphone nestled beneath the first fold of fabric. The sound quality was muffled, but we could hear them well enough to know if they were in trouble. I had very little doubt any trouble could hatch that the two of them weren't capable of handling without our involvement.

"Guess who I found," I said. "Our first target is arranging notecards beside the podium. Let's grab her in the wings. Hunter, you take the left side, and I'll cover the right."

Hunter whispered, "Moving."

Watching another operator move in a covert scenario is one of the worst tells a team can display, but not keeping an eye on my partner as he navigated the crowd of socialites was nearly impossible. None of us fit into the crowd, no matter how well-dressed we were. I forced myself to avoid eyeing the spectacle and focused on my route to the side of the stage.

I stepped through a black curtain and into a relatively dark space with cables taped to the floor and an array of sound equipment with tiny lights flickering through the darkness. The urge to unplug a few things was almost irresistible, but I refrained and said, "One's in position."

Hunter's whispering voice filled my earpiece. "Three's in position."

I asked, "Can you see her, Three?"

"Negative."

"I can't, either, so we'll need someone on the floor to report her movement."

Clark said, "I've got her, and I'll call her movement."

Hunter and I replied in unison. "Roger."

The minutes passed like hours as I waited and practiced my speech.

Hello, Mrs. Wainwright. I hope I didn't startle you. My name is Chase, and we need to have a talk. Please come with me.

Clark said, "On your toes, Three. She's moving to you."

Hunter said, "Roger."

We'd conducted snatch-and-grab operations before, but never with such a light touch. Our typical targets ended up much like I had—in the trunk of a car, gagged, bagged, and hog-tied—but grabbing Gloria Wainwright wouldn't include the use of any duct tape or flex-cuffs. Instead of sticking a pistol in her ribs and ordering her into the back of a van, Hunter would hold up his phone with a grainy photo of Gloria and Bryan Tomlinson in flagrante delicto.

My heart raced with anticipation as I departed my darkened position to join Hunter on the other side of the stage.

Unexpectedly, Skipper's voice rang in my ear. "Hey there. Why aren't you mingling with the rest of the self-important blowhards?"

I groaned as the realization of open-channel comms in a multi-part operation hit me. Skipper had found her target and dangled the bait, but Hunter and I didn't need her phase of the operation in our ears while we were confronting Gloria. Although, there was nothing I could do about it at that point, so we pressed on, conducting separate but linked operations simultaneously on one radio frequency.

I said, "I'll be there in fifteen seconds, Three."

Instead of hearing Hunter respond, Clark's voice caught my attention. "Fall back. She's moving back to the podium."

I froze, trying to decide if I should move back to the right wing or continue to Hunter's position. I could see part of the stage from where I stood, and moving back to my original spot would rob me of that advantage, so I held my position.

Gloria Wainwright tapped the microphone several times and leaned against the podium. "Good evening, distinguished guests, ladies, and gentlemen. Thank you so much for joining us this evening for this incredibly important event. Please help yourselves to hors d'oeuvres, wine, and cocktails, and don't forget the silent auction items, as well as the live auction items on display in the next room. Don't miss the opportunity to outbid the congressmen."

The jab got a few laughs, and Gloria turned left, directly toward the position I'd abandoned. I launched myself back toward the darkened area as Clark said, "She's moving to Chase."

Hunter said, "Three's in route."

Skipper's voice turned sultry. "I was thinking of slipping out back for a smoke and a look at the moon. I hear it's almost full tonight. Join me?"

I didn't listen for Tomlinson's reply. Instead, moving as quickly as my feet would carry me without sprinting, I turned the corner and met Gloria Wainwright face-to-face. In that instant, I forgot my speech, but I reached out and laid a hand on her forearm. "I'm so sorry, ma'am. I didn't see you."

She put on the practiced smile of a woman who spent too much time forcing cordiality. "It's fine, really. Where are you going in such a hurry?"

I took half a step forward, intentionally invading her space, and slid my hand from her forearm to cup her elbow. The shift served only to give her the slightest hint of being controlled. I wanted her on her heels and feeling powerless. The pitch I was about to deliver was meant to leave her shaken, not stirred.

Chapter 31
Rescue Me

I thumbed my phone to life and held it up for her to see. The first picture was of Gloria and Bryan Tomlinson strolling hand in hand through Central Park. The second was a shot of her kissing her security man in the back seat of a Lincoln Town Car. The third was a little more personal.

I hissed. "Well done, Mrs. Wainwright. You appear to have the body of a woman half your age, and perhaps prefer your lover in that same generation." I paused only long enough for her heart to quicken. "Come with me, Gloria. We're going to have a little talk, and I'll explain how you can keep Malcolm from ever seeing these pictures . . . and the six dozen more we have."

She took a defiant step backward, but I closed my hand around her elbow. "No, Gloria, not that way. Come with me."

"Take your hands off me. I demand to know who you are! If you don't let me go this instant, I'll have my private security in here in five seconds."

I continued my grip on her elbow and turned her toward the black curtain behind her. When she spun, I pulled back the curtain a few inches. "Is that the private security you're planning to summon?"

Skipper laced her hand through Bryan Tomlinson's arm and allowed her hip to brush against him as she led him from the reception hall and through a pair of French doors.

"Just so you'll fully understand what's happening, that lady in red will be entertaining your bodyguard—or should I call him your lover—for the next half hour. No matter what we call him, she's very convincing, and you can rest assured he won't hear your plea for help."

My partner appeared as if materializing from the darkness and pulled the curtain closed.

Now surrounded, abandoned, and likely terrified, Gloria Wainwright seemed to strengthen her resolve. "I don't know who you people are, and you clearly do not know who I am because you wouldn't attempt something this blatantly stupid. Unhand me immediately, and I'll have security see you out. Otherwise, I'll literally press the panic button, and you'll likely be hurt or possibly even killed in the aftermath."

Hunter leaned close to her ear and held up a device the size of a small change purse. "Do you mean *this* panic button?"

She jerked away from my partner. "How dare you touch me! Give that back to me at once!"

I pulled her elbow. "Don't worry, Gloria. We're not going to hurt you, physically. I wish I could say the same for your little boyfriend, but we're a little less gentle with the men we interrogate. Now, let's go before we have to carry you away."

She tried to jerk her arm from my grip, but I was prepared and didn't release the elbow. She opened her mouth to scream, but Hunter shoved two fingers into her abdomen just below her bottom rib, and the exhalation came out as a dry, lung-emptying huff rather than a cry for help.

She grabbed the spot where my partner had pressed and said, "You said you weren't going to hurt me."

Hunter smiled. "No, ma'am. I didn't say that. He said that.

Now, do what you're told, or this uncomfortable endeavor becomes much worse."

Her shoulders fell, and the defiance left her eyes. I led her down a long corridor and up an arched staircase to a secluded office.

Anya's seductive, Russian-accented voice dripped through my earpiece. "You are strong like iron. I like this."

Dr. Fulton should've understood why the sting of jealousy pierced his gut at that moment, but I shoved the thought from my head and plucked my earpiece from my ear. "Do you see this, Gloria? This is a secure communication system, and every member of my team is wearing one." I pulled the tiny microphone from behind my bowtie. "And this? This is a mic, so all of us know everything everyone else on the team says. You understand that concept, right?"

She fidgeted in her chair. "The two of you have no idea what you're doing or to whom you're doing it to. You'll pay for this, and that payment will be harsh."

Hunter shook his cell phone in front of the woman and recited Malcolm Wainwright's personal cell number. "I'll go ahead and send these pictures off to your adoring husband, and we'll call it an evening. How does that sound to you?"

She quivered, and her face flushed pale.

I laid a reassuring hand on top of hers. "Just relax, Gloria. We understand that you don't want your husband to see the pictures, and that's perfectly normal. We've all got secrets, and yours isn't the end of the world. It would, however, be the end of your marriage, and that pesky little prenuptial agreement you signed has a specific exclusion for adultery. I know Malcolm is a wealthy man, and you've come to enjoy the lifestyle his wealth provides. I'd hate to rip that away from you, but I will if you make me."

An errant tear escaped her eye, and she quickly wiped it away. "What do you want? Why are you doing this to me?"

I pressed my earpiece back in place and tried to ignore the affections pouring from the mouths of both Skipper and Anya. My desire to ignore them was rooted in two very different foundations: I didn't like hearing Skipper, my little sister, seducing a dangerous man. And hearing Anya gush over her target with many of the same phrases and expressions she used on me over a decade before left a bitter taste on the tongue she'd sliced in two.

"What we want is very simple and very easy for you to provide, but there's a cherry on top for you. We'll get to the crowning jewel in a few minutes, but for now, we have to tell you a story about your husband."

Hunter took the reins. "You see, Mrs. Wainwright, your husband had become a rotten egg. I'm sure, when you met him, he was a patriotic, brave, fascinating man, but he let himself become a victim of the system under which he thrived." My partner looked up at me. "Show her the video."

I punched the play button and slid my phone across the table. The security camera footage of my boathouse exploding played in slow motion on the screen.

Gloria watched the video and furrowed her brow. "What is that, and what does it have to do with me?"

"That is—or more correctly—was my boathouse. Your husband blew it up."

"He did no such thing."

"I'm sorry to be the bearer of bad news, but he most certainly did. Ah, I suppose in the interest of complete honesty, he didn't actually plant the explosive and press the plunger, but he did order a man to do it. That makes him guilty of two federal capital crimes. The first is conspiracy to commit murder, and—"

She almost yelled, "Murder? Are you telling me that explosion took someone's life?"

I shrugged. "I'm not the attorney general. I'm just a guy who your husband directly attacked. I'm the victim, Mrs. Wainwright, but that condition is temporary. I won't remain the victim. Thanks to you and your sordid little affair with the man who is supposed to be protecting you, it's Malcolm's turn to taste the bitter pill of the victim."

Anya cooed her seduction, and I plucked the earpiece from my ear and tossed it onto the table. "Go ahead. Have a listen."

She stared down at the device but didn't move.

I motioned toward it. "Go ahead. It's just the rest of my team at work. I think you'll find it interesting."

Reluctantly, Gloria reached for the earpiece, wiped it clean as if my ear contained the Ebola virus, and held it against her ear. The light drained from her eyes, and she swallowed hard. In the voice of a child, she said, "Why are you doing this?"

I held out my hand, and she laid the earpiece in my palm. "I'm doing this to protect innocent people from the wrath of a wealthy, pompous threat to honest, hardworking people."

The tears came on the leading edge of her submission, with no cruel threats, no infliction of physical pain, and nothing nasty. Interrogating noncombatants, I learned, is a lot more boring than breaking legs and sending bullets through kneecaps.

"Listen to me, Gloria. I know this is overwhelming for you, and it's perfectly normal for you to cry."

She slammed her hand onto the table. "How? How can you do this to people? I don't understand."

Once again, I covered her hand with mine. "This isn't what we do. We find enemies of freedom and eliminate them. *That's* what we do. What we're doing here is a sickening necessity brought about by your husband and his partner."

"Which partner? Are you talking about Gibson Richardson?"

I caught Hunter staring at me, and I asked, "What do you know about Gibson Richardson?"

Gloria wiped a wall of tears from her face. "He's a snake. That's what I know about him. And he's the one who got Malcolm into this."

"Into what?" I asked.

"The whole thing with Korea."

I froze in my seat, determined to do nothing that might interrupt her stream of consciousness. I wanted her to keep talking. I needed her to keep talking because I had just plunged into a pool way over my head, and I didn't know which questions to ask.

I shot a glance at Hunter, and he slowly backed away. I prayed he was on the verge of doing what my glance implied.

"Are you getting this, Tony?" Those words whispered by my partner solidified my faith in our ability to communicate without a sound.

"I'm recording every word," Tony said. "Keep her talking."

Although our analyst was somewhere in the same house as Hunter and me, she could've been a thousand miles away. Fortunately for us, she'd turned her fiancé into our temporary ops center analyst, and he was obviously up to the task.

Gloria continued as the tears kept falling. "I tried to tell them, but they wouldn't listen."

The previous two years, sitting with a legal pad on my lap and a psych patient before me, had taught me two things: shut up when you want to talk, and more importantly, shut up when you want to talk. So, despite my yearning to ask who *they* were, I held my tongue, praying she'd keep talking.

Instead of continuing, she lifted her chin and glared at me in horror. "Oh, my God. That's who you are. You're them, aren't you?"

I didn't change my expression, but something inside my skull made me tilt my head ever so slightly.

She said, "That's it. You're going to kill us, aren't you? I knew it. I knew I should've played the ignorant fool, but I couldn't. You've got to understand. I was scared. Bryan warned me. He said you'd come for me, but why here? Why at such a crowded event?"

She widened her stare. "You're making an example of me . . . of us. That's it, isn't it?"

I remained silent, and her defiance returned. "I hope Bryan tears you apart. He will fight, and you will hear him kill your women in that earpiece of yours. In fact, I'd like to listen when it happens."

Mistaking interrogation for counseling had just gone terribly wrong, and I was left with no choice other than to redirect the conversation and bring back the tears.

"We're not here to kill you, Mrs. Wainwright. We're here to rescue you."

"Rescue me? From what?"

"We'll get to that," I said. "But let's talk about Bryan first. I'm not sure who you think we are, but we're not interested in killing the man you love, either. As long as he doesn't force us to do so, we will not hurt him."

She let out a huff. "You have no idea who and what Bryan is, do you?"

"We know exactly who and what Bryan is, but we're well-prepared to deal with him if he gets out of hand. We also know he's smart enough to know when he's outgunned. He won't break. He'll keep his secrets. But he won't put himself in a situation to get hurt. That's not what this is about."

Her look became one of confusion rather than defiance, and that was a victory for the good guys.

"Then who are you?"

"Believe it or not, Mrs. Wainwright, we're the good guys."

She didn't react other than to say, "Please don't call me that."

"Okay, Gloria. Here's the bottom line. We want to know everything you know about your husband's misdeeds involving the North Koreans. Give us what we want, and all of this ends. You'll be free to return to your gala and Mr. Tomlinson."

Her shoulders rose and fell with a long, deep breath. "Along with Gibson Richardson, Carl Burlingame, and Malcolm Wainwright, he's funneling money and missile technology into Pyongyang."

In disbelief, I asked, "Senator Carl Burlingame?"

She nodded.

"And you have proof of this involvement with Pyongyang?"

"Yes, of course. That's what I told the agent from the NSA."

"How long ago did you speak with the NSA?"

"Forever ago, that's when. My husband, his coconspirator, and the senator are powerful men. Probably more powerful than you know. They had the NSA agent killed before . . ." She squeezed her eyes closed. "You said you were here to rescue me."

Chapter 32
Not Tonight

I relaxed in my seat and gave Gloria Wainwright my most sincere look. "I did say that, didn't I?"

"You did, but you still haven't told me from whom or what you're willing to rescue me."

The interrogation had taken a pair of drastic turns I never considered during our planning, and the latest switchback had me wishing anybody other than me was sitting across the table from Gloria Wainwright. It was time to gamble, and I prayed I didn't draw a bust card.

"From Malcolm Wainwright," I said with far more confidence than I felt.

Gloria threw back her head and laughed as if I'd claimed to be the Pope. "That's a good one. Clearly, you don't know Malcolm."

My eyes turned deadly. "Clearly, you don't know me."

The game became who-blinks-first, and I wouldn't lose.

She said, "Okay. If you're telling the truth, let me walk back downstairs, enjoy the gala with a thousand people pretending to be sincere, and then we'll talk, Mr. Rescuer."

Clark's voice pulled me from my deliberation. "Don't do it, Chase."

I still had a pair of aces up my sleeve that Clark couldn't know I was willing to play. "How well do you know Mrs. Richardson?"

Her eyes became saucers. "Gibson's wife? That was you?"

I nodded, and she sighed.

I checked my watch. "It's eight o'clock. You have exactly two hours and not a second longer. You'll be back in that chair, telling us everything you know."

"What about Bryan?"

I spoke into my mic. "Is Tomlinson still alive?"

Clark said, "Chase, don't do it. She'll disappear."

I played my first ace. "He's still alive, for now, but at ten oh one, he'll find himself bleeding out in the park across the street if you and I aren't right here in this room. Is that perfectly clear?"

She looked down at her folded hands, and I played my second ace. "Tell me the NSA agent's name you spoke with."

"Gill McKnight is how he introduced himself and what was printed on his credentials. That's all I know."

Tony said, "I'm on it. Give me sixty seconds."

Gloria moved to stand from her seat, and I waved a finger. "Not so fast. We're checking on Special Agent McKnight."

Tony said, "Killed in the line of duty eleven months ago."

I stood. "Lay your cell phone on the table, and enjoy the party, Mrs. Gloria. I'll see you at ten, and not a second later."

Clark barked orders. "Reposition to keep eyes on the woman. Never let her out of your sight. If she touches a telephone or makes any move to leave the building, roll her up."

Everyone acknowledged his orders, then he continued. "Mongo, get the vehicle to the north lawn, double-quick. I want Tomlinson inside the vehicle in less than three minutes. Make it happen."

Mongo said, "I'll be at the north entrance in twenty seconds."

Skipper whispered in Bryan Tomlinson's ear. "Let's go some-place where the three of us can have a little fun and no one can hear either of us girls scream your name . . . whatever it is."

Before Gloria Wainwright reached the staircase, her boy toy was inside our Suburban, snuggled between two of the most beau-tiful women in DC.

I motioned toward the staircase. "Let's get downstairs so Clark can fire me."

Hunter chuckled. "He's not going to fire you until this thing falls apart underneath us."

My earpiece came to life with Clark's voice. "Don't be so sure about that, Hunter."

We made our way back to the first floor and rejoined the party. Gloria never offered to escape, but she checked her watch every five minutes as if she were the town crier.

I accidentally bought and paid for two items in the live auction and immediately donated them back to be sold again. Apparently, my re-donation became a trend, and the auctioneer made great sport of reselling items.

At five minutes before ten, Hunter and Singer shadowed Glo-ria back up the staircase, and Hunter held the door for her.

She eased herself into her chair across from me. "I'm here on time, and I want to hear Bryan's voice before we go any further."

I said, "I trusted you, and now you have to trust me. Bryan is alive and unhurt, but he's not free to roam about. You'll give us what we want, and then you can talk with him. I'm sure you have a few questions about his evening with the ladies."

She ignored my sarcasm. "I need a computer."

"Why do you need a computer?"

"You want proof, and I have it, but it's encrypted in the cloud."

I looked to Hunter, and he said, "I don't know what that means, either."

Skipper came to our rescue. "I'll be right there."

"Our analyst is on the way up with a laptop."

Gloria lost the composure she'd forced into place for the previous two hours. The tears came again, and with them came the reality of the moment. "Can you really protect me? Is that even possible?"

"Not only can we protect you, Gloria, but we can make certain the men who you see as a threat are no longer a threat to anyone, especially you."

Skipper glided through the door in her stunning red dress with her laptop tucked beneath one arm.

Gloria looked up. "Were you one of the women with Bryan?"

The analyst never missed a beat. "I have no idea what you're talking about, ma'am. I'm simply delivering a laptop." She opened the computer and slid it across the table.

I rose, circumnavigated the table, and watched Gloria Wainwright access her secure account. I stared down at the laptop, then back up at Skipper, and she smiled. The look on her face told me every keystroke was being recorded.

After thirty seconds of clicking her way through the prompts, firewalls, and roadblocks inherent to the world of encrypted file storage, Gloria slid the machine toward Skipper.

More clicking and scrolling ensued, and with every keystroke, Skipper's face grew more dire. She finally looked up and said, "You have to see this."

I took a knee beside her and watched as records of massive financial transactions filled the screen and scrolled for pages before decrypted emails appeared between Kim Hyok-ji—the North Korean chairman of state commission of science and technology—and Gibson Richardson and Malcolm Wainwright, with voluminous attachments detailing missile design, guidance system technology, and nuclear warhead configuration data. Finally, it revealed audio recordings of conversations between Wainwright, Richardson, and Senator Carl Burlingame discussing the allocation of funds into individual offshore accounts.

We read and listened for almost an hour before I said, "Stop. We have some things to take care of before we go any further. Do you have any evidence that these men had anything to do with Agent McKnight's death?"

Gloria pulled the laptop from beneath Skipper's fingers and clicked to another audio file. "Listen to this."

Gib, it's Malcolm. We've got to do something about this agent from NSA. I don't know how he got inside, but he knows far too much about what we're doing.

Relax, Malcolm. You're too jumpy. It's already taken care of. I put Valeska on him this afternoon. He'll never see another sunrise. Now, stop worrying so much.

Gloria hit the pause button and looked up expectantly.

I leaned across the table and stared directly into her eyes. "Listen closely. If you have the ability to move any holdings, cash, or anything of value into accounts only you control, do so now."

Without hesitation, she buried her face in Skipper's computer and spent several minutes moving assets. When she was finished, she closed the laptop and leaned back in her chair. "What are you going to do now? Do you still believe you can protect me?"

As if on cue, Mongo darkened the door of the room blocking the space almost more fully than the door itself. "It's not a belief, ma'am. It's simply fact. We'll protect you . . ."—he stepped aside and waved Bryan Tomlinson into the room—"and him, too."

Gloria rose and opened her arms. Bryan took her in a long, powerful hug until she pulled away and slapped him solidly across the face. "I still love you, but this is far from over. What were you thinking letting those women lead you away from me when I needed you most?"

Hunter said, "He wouldn't have stopped us from taking you, even if he hadn't been lured away. We had a contingency plan for dealing with him if our honey trap didn't do the trick."

I spoke into my mic. "Tony, how's our exfil plan coming together?"

"Right on time," he said. "Disco will be on deck at Gaithersburg, Maryland, inside an hour."

"Good work, Tony. I think we may have finally found an analyst we can rely on to get things done."

Skipper glared at me. "Good luck paying him enough to drag him away from his painting gig, but if he's what you want, I can bow out."

"On second thought," I said, "I think we'll stick with the one we've got." I pulled my phone from my pocket.

Skipper said, "Who are you calling? Everybody's on comms. Just talk."

I held up a finger and listened to the phone ring on the other end of the line. When he answered, I said, "Special Agent White, I'm sorry to bother you at this hour, but I've got something you'd like to have."

"Please tell me you're not talking about our Russian. Sometimes I feel like you and I have shared custody and I only get her every other weekend and holidays."

"As you know, she was involved in this one, but she's not the big box with a nice red bow on top."

"Tell me about the box, Chase. It's past my bedtime."

"I have emails, recorded telephone conversations of conspiracy to murder a federal agent, the actual murder of that agent, and financial transaction records in the hundreds of millions with the North Korean government."

He said, "So far, I've not heard anything worth getting out of bed for. I'm slightly intrigued by the conspiracy allegation, but why would I care what the North Koreans are doing?"

"Because the North Koreans are only one fourth of the parties involved. The other three are powerful American citizens, including a sitting U.S. senator."

He cleared his throat. "You've got my attention now. Is my agent still with you?"

"She is, but she's not in the room at the moment."

"This evidence you have . . . Is it actionable?"

"It is. The wife of one of the perpetrators gathered it, and she's willing to testify in return for protection."

"Get the evidence to me, and find my agent. I want her on the phone."

"Stand by," I said. "Anya, are you on comms?"

"I am here, Chasechka, inside house. You are on second floor in back, yes?"

"That's right. I've got Agent White on the phone for you."

Seconds later, the Russian slipped through the door in her little black dress, and Gloria deflated. "Oh, for God's sake. You've got to be kidding me. She's the other one?"

Bryan stepped away from her before the second slap could come, and I tossed the phone to Anya.

She pressed the speaker button. "Is Anya."

White said, "Tonight, you're not Anya. You're Special Agent Ana Fulton."

Chapter 33
I Can Kill?

Skipper gave DOJ Supervisory Special Agent Ray White access to Gloria Wainwright's secure cloud and waited. White examined the files for several long minutes, and the satellite phone stayed on speaker while he read.

White growled. "Fulton, are you still there?"

Both Anya and I answered simultaneously. "Yes."

"I was talking to the Russian," White said.

Anya leaned toward the phone. "I am here, Agent White."

"Do you have eyes on the witness?"

"Yes, she is here, but also her bodyguard, Bryan Tomlinson, is here."

"Take them both into protective custody, and they are your responsibility until we can get them into the hands of the marshals. You are to take them someplace safe and keep them alive. Do you understand?"

Anya's eyes shot to mine, and I said, "We'll have a Citation on deck at Gaithersburg in minutes."

She turned back to the phone. "I can do this. We have two strong vehicles and fast airplane."

White said, "Keep them alive, Anya. You got me?"

The Russian put on that terrifying smile she wore so well. "This means I can kill anyone who tries to hurt them, yes?"

White didn't hesitate. "Absolutely. I'm waking up a federal judge, and we'll have a warrant before midnight. Get the witnesses out of DC, and call me on one of Chase's magic phones that can't be traced when you get wherever you're going."

Before the conversation was over, Mongo and Clark sprinted from the room, and minutes later, Clark reported, "Both vehicles at the south exit. Put one in each."

Anya gave the order. "Mrs. Wainwright is with me, and Bryan is with Chase. I am in lead vehicle. Move now!"

We powerwalked to the south exit and surrounded the two witnesses between the exit and the back seats of the Suburbans. Once rolling, I conducted a comms check, and everyone reported loud and clear. "We're thirty-five minutes from Gaithersburg. I'm not expecting any resistance for at least two hours. I can't imagine anyone getting tipped off quickly enough to hit us before we're wheels up. Tony, how far out is Disco?"

"He's ten minutes out."

"Perfect," I said. "Put him someplace dark, and douse the lights. We don't want any unnecessary attention."

"Already briefed," Tony said.

Anya cleared her throat. "Chase, I believe you have forgotten that you are not in charge. I am now responsible."

I grimaced. "I'm sorry, Anya. You're right. It's all yours."

She said, "Almost everything Chase said is what I would have done, so continue mission, but now I am commander."

Almost? I thought. *What order did I give that Anya didn't agree with?*

My answer came earlier than I expected when Anya said, "I believe we must be prepared to repel at least small force of men. Is possible Agent White will wake up judge, who will not give to him warrant and who might warn senator or others about our attempt to have warrant. This is likely, so do not relax. Everyone must remain on front of feet."

I eyed Clark. "Front of feet? That sounds like something you'd say. What do you think she meant?"

He rolled his eyes. "For Pete's sake, College Boy, try to keep up. She meant to say, stay on your toes. Sometimes I think you don't have any clue what's happening around you."

"Yep, that's me . . . Ol' clueless. What do you think about Anya's theory?"

"I think she's probably right. These aren't street-corner drug dealers. These guys are seriously high-placed power brokers."

Bryan Tomlinson said, "I don't have comms, so I'm not hearing what you guys are, but if you're talking about how well-connected Wainwright and Richardson are, they have the president's cell phone number."

My sat-phone chirped ten minutes into the ride, and I thumbed the button. "Go for Chase."

Special Agent Ray White said, "Put Anya on."

"She's not in my vehicle, Agent White. She's in the lead."

He huffed. "Can you patch this call into your comms?"

"Give me a minute," I said. "It can be done, but it'll take me a minute to remember how to make it work."

"We don't have a minute!"

Ignoring his impatience, I dived into the menu options on my phone. Twenty seconds later, I said, "Sat-phone comm checks. Give a test count, White."

Agent White said, "One . . . two . . . three . . . Three . . . two . . . one."

Anya said, "Loud and clear."

White exploded into a rapid-fire situation report. "HRT is en route to Gaithersburg to provide cover. Judge Phillip McCord shot down my warrant application, but I dug up another judge who gave us the green light. I'll pay for that one, but we have to consider the possibility that McCord will notify Wainwright, Richardson, or the senator."

I opened my mouth to respond, but Anya beat me to the punch. "We are inside two black Suburban, fifteen minutes from airport. Tell to Hostage Rescue Team we will be in close, two-car formation. Have HRT open gate for us."

White asked, "Can you defend yourselves?"

This time, I was first to speak. "We have M-Fours and sidearms, but our vehicles aren't hardened. We can fight, but if they come hard with heavy weapons, we may be in one hell of a firefight."

White said, "Lock and load, and don't lose my witnesses."

We broke the connection, and Mongo hit the gas in the lead SUV.

Clark sent his foot to the floor. "It looks like Anya's not worried about speed traps."

Hunter leapt over the back seat and uncased our rifles. He passed two of them forward to Clark and me and then stared at Tomlinson.

I saw Hunter's hesitance and said, "Whose side are you on in this thing, Bryan?"

His one-word answer spoke volumes. "Gloria's."

"Give him a rifle."

Hunter passed the M4 to Tomlinson and cursed.

I spun in my seat. "What is it?"

He said, "Singer's three-oh-eight is here, but he's not."

"If this thing turns into a gunfight," I said, "it's not going to be a sniper's battle. We're all ground-pounding grunts in this fight."

We raced northward with the needle hovering near the one-hundred-mile-per-hour mark and our heads on swivels. We scanned every intersection, every vehicle that looked out of place, and every pair of headlights that lit our mirrors.

Everything looked like a potential threat, but we didn't slow down for anyone or anything.

Mongo said, "Airport in sight, but the gate's not open."

"Do you see any HRT?"

"Negative," he said. "I'm blowing through the gate."

Seconds before the front bumper of Mongo's Suburban knocked the airport gate from its hinges, a pair of commandos materialized, and two small explosive charges saved the SUV's grill and rendered the airport gate meaningless.

"I guess those were the HRT guys, huh?" Mongo said.

I said, "I hope so. I can't imagine anyone else blowing up a gate for us. Turn right. The Citation is two o'clock and eight hundred yards."

"I got it," Mongo said as his speed climbed through sixty on the parking apron.

We trailed only feet behind him, racing for the stairs of the waiting airplane. We slid to a stop at the bottom of the stairs, and Anya leapt from the lead vehicle with Gloria close by her side. Taking the stairs as fast as their dresses and heels would allow, they hustled through the open door and turned down the aisle.

I was first out of the Suburban, and Hunter practically threw Bryan Tomlinson from the vehicle. As we hit the first step of the airstairs, I glanced up to see a bright-red placard in the window of the cockpit that read "Brakes Set" in large white letters. The sign was used to let airport ground crews know the airplane couldn't be towed until the brakes were released, but there was no reason to believe anyone would try to tow the airplane anywhere in the middle of the night. In that instant, my blood ran cold, and I spun on a heel and shoved Bryan back toward the Suburban.

"Get him out of here!" I yelled. "Something's not right."

The tires squealed as Clark powered away from the plane.

"What's going on?" Hunter yelled.

I pointed toward the cockpit window bearing the sign, and we drew our pistols simultaneously. Singer was out of the lead vehicle in seconds and following us up the stairs.

I led the entry through the door to find Anya facedown in the aisle and Gloria Wainwright in the clenched arm of a gunman with an MP5 pressed to her skull. Two more muzzles showed around the edges of a pair of seats, and I was instantly in what could've become the deadliest gunfight of my life. We were trapped inside an aluminum tube facing three armed gunmen, one with a high-value hostage in his arms.

If these guys were good enough to overpower Disco and put Anya on the ground, they weren't amateurs, and the grip the standing gunman had around Gloria's neck was practiced and precise. We were facing at least our equals, and likely our superiors. Decisions were on the verge of being made, and I was finished allowing other people to shape my life.

I focused on the hostage taker's left eye and pressed my trigger twice. What had been his skull plastered the bulkhead behind him, and Gloria collapsed to the floor, screaming as if she were on fire.

Hunter and Singer pumped two pairs of rounds into the seats the remaining gunmen were using as concealment, and their weapons fell to the deck.

"Clark, are you there?" I bellowed, my ears ringing from the six shots.

"Go for Clark," he said.

"Three gunmen down. Disco is unknown, and Anya is down but breathing. All the shots were ours. Get the Hostage Rescue Team in here now."

Hunter squeezed by me, knelt, and checked pulses. "Three

dead bad guys. Anya took a nasty blow to the forehead—probably the butt of a pistol."

"Clear the rest of the plane," I said. "I'm going for Disco."

I found our chief pilot slumped over the captain's seat on the left side of the cockpit with blood trickling from his ear.

Hunter's voice poured from my earpiece. "The plane is clear. What do you want me to do with the bodies?"

"Get Mongo up here, and throw them on the tarmac. Disco's hurt, but I've got a strong pulse and steady respirations."

"Should we call EMS?"

I carefully pulled Disco from his seat and laid him on the deck, cautious to move his neck as little as possible.

A booming voice rang through the entry door. "FBI Hostage Rescue! We're coming in. Identify yourselves."

I looked up as the muzzle of an M4 cleared the doorway. "I'm Chase Fulton. This is my airplane. This man is the pilot, and the screaming woman is our protectee. The woman on the deck in the aisle is ours."

Almost before I could finish, a belch of automatic-weapons fire filled the air, and the interior of the Citation pulsed as the rounds pierced the skin of the airplane and tore the leather of the over-heads and seats. The lead HRT man dived through the door and onto the deck. The second man slumped where he stood, and blood poured from his body. Another HRT commando stumbled across his teammate's body and rolled onto the floor of the plane.

"Are you hit?" demanded the lead man.

The other nodded. "I'm just winged in the left arm, but I'm still in the fight."

The automatic fire continued and tore into the airplane. We were pinned down with no way to know where the fire was coming from, and we were unwilling to fire blindly into the dark.

The lead HRT man yelled, "Where's the emergency exit?"

I said, "It's over the right wing, just behind you."

He spun and studied the exit from his position on the floor, then shook his head. "I'm not standing up to open it. Is there any possibility of getting this thing started?"

"I can try," I said as I crawled over Disco to the cockpit.

There was no time for a checklist. I needed at least one of the two turbines to spool up so we could taxi anywhere other than where we were. I ran through the start procedure from memory, and both engines whistled to life. Despite Disco's sign, the brakes weren't set, and the jet rolled as soon as I pressed the throttles forward. With us moving, I shimmied into the right seat, as far from the gunmen as possible, and raised my head barely enough to see through the windshield.

We taxied slowly at first but picked up speed as I made the first turn onto a taxiway. I couldn't hear the rifles, but that didn't mean they weren't still shooting.

I saw movement and turned to see the FBI agent poking his head into the cockpit from his position on the floor. "Any chance it'll fly?"

"Close the door, and we'll find out."

He crawled away, and the light indicating the main cabin door was closed came on. We rolled onto the taxiway, and I shoved the throttles forward. The plane accelerated, but red lights filled the cockpit as if the panel were a Christmas tree.

I pulled the throttles back. "It might fly, but there's no way to know how badly it's damaged. It's not worth the risk."

He said, "There's a ramp at the northwest end of the field. If you can get us there, we can get into a defendable position in the tree line."

I reached for my mic beneath my collar. "Clark?"

"Go ahead, Chase."

"We took a barrage of automatic-weapons fire, but I got the airplane started. We're taxiing to the northwest end of the airport. The HRT guy says there's a parking apron there and a tree line. Can you get there?"

"Any casualties?" he asked.

"I don't know for sure yet, but I think we lost at least one of the HRT agents. Another is injured on board. Can you get to the ramp at the northwest end or not?"

"Yeah, we're on our way. It looks like we're two minutes out."

I looked over my shoulder. "Are they still shooting?"

The agent said, "My team on the ground rolled up five of them, but there's no way to know if there's more. We're not taking any fire right now."

I wiped sweat from my brow. "We'll be on the ramp in thirty seconds, and my team will be there inside two minutes. How's your man?"

"He's bloody, but I set a tourniquet."

"Is anybody else hit back there?"

"No, and the blonde woman is coming around."

"Good," I said. "She's one of us, but she's Russian, so don't be surprised if you can't understand anything she says. Check on my man, will you?"

He examined Disco and looked up. "He's out cold, but he's got a good pulse."

I focused on getting the crippled airplane onto the ramp and made the turn from the taxiway without any issue—until I pressed the toe brakes and nothing happened.

With far too much speed to coast to a stop on the ramp, I yanked the throttles across their stops, deploying the thrust reversers. One of them worked and yanked the plane to the left.

"Hold on!" I yelled. "We're going into the trees."

The nosewheel left the pavement a second before the main landing gear, and we careened down an embankment toward

Cabin Branch. When the wings contacted the trees, the heart-breaking sound of aluminum being crushed sickened me, but the airplane was lost the instant somebody began pouring bullets into her.

We came to a jolting stop, and I shut down the turbines and called Clark. "We're in the trees, off the end of the ramp."

"Roger. We're thirty seconds out."

I climbed from the cockpit and opened the main door. "Get out! There could be a fire."

Could be turned into *there is,* and flames lapped at the tail section of the jet. Hunter threw Disco over his shoulder and bounded down the stairs. The HRT agent pinned Gloria to his side and hit the stairs. The wounded agent followed his team leader while I gathered Anya into my arms and carried her down the steps.

The uneven terrain was slick, challenging, and dark, but we climbed the slope to the ramp just as two pairs of headlights burst into sight. Mongo and Clark brought the Suburbans to a skidding stop, and everyone piled inside except the FBI agents.

"Get in!" I ordered.

The lead agent shook his head. "No, just go! We've got a vehicle on the way, and my partner's stable."

As much as I hated leaving the agents behind, there was nothing more important than getting Gloria Wainwright and Bryan Tomlinson someplace safe.

Ten minutes later, we were on Interstate 270, toward Frederick, Maryland.

Epilogue

Ten days later, Clark Johnson and I sat in a mahogany-paneled study in a mansion near Manassas, Virginia, with five other men and one woman, each wearing sophistication and undeniable power on their sleeves.

"Gentlemen," began the woman. "As you probably know, I'm the attorney general of the United States, and the reason you're here—instead of in my office on Pennsylvania Avenue—is because neither of you two exists, and this meeting never happened."

Clark and I nodded without a word, and the AG continued. "Your efforts over the past month have revealed an ever-widening crevasse in the fabric of an essential element of this country's security. The men you know as the Board are men of enormous insight, experience, and patriotism. When treason and greed take root in such a crevasse, they serve only to weaken the foundation of this nation. Men and women like you and your team are the sutures that close wounds in our fabric, and without you and people like you, the blanket of peace, security, and comfort the citizens of this country enjoy would be rent from end to end, and democracy would fall into the pits of darkness, never to be seen again. Gentlemen, we are the world's only remaining bastion of freedom and democracy."

A man in a dark suit with a pipe clenched between his teeth cleared his throat. "I hate to interrupt our learned attorney general, but I'm a busy man, and I'd like to get back to work before another century turns. To that end, let me summarize what may have taken our AG a month to spit out. You boys done good. Those bastards, Malcolm Wainwright and Gibson Richardson, will spend the rest of their lives in a Caribbean paradise known as Guantanamo Bay, and as for the revered Senator Carl Burlingame —that cowardly rat—he put a bullet in his mouth before the FBI could take him into custody."

He coughed and wiped his mouth. "As far as one old man is concerned, Hell is too good for his rotten soul . . . if he'd had one. To further ease your minds, boys, Gloria Wainwright and Bryan Tomlinson are safe and sound with new names and a new address that's much more comfortable than Guantanamo. I don't know how you did it, but I know why the rest of the Board members and I consider you to be the most valuable team of operators we've ever had the privilege of directing. Our days of hiding behind a veil are over as far as you and your team are concerned. You'll hear from all of us or none of us, and we'll speak with one voice. You'll never again be sent on an assignment by one or two of us to accomplish a personal vendetta. You have my word and the word of everyone in this room."

A slightly younger gentleman wearing an open-collared shirt under a navy blazer tapped his foot and said, "It looks to me like the attorney general isn't the only long-winded blowhard in this room, so let me sum it up. We're deeply sorry for what happened to your team, especially to your Coast Guard rescue swimmer. The actions of Wainwright and Richardson tore a warrior from our battlefield, and that's unforgivable, but I just happen to know that young man is going to live a long, full life creating art that will find its way onto a lot of walls just like mine."

He motioned toward the fireplace, above which hung a massive oil on canvas of Lord Nelson's *Battle of Trafalgar*. "From my understanding of things, painters are rarely shot at, so your man can at least enjoy that benefit, such as it is. Now, concerning the airplane you lost . . . We'd like for you to visit some friends of ours in Wichita, Kansas, at the Cessna headquarters and pick out the one you want. Tell them to send us the bill. How's your pilot, by the way?"

Clark deferred to me, and I said, "He's doing fine. Thank you for asking. It was a nasty concussion, but he's as hardheaded as the rest of us, so the flight surgeon cleared him to fly within a few days of the, uh . . . accident.

"That's good to hear," the man said. "Oh, and just one more thing. What about the Russian? I pray she's recuperating from her injuries."

It was my turn to defer to Clark, and he put on that crooked Clark Johnson smile. "What Russian, sir?"

About the Author

Cap Daniels

Cap Daniels is a former sailing charter captain, scuba and sailing instructor, pilot, Air Force combat veteran, and civil servant of the U.S. Department of Defense. Raised far from the ocean in rural East Tennessee, his early infatuation with salt water was sparked by the fascinating, and sometimes true, sea stories told by his father, a retired Navy Chief Petty Officer. Those stories of adventure on the high seas sent Cap in search of adventure of his own, which eventually landed him on Florida's Gulf Coast where he spends as much time as possible on, in, and under the waters of the Emerald Coast.

With a headful of larger-than-life characters and their thrilling exploits, Cap pours his love of adventure and passion for the ocean onto the pages of the Chase Fulton Novels and the Avenging Angel - Seven Deadly Sins series.

Visit www.CapDaniels.com to join the mailing list to receive newsletter and release updates.

Connect with Cap Daniels:

Facebook: www.Facebook.com/WriterCapDaniels
Instagram: https://www.instagram.com/authorcapdaniels/
BookBub: https://www.bookbub.com/profile/cap-daniels

Books in This Series

Books in the Avenging Angel – Seven Deadly Sins Series

Other Books by Cap Daniels

Made in the USA
Coppell, TX
10 April 2024

31123710R00162